I0691549

Acknowledgements

It seems like we just did this, right? Well, here I go again. Can't stop, won't stop. I'm feeling myself like Bad Boy in the early nineties. We at fifteen books. Fifteen, not including Ghostface Killaz and Bossy. Can't stop, won't stop. Hope you enjoyed part three of this series. If you did, welcome to part four. Strap on your seat belt and get ready to ride with the characters in this book. I try to give y'all a little bit of everything, sex, betrayal, murder and love. I try to wring out your every emotion. I endeavor always to make you laugh, to shed a tear, and to hate somebody. Most of my loyal readers already know to expect a wicked twist in the story. I won't let you down. These acknowledgments will be brief. I promise. To all the people I've named in the book or made a character, either I mess with you or you've violated my trust and I had to kill you! :) One thing I understand is that you can't please all the people all the time. So, before you write me and tell me that I shouldn't have wrote this and shouldn't have wrote that, understand that this is all entertainment. This is for all the good men from D.C. who recognize a sick pen game and depend on me to 'take them out there.' I do this for you all. To all the men who want to read these books, but it's a sucka in your ear saying, "They got a bad bone out on Buck," pay them no mind and read the books anyway. Then ask them, those who spread rumors and slander without cause or proof, "Why are all of Buck's co-defendants home and he's not, if he told?" Ask them that and see what answer you get. And that's all I'ma say about that, besides the fact that I'm still standing, still controlling my environment and still daring a muthasucka to disrespect me or play with me with that bull jive. With that said, shout out to all of the people I love. You know who you are. F— K you to all the people I hate. You know who you are. Shout out to all the good men in the streets and still behind bars. Shout out to all the women who support me, in jail and out. I appreciate it. Thanks to everyone who supports me. And stay tuned for Angel 5. It's up next. Then look out for AMEEN: The beginning. Until next time. P.S. Rest in peace Lonneel Nunn

D.C. Stand up,
Buckeyfields

Lock Down Publications and Ca$h
Presents

IF YOU CROSS ME ONCE 4
Let the Truth be Told

Written By
Anthony Fields

First Edition 2024

Printed in the United States of America

This is a work of fiction. Names, characters, places, and incidents either are products of the author's imagination or are used fictitiously. Any similarity to actual events or locales or persons, living or dead, is entirely coincidental.

Lock Down Publications
P.O. Box 944
Stockbridge, GA 30281
www.lockdownpublications.com

Like our page on Facebook: Lock Down Publications
www.facebook.com/lockdownpublications.ldp

Stay Connected with Us!

Text **LOCKDOWN** to 22828 to stay up-to-date with new
releases, sneak peaks, contests and more…

Like our page on Facebook:
Lock Down Publications

Join Lock Down Publications/The New Era Reading Group

Visit our website:
www.lockdownpublications.com

Follow us on Instagram:
Lock Down Publications

Email Us: We want to hear from you!

Dedication

This book is dedicated to my youngest son, Amari Tariq Fields-Gardner. I pray that one day our bond increases and is strengthened through love and sacrifice. Love you, Kiddo.

Chapter 1
Quran
The Tyler House
1200 North Capitol Street
Norwest, D.C.

"Fuck," I exclaimed to myself. I pulled my dick out and took a piss out of frustration. It was times like these that I would've called Jihad and Lil Bo. But Bo was dead and Jihad sat in a cell at CTF, while awaiting an indictment for murder. After answering nature's call, I washed my hands in the sink, mind completely on Joseph 'JoJo' Morris. The dead man walking in the next room. Pocketing my cell phone, I exited the bathroom and found Andy Daniels where I left him, in the living room of the apartment on the third floor, in the company of KD and her friends. Each of the women with KD were in the process of rolling weed into blunt papers. I observed Andy's eyes as they went back and forth from the three women to JoJo Morris. My eyes did the same. Only I wasn't as obvious as Andy. Once the blunts had been rolled, I grabbed the blunt from the hand of the woman to KD's right.

"What's your name again?" The woman asked.

"Que," I replied and pulled out a lighter to light the blunt.

"I'm Day Day."

"Hey, Day Day. This is KD, and you are?" I asked the other woman.

"Morshay. My name is Morshay."

"Morshay, Day Day and KD I like it. But not as much as I like good weed."

"Fire it up, then," KD said.

I hit the blunt and inhaled, then held the flame of the lighter up to light the blunt in Day Day's hand. I inhaled the pungent, acrid smoke and almost coughed up a lung. Looking at the blunt, I said, "Damn, what the fuck?"

All three women laughed at me. KD said, "Best weed in the city. Facts."

"No bullshit," I said in between coughs.

"You like it, huh, pretty boy?" Morshay asked.

"Love it, pretty girl."

"Glad you like the tree, baby, but it's the price you might not like," Day Day said.

KD smiled and said, "It's three thousand a pound. No exceptions."

"Three band's is some skinny shit. I need ten of 'em ASAP."

"Is that all?" KD asked.

I hit the weed again and then put it out. "Make it twenty pounds, then. Sixty racks is light shit. I need that."

KD reached out and took the unlit blunt from my hand. She turned to her friend, who had the other blunt. She took the blunt from her and used it to relight the blunt she'd taken from my hand. KD slowly inhaled the weed several times and held in the smoke.

She never coughed, not one time. Her eyes on mine, KD exhaled smoke. "I'm ready to meet whenever you are."

I glanced over at JoJo Morris and couldn't hold back my ill feelings. My face told the story as I tapped Andy. "Cuz, let me holla at you for a minute," I told Andy. To KD, I said, "Excuse me for a minute."

Once me and Andy was away from the three women and out of everybody's earshot, I asked Andy, "How well do you know this building?"

8

"I grew up in it, running around it. I know it well. Why? What's up?"

"How many exits are there?"

"Just two. No, three. But one is never used. The side joint on the bottom floor is for emergencies, like a fire exit. It's always locked, so that leaves two exits, back and front."

"JoJo could use either one, right?"

Andy nodded.

"A'ight, look, JoJo is the priority now. KD is gonna have to wait. Do you fuck with slim?"

"He's the homie. We ain't never been buddies, but we always been cool. Why, what's up?"

"I need you to disarm JoJo."

"You want me to take his gun from him?"

"Naw, slim, not like that. I need you to talk to him. Holla at him and make him feel comfortable with you. Since you just got home, act like you need a hand out, or something. Reminisce about the good ole days, or something. Just gain his trust for a little while. I'ma go ahead and bounce. After I leave, find a way to get him to leave. I don't care how you do it, just do it. See if you can find out where he's parked at, front or back. Once you know, I need you to text me one word, front or back. I'ma take care of the rest. Do that for me and I got a couple rocks for you."

"What about Kendra?"

"I told you that she's secondary. JoJo is the most important one now. I can get KD another day. As a matter of fact, I'm 'bout to go holla at her now and set up something for one day this weekend. You go and get on JoJo for me."

"Got you, homie. Say less."

Andy turned and found his way over towards Joe Morris. I slid back over to KD and her two friends.

"We thought you forgot about us," Day Day said.

"How could I ever do that?" I replied.

"Where are you from, Que?" KD asked.

9

"I'm from Glass Manor. But I was raised in D.C. in Kenilworth."

"That's what's up. Just wanted to know who I'm dealing with."

"I can respect that, baby girl. I'ma official nigga. And my men are official, Ish, Frye, Tay and J Rock. Ask about us."

"No need. If Andy vouched for you, that's all I need."

"Cool. Like I said, though, I need twenty of them, as soon as possible."

"Whenever you ready. Put my number in your phone."

I programmed KD's number into my phone. "I might need more than that. I'ma let you know when I hit you. My man that I copped from got killed recently so, I definitely need a new connect. Me and my men, we gon smoke twenty in like ten days. Can you handle more than twenty?"

"I can handle whatever you need, pretty boy," KD replied.

"I'ma hold you to that. Y'all have a good night. I'm out."

"Bye, pretty boy," Day Day and Morshay called out.

Smiling, I waved at them. Then I turned and saw Andy talking to JoJo. I left the apartment and quickly descended the stairs. On the side of the building, I waited.

"Come to papa, big boy. Come to papa."

Chapter 2
Zin

The revelation that Quran was the person that killed Dontay Samuels hit me like the green line train during rush hour. They were friends, close friends. According to Delores Samuels, they were best friends. Why would Quran kill Dontay? Was it for my father? I thought about my mother's letter locked away inside my purse. She had put Quran and Dontay together, said they rode with my father everywhere and killed for him. "Quran killed Dontay?"

Delores nodded. "Everybody witnessed it. He walked up to Dontay on the front porch, pulled out a gun and shot him."

"But if they were friends…"

"Best friends."

"If they were best friends, then why would Quran kill Dontay?"

"Now, that's what we don't know. No one knows why."

"From the very beginning, my father always said that he was innocent. He maintained that for years, but I always thought he was lying to protect my feelings. I thought that he didn't want me to look at him differently, like a crazy killer."

"There's a lot of things that you don't know, Zin. I can see the confusion in your face, in your eyes. I have a lot to tell you, a lot of truths. You asked me earlier how I knew your mother and how I knew your middle name was Marie.

I can tell you everything you need to know, if you want to hear it. Hear the truth."

"I want to hear you out, hear the truth, as you put it."

"Well, this may take a while, Zin. Would you like something to eat or drink?"

***

"Your grandmother's name was Pearl Ann Mitchel. She was five foot two but her undeniable spirit made her appear a giant. She embodied confidence and power. Her fiery personality made living in Jackson, Mississippi in the forties, fifties, and sixties a serious problem. So, she boarded a Greyhound bus in 1965 and headed north. With her were her three children, Paul Jr., Preston Earl, and Pamela Rose. Paul was 7, Preston, 6, and Pam was 4. It was on that bus that your grandmother met my mother, Deborah Louise Allen, a twenty-year-old, escaping a bad marriage to a man in Tupelo, Mississippi. All my mother had to her name was sixty-five dollars, one suitcase and one daughter, me. I was born in Tupelo in 1960. I was five years old when that bus arrived in the Nation's Capital.

"Why Pearl and Deborah chose Washington, D.C. to emigrate to, I never knew. Never asked. Being two young women, your grandmother was only twenty-three years old then, from Mississippi, they bonded together and scraped out life for themselves in the city. Then, in 1968, everything changed. Martin Luther King, Jr. was assassinated in Memphis, and that same night, your mother was born. Ms. Pearl named her youngest daughter Patricia, after one of her distant relatives, she said. I was eight years old by then and never did meet or even know who Patricia's father was. And nobody ever mentioned him. Ms. Pearl and my mother lived in the same building on Sayless Place, 2022, and they helped each other out in every way possible. The city was consumed with riots that year after MLK's death and a lot of the white

12

citizens of D.C. ran for the hills. The mass exodus of white folks fleeing to the suburbs left D.C. with a majority black citizenship. After that, D.C. was later nicknamed Chocolate City.

"I loved baby Patricia and spent a lot of time taking care of her while Ms. Pearl worked. So much so that I couldn't stand to be away from her for long periods of time. I used to pretend that Patricia was my child. In the latter part of 1968, tragedy struck. Your uncle Paul Jr. ran into the street on Stanton Road, trying to cross, and was struck by a car and killed. Ms. Pearl remained stoic and graceful, but we all knew that the death of her oldest child had ripped away something inside of her that was needed.

"Your grandmother went back to work at Savoy Elementary in the cafeteria and did all she could to maintain her composure. My mother worked in the cafeteria, too. Always there for Ms. Pearl in every way. Then tragedy struck a second time. In 1973, I was thirteen and your aunt Pam was twelve. Preston was fourteen and your mom, Patricia, was five. Me and Pam were only a year apart in age but two people could never have been more different. Pam took after Ms. Pearl in the looks department. She was a beautiful girl, a hair over five two, long black hair, big brown eyes and the body of a grown woman. She was a smart one in school, but that girl was a fast one. 'Hot in the drawers' was what my mother called her. Pam linked up with an older guy from Berry Farms, named Tony Edelin, and snuck around like nobody knew her business. One day in the summer, Pam was hugging a boy from Howard Gardens on Baven Road. Tony Edelin saw Pam with the boy. He walked up to them and shot them both, killing them. The death of your aunt Pam crushed Ms. Pearl. She was inconsolable. It was a sad, sad time. Tony Edelin went to jail for both murders, but nobody was satisfied with that outcome, especially your uncle Preston, who'd been very close to his only sister.

"One year later, in 1974, Preston, who was fifteen at the time, went to the Edelin family home on Eaton Road in Berry Farms and shot five members of the family as they cooked out in their front yard. Tony Edelin's brother's, Wayne, Ray Ray and Tommy, all died. A sister and the mother survived. Preston was declared clinically insane by a judge and never did a day in jail.

"He was sent to Saint Elizabeth's mental hospital. Two years later, in 1976, Preston killed a doctor and a nurse, then he hung himself. Preston's death did to Ms. Pearl what the other two didn't. It broke her, completely. She left her job and became reclusive and sick. My mother cut her hours at work to part time, just to care for her. Then in 1978, two things happened. I had sex for the first time and got pregnant and your grandmother passed away. My mother said that Pearl Ann Mitchel had died of a broken heart, and nothing more. My mother, who was 33 at the time, became the sole legal guardian for Patricia. Your mother moved in with us on Sheridan Road. She was ten years old. I was seventeen, about to turn eighteen. And that's when I met Donnie Samuels.

"In the sixties, a lot of men in D.C. became a part of the 'Black Muslim' movement. I think it was mostly to get away from white people's culture and their religion, Christianity. In 1975, Elijah Muhammad died, and the Nation of Islam became something else— Sunni Muslims. Donnie was a Sunni Muslim. He wasn't my child's father, but he took responsibility. So, I had my son and named him Dontay Samuels, giving him Donnie's last name. Dontay was born in 1979. Donnie and I married a year later. I converted to Islam that same year. I moved in with Donnie, leaving Patricia as the only person in the house with my mother. Living as a Muslim woman and wife was new to me, but I adapted. I catered to my husband and son. Donnie had all Muslim friends that came to our house, all except one, Kevin

Carter. Kevin Carter was Donnie's only non-Muslim friend, but they were close. Kevin had two brothers and one sister."

"My aunt, Linda, my uncle, Kirk, and my father."

Delores got up from the kitchen table where they sat. She walked over to the counter and retrieved a pie. "When you were a kid, you loved strawberry cheesecake. Is that still the same?"

I nodded.

"Good," Delores put the pie down on the table. Then she went to the cabinet and pulled out two small plates. She got out the silverware and returned to the table. After slicing two pieces of cheesecake and putting a slice on each plate, Delores sat back down. "Donnie's mentor in all things was a man named Amir Bashir. Amir was one of the most enchanting men you could ever meet, and damn was he handsome. Then there was Ameen Bashir. In 1979, Ameen was, I think, seventeen years old, and the spitting image of his father. All the girls in our neighborhood fawned over him, as if he was a celebrity.

"In 1980, I turned twenty and life was good. My husband had turned to the streets, selling drugs. Dontay was one and your mother was twelve years old. I was working at that time and was rarely seeing Patricia. My mother had met the man she'd eventually marry and was working a lot. So, that left your mother to basically fend for herself. And just like her sister, Pam, Patricia was twelve, but built like a woman grown. She had the family pretty hazel eyes, long hair, caramel complexion and diminutive height. The girl was beautiful, too. Really attractive. How Ameen Bashir got to Patricia…"

"Ameen Bashir? Back then? Before my father?"

"Yes. Ameen came before Michael. He was every bit of eighteen years old and the most sought-after dude in the hood, but he wanted Patricia. She and I were still very close, although I couldn't see her often. But we made time to get together. She was my younger sister. Patricia told me that

Ameen had taken her virginity and did things to her sexually that she had never known were possible. And over time, she confessed that she loved him more than the air she needed to live. Patricia looked like a woman but wasn't one on any level. When she found out that Ameen belonged to Katherine Ball, who was pregnant with a son, she went crazy. It made Ameen back away, but not all the way. Katherine converted to Islam, became Khadijah, married Ameen and gave birth to a son…"

"Quran."

"Exactly. Patricia was devastated by Ameen's marriage, but learned to play her position, if she wanted to be in his life at all, and she did. Michael Carter, your father, was three years younger than his friend, Ameen Bashir, and about to turn sixteen when he met Patricia at a store on the Avenue. I was working, then I was spending a lot of time at the masjid. I wanted to raise Dontay in the Islamic religion to help him become a good man and Muslim. So, I kept Dontay there with me. Another person who was always at the masjid with me was Khadijah Bashir, Ameen's wife. Her son, Quran, was ever present as well. It was there in the masjid that Quran and Dontay met and formed their bond as children. I want to say that Patricia was 14, maybe 15, when she came to me and professed her love for Mike Carter. Yet she still continued to love and sleep with Ameen, unbeknownst to your father, of course. At some point, Patricia moved into an apartment with Mike Carter. Then in 1984, she became pregnant with you.

"One day, Patricia came to my house and broke down crying. She was hysterical, inconsolable. I thought that someone else had died. It was that day that I learned of the pregnancy and the fact that Patricia feared that the baby was Ameen's. She had managed to hide her relationship with Ameen, scared her to her core. I did and said everything I could to comfort Patricia, but in actuality her concerns were real. If Michael Carter had found out about Patricia and

Ameen, he would have killed them both. And make no mistake about it, Ameen Bashir and Michael Carter were two of the most feared men in Southeast at that time.

"Ameen Bashir had gained a reputation for being sadistic and barbaric. I watched him kill two men right there by the walk bridge. Once both men had fallen, he stood over them and pumped more bullets into their corpses. He was a skilled killer, a butcher, a maniac. And while Mike Carter was more patient with people, more diplomatic and focused on money, he was rumored to be just as vicious as Ameen. Your mother's fear was that the baby would be born with light grey eyes, thereby revealing her deceit and Ameen's betrayal of Mike. Something happened one day to make her almost tell Mike about her and Ameen. Patricia told me one day that she had went to Mike's apartment only to find Khadijah Bashir leaving it. She said that it happened a few times before and that Ameen was never present. Patricia said that she dismissed Khadijah's visits as business or her handling something for Ameen. Then Khadijah got pregnant with the third child and Patricia always wondered. But she kept quiet about Khadijah, and about her and Ameen. How's the pie?"

"The cheesecake is delicious. Made it yourself?"

Delores nodded. "I did, actually. Suddenly, I feel like ice cream with my cheesecake. How about you?"

"I'd like some."

Chapter 3
Quran

The phone in my hand vibrated, alerting me to the incoming text. I read the text. There was only one word. The one word I'd been waiting for.

Back.

I pulled the hat down low onto my head and zipped up my coat. I pulled the FNN from my waist. Slowly, I made my way to the rear of the high rise building. For a brief second, I thought about the shot spotter's gun fire detection system that was mounted on all the buildings in the city. But I was determined to make the kill and get away with it. The bounty on JoJo Morris's head was fifty bands, and I needed that. That, and the fifty that was on Kendra's head, too. It was cold and getting colder by the minute, but in a few minutes, things for JoJo would get hotter than summer.

The rear door of the Tyler House building let out onto a raised platform. You had to walk down a winding staircase to reach the ground level. There was a playground and basketball court next to a pool. Adjacent to all that was the parking lot. I skulked on the side of the building with the entire area in my sight. There was no way that JoJo could get away from me, without me seeing him. In the heart of winter in D.C. it was always overcast skies, darkness and cold. People in every neighborhood usually stayed inside to avoid the bitter cold. I looked around the entire area at the rear of the building and saw no one. The day was a perfect day for killing. I couldn't see the rear exit door, but I could hear it. I heard the door open and close. I could vaguely hear voices. The two men were JoJo and Andy. They descended the winding staircase as they talked. Whatever Andy was saying, he definitely had JoJo's attention. I crept from where I hid and came out into the dimly lit night. I walked up on the pair of men as they headed for the parking lot.

"What the...?" JoJo Morris uttered and reached for his waist.

I upped the FNN and said, "Uh uh, bitch."

JoJo looked from me to Andy. Andy calmly walked away.

"Say his name."

"What? Who are...?"

"Say his name," I repeated.

"Say whose name, slim?" JoJo asked.

"The name of the good man you told on. Say his name."

"Which one?"

"Donte Bailey," I told him. "Say it."

"Baltimore Gutta. The Blood nigga. Fuck h..."

I shot JoJo in the face and watched his body drop. "Naw, nigga. Fuck you."

***

Miles away from the JoJo Morris crime scene, I pulled the car over and checked to see had I been followed. I hadn't been. I reclined my seat and closed my eyes. Staring in the face of death, JoJo Morris had bravely. The nerve of the rat to not show fear in his last moments on earth. Rats were getting bolder and bolder. Quickly, I disassembled the Galaxy phone in my pocket. I extracted the sim card. Letting the window down, I tossed the sim card out the window. Searching in the center console of the Cadillac, I found the new sim card and inserted it where the old card had been. I reassembled the phone and dialed Zin's phone. No answer. I sent her a text to let her know that the caller was me, then I called her again. Still no answer. Thoughts of Zin with another man crossed my mind, but then quickly left. My next call went to a number that I knew by heart. Before I made the call, I sent a text to the number.

Mike Carter answered on the third ring. "What's up, youngin?"

"I'm good, old head."

"Good news, I hope. What's good?"

"Scratch another one off the list," I informed Mike.

"Which one? Male or female?"

"Male, but the female is lined up. She'll be gone soon."

"Definitely great news. How did you find the guy that was so hard to find?"

"Caught a helluva break and ran into him when I wasn't looking for him. A 762 bullet fucked him around. Closed casket shit."

"Say no more, youngin. Gutta will be pleased. The money will be in the account by eight a.m. tomorrow. Text me to confirm when you get it."

"Got you."

"Do I lock this number in or what?" Mike asked me.

"Yeah, you can. It'll be good for about a month or so."

"A'ight. What's up with all the men?"

"Jay is recovering over CTF. He good. It's the beginning of round one. We prepared for nine rounds. I'ma do what I do to make sure he good. Dave got hit over the jail. A friend of the dude he butchered last month. I'ma go and see his folks as soon as I get his info. Dave got hit bad, but he good, too. Recovering. I send them both the kiss of like, so they good on all levels."

"Where is Dave at? The jail?"

"Naw. He's over CTF, too. In the medical unit."

"What about Sean?"

"What can I say, old head. You know how the big homie is. Lunchin' good as shit. One track mind. Revenge."

"Still on one, huh?"

"You already know. Both of y'all throwing me off, though. No bullshit."

"He throwing me off."

"Y'all both lunchin'. Let me bounce, old head. Gotta go and clean up. I'ma hit you tomorrow. The woman on the list should be gift wrapped soon. KD shouldn't be with Golden State for too much longer."

"A'ight, youngin. You be safe."

"You be safe. Make sure none of them Aryan Brotherhood crackas don't kill you in there."

Mike Carter laughed. "They'd rather fuck with a thousand pound grizzly bear than fuck with me."

"That's what I like to hear. Later."

"Later, youngin."

Ending the call with Mike, I tried Zin again. Still no answer. I dialed another number that I had memorized. Halina Ndugu's phone rung five times then went to voicemail. Smiling, I said to myself, "Ain't none of the women in my life fucking with me right now."

Tossing the phone into the passenger seat, I drove to Haynes Point. I parked the car and got out. At the railing that overlooked the water, I pulled the FNN from my waist. I tossed it into the water.

Chapter 4
Zin

Delores Samuels sat both plates and the silverware in the sink, then walked back over to the table and sat down. "Now, where was I? Oh, I remember. In the summer of 1985, you made your entrance into the world. Seven pounds, five ounces. And the spitting image of Patricia. I held her hand as she pushed you out of her. The both of us holding our breaths as you opened your eyes. Your father was not in the room. He didn't want to witness your birth. He was outside the room in the hallway. When we saw that you had the hazel eyes of the Mitchell women, we both exhaled in relief. Your mother loved you so much, more than Mike, more than Ameen, more than herself. A year later, Patricia Mitchell became Patricia Carter or Patricia Mitchell-Carter as she liked to say. Your mother gave you the middle name of Marie to honor Mike Carter's mother, who had recently passed away…"

"She named me Zinfandel after her favorite wine."

Delores laughed. "Your mother told you that, but it wasn't true. Patricia never even drank wine. Zinfandel was her mother's favorite wine. Your grandmother, Ms. Pearl's. Okay, where was I again? At your parents getting married when you were one years old. In the neighborhood, Mike Carter's status grew. And so did Ameen's. They became large level drug dealers. Their meteoric rise to street fame came because of a rumored connection to the Carlos

Trinidad drug organization. As time went on, Ameen Bashir's role became more about security. He did all of the beatings and killings. I guess with so much going on in the streets, it became easier for Ameen and Patricia to hide their secret relationship from Mike. And so it went all the way to the nineties.

"In 1991, I started a new job at Goodwill Industries on South Dakota Avenue. The money was better and my workload increased. I hadn't spoken to Patricia in months, nor had I seen you in a minute. I think you were about what, six, maybe. Yeah, six. Dontay and Quran, by then, were inseparable. Quran Bashir spent so much time at my house that people thought he was a part of the family. At that time, Dontay was twelve and Quran a year younger. Then one day, your mother showed up at my job, your hand in hers. She told me that she couldn't speak about things at home to anyone, but she was desperate to talk. She told me that Mike went on a business trip to New York and was supposed to be gone a day or two. Ameen came to their house. Patricia said that she had heard noises in the house but paid them no mind. Your mother said that she believed that Mike had come home early and seen her and Ameen together. She believed it wholeheartedly. When Mike came home, she noticed a change in him. According to her, he wasn't the same Mike Carter that had left her days before.

"Then Ameen Bashir was killed, and that devastated her. His death, she said, proved her theory about Mike seeing her and Ameen together. Your mother couldn't prove it, but she was convinced that Mike Carter killed Ameen. And she also believed that he was going to kill her. I tried to convince her that she was just being paranoid, but her mind was made up. I told her that the streets had come back to claim Ameen Bashir's life. Patricia wouldn't hear of it. That was the last time I ever saw you. Your mother became reclusive after that. After Ameen's death, his son, Quran, changed. Something inside of him died with his father. Maybe it was his moral compass and simple humanity. Or, maybe he was just destined to become just like his father. A year after Ameen's death, Quran started hanging out with your father. Not long after, word around the neighborhood was that Mike groomed Quran to kill, to replace his father.

"Dontay was impressionable and a year older than Quran, but for some reason, he followed behind Quran and not the other way around. Dontay's father and I had long since separated, but hadn't divorced, and Dontay was never really close to his dad. So, at some point, Dontay became the third wheel to Quran and your father. I was a single mom working hard and going through it mentally about Donnie, so I wasn't overly protective of Dontay. I kinda let him find his own way. If he wasn't with Quran or Quran and Mike, he'd hang out on Dexter Terrace with his father's family. Despite our distance, me and my son were especially close.

Not long after, I began to hear stories about my son. The people he robbed, beat and then killed. The combination of Dontay and Quran in the streets was like Ameen and Mike Carter as teens. In 1995, your mother was killed. Her death was broadcasted all over the news. But the neighborhood spoke of the crime the most because of who Patricia was, Mike Carter's wife. Nobody knew who was responsible. My mother and I took Patricia's death extremely hard, but her more than me. To lose Pearl Ann Mitchell and all four of her children, after leaving Mississippi for a better life in D.C., hit my mother to her core. Although you and your mother was my family, Dontay had never really gotten to know and love Patricia. But he loved me. He saw how much Patricia's death affected me. It was then that he told me the truth…" her eyes filled with tears.

My eyes had filled with tears, too. Tears rolled down my face. "That him and Quran killed my mother."

"What? Dontay didn't. Where did you get that?" Delores said, befuddlement etched across her face. "You got that from the trial, when the prosecutor said that Mike killed Dontay because he killed Patricia. That's not true, Zin."

I reached into my purse and pulled out the letter that my mother had written - I passed the letter to Delores.

Delores stared at the letter, then began to read. "Things grow progressively worse each day now. Our relationship has changed drastically in the last year or so. The way that he looks at me, touches me, it's all foreign to me now. It's as if I'm living with a stranger. Gone is the loving way that he used to touch me. Sex is bestial and degrading. I feel as if I am his whore, instead of his wife. I believe that he knows. He has to. That is the only explanation for the cold look in his eyes, and the distance between us. I feel like a prisoner in my own home at times, and my husband is my jailer. The way he watches me, it's spooky. When he's home, it's as if he's far away. And when he's far away, it's as if he's here, staring at me, accusing me. Is it possible that he can see the stain of betrayal in my eyes? In my heart? Is love that powerful? I cry myself to sleep at night and pray that our daughter doesn't hear me. My sweet, precious daughter. I love her so and so does he. Without her, I'd go crazy. Cooking, cleaning and caring for Zin is my perpetual nirvana. Her smile, her voice, her laugh, it comforts me.

"It's been four years since Ameen's death and I still feel his absence, his loss. I know that having an affair with my husband's best friend was dangerous and wrong, but the man was like a forbidden fruit that I had to taste, often. His body, his demeanor, his sex appeal, his light grey eyes, they were too much for me to resist. I believe that my husband knows of my infidelity. He knows and he's mentally punishing me. As me and my lover made love in my bed, while my husband was away, I heard noises in the house, but dismissed them as things that go bump in the night. I was too caught up in the act of my betrayal to think clearly and investigate the sounds that I heard. But as sure as I sit here and write this down on paper, I know what I heard. I believe that my husband was here that night. He was here and he saw us. I may be delusional or may just be paranoid, I don't know. But I believe that my husband saw us and that he killed my lover, his best friend. These are words that I can never speak to a soul." Delores got up from the table and walked over to the sink. She put both hands on the counter and cried.

I could hear her sobs and they broke my heart. I cried openly. Delores Samuels took several minutes to compose herself. "She told me. She spoke these words to me. I can still hear her voice talking to me. As I read this letter, I can hear her voice. My sister. My friend."

I wiped the tears from my eyes and tried to steady my reserve. I never meant to break down in front of this woman in front of me. I dropped my head. Then I heard Delores start to read again.

"So, I must write them down to get them out of my head, my heart and my soul. As sure as I write this today, I'm sure that Mike killed Ameen. And I also believe that one day, soon, he's going to kill me."

"She predicted her own death."

I nodded my head, struggling not to cry again.

"My husband has taken to disrespecting me publicly. He brings the reminder of my betrayal to our house from time to time. Every time I see Ameen's son, Quran, I think of his father and our infidelity. Quran has a friend named Dontay and they ride with Mike everywhere. They kill people for Mike. That I know for sure. And for some reason, I believe that they will kill me. It's in their young eyes, both are teenagers, teenage killers. When I die, and I believe that I will die soon, my husband and his boy assassins will be my executioners."

"She was wrong." Delores walked back to the table, her eyes focused directly on mine. "Dontay didn't kill your mother, and neither did Quran."

"How do you know that? How can you be so sure?"

"Because me and Dontay had this weird kinda bond. He may have been a lot of bad things around everybody else, but to his mother, he was just 'Tay' and he never lied to me. Ever. He was so brutally honest that I never asked him about his life outside my house. I was always afraid of what his answers would be. I think I ignored the rumors about Dontay because I had to. I never wanted to feel like I failed him, never wanted to think I was the mom of a monster. When Dontay came home and told me that Mike Carter killed his wife, killed Patricia, I believed him. Number one reason was because Dontay never lied to me, and the number two reason was because, just like in the letter here, Patricia said that Mike would be her killer. I had ignored her words to me as paranoid ravings, but they proved prophetic."

"Wait. So, Quran and my father killed my mother, then?"

Delores laid the letter on the table. "No, Zin. Quran Bashir didn't kill Patricia. It was your father alone. Dontay told me that Mike Carter called him and told him to get Quran and for the both of them to come to his house. Dontay picked up Quran from Oxford Manor and drove to Mike's house. When they got there, Patricia was already dead, naked and beaten on the couch. They were ordered to help him, Mike, move the body. Mike told them that Patricia was a snitch and had had an affair with a cop, so he killed her."

"They helped my father throw my mother's body away, like trash."

"Your father made them do it, Zin. Mike Carter was in control. When I learned that Mike had killed Patricia, I wanted to do something. But I didn't. I never went to the cops. I never told a soul. Why? Because I feared what Mike Carter would do to me, my mother and my son. I was a coward, Zin. I did nothing. So, three weeks later, on April 17th, when Quran Bashir walked up to my front porch and killed my son, I died that day, too. Because I could've prev…"

"You couldn't have, Delores."

Delores Samuels dropped to her knees. I rushed to her side, leaned down and held her as she cried, tried to console her. Console myself. We were two broken women crying uncontrollably on a kitchen floor in a house on Banger Street.

"They were best friends, like brothers. I fed him. I nursed his wounds. I treated Quran Bashir like a son. I wiped his tears when his father was killed. He said that he couldn't cry at home in front of his mother, younger brothers. I cried with him for Ameen. My son loved him, trusted him, and was loyal to him. And he killed him like he was nothing, as easily as you'd kill a bug. They'd been together since they were toddlers. They prayed together, learned Islam together. They fasted Ramadan together. They believe in one another. And he... he just... he just killed him. Had I gone to the police about Mike..."

"Then you'd be dead, too. You'd be dead, too."

"If I could have saved my son, I would have gladly died. I'm fifty-three years old, Zin. I was thirty-five when I lost my son. For eighteen years I've been a walking dead woman inside. I've had no other children for fear of losing them. I've never allowed myself any other relationships with men. I still mourn for him, for my son. Always wonder what he would have been. Who he could have become. Dontay's father was a coward, too. He knew that Quran Bashir killed his son yet did nothing. Seven months after Dontay's death, Donnie overdosed on heroin. People say that he killed himself, binged on what he could get until it killed him. I still see him, you know? Quran Bashir. He still hangs out in the old neighborhood, on Howard Road. He and his brother Jihad, the youngest one. Khitab got killed. He was the son, the one that..."

"The one that what?" I asked.

"Nothing." Delores replied. "Just something I heard."

"Delores, do you know why Quran killed Dontay? I already asked that."

28

Delores picked herself up off the floor. She wiped her eyes and fixed the hijab on her head. "There was a lot of speculation, but no, I never found out why he did it. I don't mind answering again."

"Well, let me ask you this. Do you know of any connections between my father and Greg Gamble?"

"None. What makes you think there is one?"

I told Delores about the affidavit from Maryann Settles.

"Did you ask your father that question?"

I nodded my head.

"And what did he say about it?"

"The same thing that you just said."

"I know Maryann and all of her family. Heard that she straightened up, but back in the day, woo-wee, that woman was vicious. A crackhead and a dope fiend, she was stealing them dudes stashes and tricking."

"Tricking?"

"Yeah, tricking. That's what they called exchanging sex for drugs back in them days. She's younger than me. I think she's maybe a year or so older than your mother. When I heard that her and T.T. testified against your father, I was confused as to why they had lied on Mike Carter. I never found out why they did that. I never attended the trial. People told me about certain aspects of it, though. After your father…"

"I wonder why Quran didn't kill them."

"Kill who?"

"The witnesses. Maryann and Thomas Turner."

"Good question."

"But the better question is why Greg Gamble paid them to lie on my father."

"Even though I knew that Mike Carter didn't kill Dontay, that an innocent man had gotten found guilty and sentenced to a long time in jail, I never felt bad about it. Why? Because of what Dontay told me, that Mike killed Patricia. I believed it was justice. Justice in a twisted form but justice nonetheless. Are you close to Mike, Zin?"

"Unfortunately, yes. Other than my aunt, I'm all that he has left. All my life I've been a daddy's girl. He was my hero. Growing up, thinking that he avenged my mother, that made me love him like no other. I have always supported him, believed in him, stood by his side. I found that letter in a box of my mother's things that I had in storage. I had never went in the box before, until about a month ago. Reading that letter messed my head up. It still does. And now to hear all that you've told me…"

"It's a lot to process, I know, especially the part about what your father really did to your mother. I know that hurts."

My tears started again, and I hated myself for being so weak, so vulnerable. I wiped my eyes with both hands while nodding my head. "It does hurt. Too much. And I really, really miss my mother."

"I miss her, too, Zin. I miss Patricia more than you can know," Delores said, her eyes full of tears to match mine. "And I hate that I'm crying so much and ruining my makeup. My hijab won't stay on right."

Despite the immense sadness I felt, I laughed. Delores did too.

"My mother never talked about them to me. Never told me about her family. I vaguely remember hearing your mother's name, and your name. Is your mom still alive?"

"Alive," Delores shrugged. "But she's still here, Zin. All praises due to Allah. Her mind has left her, though."

"Alzheimer's? Dementia?"

"Both. After Dontay died, her health failed her. Grief and life's tragedies robbed her of her vitality. I cope with my mother's condition by telling myself that Deborah Allen has seen too much, been through too much, cried too much, lost too much and that she just wanted to forget it all."

"My grandmother, aunt, uncles... She never... I don't even know where they are buried."

"Maybe your mother just wanted to forget everything, too, Zin. The memories, the pain could have been too much for Patricia. But, don't fret, I know where they all are buried. They're all at Harmony Cemetery, just like your mother, and Dontay."

"I'm sorry about Dontay, Ms. Delores. Really, I am."

"Please, Zin, call me Delores or Dee. And what are you sorry about?"

"I'm sorry that he got killed before he could become a man. And sorry that I hated him my whole life because I really believed he killed my mother."

"No worries, Zin, and please no more apologies. I don't want us to be forever stuck in the past. I wanna focus on the future, a future where you and I get to know each other, to grow to love one another. Can we do that, Zin?"

I covered the space between myself and Delores with my arms outstretched. I hugged her. "I'd really like that. You were close to my entire family, I need you in my life."

Delores hugged me tight and rubbed my back. "Thank you, baby. Thank you."

"Life is funny, huh? I come here hoping to get answers about Dontay and why he'd take part in my mother's death, and I gained an aunt."

"Speaking of such, how is your aunt Linda doing anyway?"

I broke our embrace and sat back down at the table. "Can I have another piece of that cheesecake?"

"Sure, baby," Delores replied, and got me another slice of cheesecake.

"My aunt is crazy, but I love her to death. She raised me after my father went to prison." I ate half of the pie before continuing. "I was about to go and see her to give her my news, but since I'm here and you're family now, I guess you'll have to be the first person to hear it."

"News? What news, Zin?"

"I'm pregnant. I found out today that I'm pregnant."

Chapter 5

Sean Branch
Later that night …
MGM Grand Hotel and Casino
National Harbor
12:10 a.m.

"How do you know that they are in there for sure, slim?"
I opened my eyes and glanced over at Quran. "Dudes like Rodney are creatures of habit. He's predictable with his routines. Rodney loves to gamble. Ceelo, two dice, lottery tickets, it's his rush. He doesn't use drugs or drink alcohol. All he wants to do is gamble. Before they opened the MGM Grand, he went out Baltimore to the Horseshoe joint or Casino live at Arundel Mills. How do I know that since I only been home a few months? Because he told me. I used to talk to Rodney all the time. In the joint, he always looked out for me and Big Dawg. Since I been home, I come here with him. It's Friday night…"

"It's Friday? Damn. That's crazy. Time be flying like shit. I wanted to go to Jummah today. I ain't been in a minute. I offered the prayer for the first time in a long time this morning."

"I feel you, Uck, but let's keep it a buck, dudes like us ain't getting into paradise. Ain't gon happen."

"So, what're you saying, old head? We just stop believing? Stop praying? Stop reading the Quran and fasting? We gotta just let the rope of Allah go because we living fucked up?"

Shaking my head, I told Quran, "Never said that, youngin. None of that shit. There's a hadith about a man who had killed ninety-nine people and was on his way to a place to seek forgiveness and repentance, but he died before he could get there. The hadith says that Allah forgave him anyway because he was close to where he was headed. But here's the thing, though, that man had killed and sought forgiveness and was on his way to repent. Are you ready to repent and seek forgiveness for all the lives 'you've taken?"

"Naw, not really, because I still got a lot more killing to do," Quran replied.

"Exactly. There's no way I can repent and ask forgiveness before I kill the one person who needs it most."

"And who's that, old head?"

"Michael Maurice Carter."

Quran's head turned quickly, as if it was attached to a swivel. "Mike Carter? You gon' smoke Mike?"

I nodded my head. "I just decided that today."

"But why? Why would you cross him like that?"

"If you cross me once, you'll cross me twice. That's what Mike and Ameen use to always say. But nobody really lives up to those words. Nobody."

"Nobody lives by the saying? How do you figure that? I'm lost, big bruh."

"Everybody who has ever said that 'if you cross me once' shit' has crossed people and been crossed more than once, more than twice."

"I'm still lost, though, old head."

"Your father always said 'If you cross me once, you'll cross me twice.' Said he'd gotten the saying from Carlos Trinidad and told it to people."

"People like me and my brothers. But still…"

"Mike Carter also said that he got the saying from Carlos Trinidad. And even though Ameen and Mike both said 'If you cross me once, you'll cross me twice', they both crossed everybody more than once, even each other."

"My father never crossed anyone who didn't deserve it, and he never crossed Mike Carter. That was his man."

"Earlier today I told you that there are a lot of things that you don't know. I guess it's time we talked. I mean, really talked. Remember the day I killed Kenny Sparrow and Crud?"

Quran nodded. "Cut both of their heads off and kept them. Talkin' 'bout that's gon let niggas know that Sean Branch is back. How could I forget? Speaking of which, what did you do with them heads?"

"What do you think I did? I peeled the skin off the faces, cooked them in oil and made cracklings. The meat I ate with cheese eggs and home fries. Rat taste good as shit fried." I smiled. "Ask Hannibal Lecter."

The look on Quran's face was priceless. It was a look of horror. "Get the fuck outta here."

"When you ask stupid questions, you get stupid answers. They started stinking and shit, so I had to get rid of 'em. What I'm tryna get to is the conversation we had in the Dodge while we was waiting for Trinaboo to pull up."

"The conversation about hot shit, the books or my father?"

"The part about your father. How he was really a ladies' man and had all the bitches, even my mother."

"You never talk about Ma Dukes. Is she still alive?"

"Yeah. We just not that close. My daughter stay with her."

"That's what's up. Go ahead, though. You were saying something about the conversation we had in the caravan before Trinaboo pulled up."

"We talked about a lot of shit that day, but there are things I didn't tell you, couldn't tell you, especially not before what we were there to do. Afterwards, I just decided that certain things were just better left unsaid. Tonight, I feel different. There's shit about Mike Carter and your father that you don't know. You wanted your boots laced, here goes. In the relationship dynamic with Ameen and Mike, everybody saw

Ameen as the ladies' man, which he was. He was better looking and had the hair and grey eyes. But what people didn't know was that Mike Carter was a ladies' man, too. What Mike Carter lacked in looks, he made up for in charisma, charm and wealth. He had the bag and all the ladies wanted a piece of him. He had all the drugs and all the women who used drugs wanted that from him. Mike Carter fucked a lot of mothers, aunts, sisters, wives, old bitches, young bitches, church bitches, you name it, he nailed 'em. Keep in mind that Mike Carter is a super slick, manipulative, smart motherfucker. He's the type that won't let his left hand know what the right hand is doing. What I'm about to tell you is gonna upset you, youngin, but what the fuck. You asked for the truth, pressed me for the truth, so that's exactly what you are about to get. Do you want me to continue or not?"

"I'm a big boy, Ock, I can handle the truth. Continue."

"I went to jail in 1993, two years before Mike did. And in those days, I was with Mike a lot, but you already know that. We got closer after Ameen was killed. In a lot of ways, I took the place of your father. We were together one day when Mike stopped at a house on Sheridan Road. He jumped out and went into the house. He came back about fifteen minutes later, fixing his clothes, and smelling like perfume and pussy. Before I could pull away from the curb, a woman came outside. A Muslimah with a hijab on her head. She stared at the car as two kids walked up. She embraced both kids and disappeared inside the house. You were one of those kids."

"Me? A house on Sheridan Road? Embraced by a woman in a hijab? Damn! That had to be me and Dontay. The woman in the hijab was his mother, Delores. Wait, you tryna tell me that Mike Carter was fucking Dontay's mother?"

I nodded. "Yeah. He said that her pussy was torch, but her head was a missile. The kid with you was dark skinned and chubby with bubble eyes. The woman was brown-skinned and pretty."

"That's them, but how do you know the other kid was me, when I never met you until the day Mike introduced us?"

"Although we never officially met until the day Mike linked us together, doesn't mean that I hadn't seen you before. I'd seen you several times before the day we met. I knew that Ameen had two sons, you and Jihad, and I'd seen you both a lot. I told you that Ameen was my father figure before Mike. On Sheridan Road, when I saw the two kids walk up, I knew immediately who you were. Then Mike mentioned you anyway that day, told me that you and the lady's son were tight. He told me that shorty's name was Dontay and that his mother, the lady on the porch who he'd just fucked, was tight with his wife, but neither gave a fuck. They'd just started fucking because Delores was getting high. She had just started getting high after she broke up, well separated from her husband, Dontay's father. According to Mike, Dontay's father had other children out of wedlock and Delores found out about it. It unraveled her. She wanted drugs. Mike seized the time and started fucking her in exchange for drugs."

"Damn. That's crazy. Mike Carter was fuckin' 'Dontay's mother and we never knew it," Quran said and smirked. "Damn."

"Youngin, Mike Carter was messing with your mother, and you or Ameen never knew it."

"Aye, slim, hold on, hold on, now you're going too far. You tryna tell me that my mother was cheating on my father with Mike? That he was tricking with my mother for drugs? Is that what you're telling me right now?"

I could see that Quran was visibly upset and I understood, but he had to understand also that his energy didn't intimidate me. "Youngin, you asked for the truth, and I'm giving it to you. I told you that you wasn't gonna like the truth. But all that you rising up out of that seat aggressively is the wrong thing to do with me. You know what's up with me, what I'm made of. So, either pipe your ass down, or we end this conversation before shit go all the way left. Your choice."

Quran recognized the lion inside me that roared. The light in his eyes came back on as he calmed down. "My bad, big homie. I didn't mean no disrespect. What you said fucked me up, but 'I'm good now. I need to hear what you were about to say. Go ahead. I'm good."

"I didn't say nothing about your mother being on drugs, or Mike tricking with her. According to Mike, your mother had come on to him back in the day, before she married your father, but he rebuffed her. He said that she came to him one day, after you and our brother were born, and she complained to him about Ameen, the way he was treating her, fucking with a lot of women. She said he'd gotten another woman pregnant. She cried on Mike's shoulder several times and then one day, he said, one thing led to another. He said they slept together three or four times before breaking the affair off completely. But when your mother got pregnant with her third child…"

"Mike thought the baby was his. That's why you asked me that earlier, about Khitab and the fact that he didn't have our eyes."

I nodded my head, "Exactly. I was telling you that there's a lot of shit that you don't know about Mike. He told me everything I'm telling you. He believed that your brother was his son. He said that Khitab had his eyes and not Ameen's."

"I just thought about something slim. Now that you say that, I remember how Mike sounded on the phone when I told him that I killed Tabu. His initial reaction was like… I can't put my finger on it, but he didn't sound too happy about it. He didn't sound upset, either, but his demeanor was off. He told me that if Khitab had become a rat, then I did the right thing. That's crazy. Whenever Mike asked me about Khitab, I just thought it was because of him being my brother. That's crazy as shit. That nigga been like another father to me for years, and all the time, he kept all this shit from me. Un-fucking-believable."

"Don't kill the messenger, youngin. I'm just delivering a message."

"I can't believe this shit. My mother. Mike Carter. Unbelievable."

Chapter 6
Quran

"Don't kill the messenger, youngin'. I'm just delivering the message."

"I can't believe this shit. My mother. Mike Carter. Unbelievable."

An uncontrollable rage built inside me, to imagine my mother with someone other than my father. If what Sean was telling me was true, then everything that I believed in my life was based on lies. How could I ever believe that my mother, the good sister, Khadijah Bashir, had betrayed my father and slept with his best friend? And given birth to his child? How could my brother not be my father's child? I thought about the time when I was young, about nine or ten, when I asked my father a question…

"Dad, why are my eyes grey like yours?"

"Because I have strong genes, Quran, just like my father, who also had these eyes. His father had them, too. But these eyes are not the eyes to be proud of, son. Our eyes came from the white slave master who raped our great, great grandmother. These grey eyes come from him. They were passed down to the first-born child, at the time, and they're continued to our line until now."

"So, whose eyes do Khitab have, Dad? His eyes are brown."

"Your little brother's eyes are your mother's eyes, son. His hair is her hair. You and Jihad have my eyes and hair. But that doesn't matter because you are all my blood.

"You are all my blood," I repeated to myself.

"What?" Sean asked.

"Huh? Oh, my bad. Go ahead."

"There was a chick that lived in Ambassador Square named Sherry Hailey. A lil bad, red bitch with light hair all over her. She was like that. Young at that time, like seventeen or eighteen. Everybody wanted her, even me, and I was young as shit then. Think of the baddest joint that you could think of, on every level, and that was Sherry. I don't know how Mike got her, but he had her. I was in the hotel room, in the closet, one day when he fucked her. I was in that closet… Anyway, come to find out, she had a boyfriend the whole time. A wild, young nigga that was bodying shit all over the city. He found out that Mike was fuckin' Sherry. Him and Mike exchanged words one day on Stanton Road. Mike was offended that the dude would even talk aggressive to him in any way. He tried to put your father on the dude, but Ameen said he knew the dude's family and declined the job. Mike came to me and told me what I'm telling you now. He wanted me to kill the dude, but the timing was never right. We couldn't never catch him in the right place. Your father got wind of it and outright told me not to do it. He said, 'If Mike wants it done that bad, let him do it himself.' I was more loyal to Ameen. After all, he raised me. But when I came clean and told Mike I couldn't do the killing because Ameen said not to, Mike was livid, mad as shit. Then it just got left alone. Shortly after that, your father got killed. Niggas assumed that, without Ameen, Mike Carter couldn't hold his position in the streets. But we proved them wrong. Me and Mike killed so many people that we single-handedly made D.C. the murder capital back then. The one dude from the past, Sherry's boyfriend, never left Mike's mind, and vice versa. Over time, the dude grew in power and stature. He didn't see Mike in any way. Disrespected Mike in every circle. Called him out on every level. Robbed his workers. Fucked his bitches and did all kind of wild shit to them, then told them to tell Mike he did it. The dude had become Mike's only op. And he was hard to kill. He couldn't use me, even though Ameen was dead, so Mike used the next best thing, you."

"Me? Mike used me, how?" I asked, confused.

"Mike used you to kill the dude. It was the first murder you ever committed."

"The dude was Tony Wells?"

Sean smiled and nodded.

"But, I thought I killed Tony…"

"Because he killed Ameen. Mike lied to you, youngin'. Tony Wells didn't kill your father. I know because I checked. When your father got killed, I felt it deep. I cried like a baby for three days straight. Ameen Bashir had made me the man I was. Your father was my father. I couldn't eat or sleep. I promised myself that I'd kill whoever was responsible for Ameen's death. I hunted and checked every angle. Every person who Ameen hated, I killed. It was Mike who threw a smoke screen. I investigated and found out that Tony Wells wasn't even in the city when Ameen got hit. Tony Wells and all of his men were in North Carolina at the Aggiefest. It was an annual festival like Freaknik that they had down there. All the hustlers in D.C. went every year to show off their wealth and to fuck them country bitches. Mike knew that Tony Wells didn't kill Ameen. He wanted Tony dead and used you to do it. Mike couldn't get near Tony, but a twelve-year-old kid could.

"Mike used you the same way that Ameen used me, to kill niggas he couldn't get close to. When we was at the gym, I told you that Mike wanted me out of the way. Remember that?"

I nodded. "You said you believed that Mike paid Reese the key to say you killed Raymond, to get you out the way."

"Right. And you asked me why he would want me out the way. Why would he give the game a black eye and be complicit to some hot shit? I never told you why Mike would do that. But the answer is simple. Mike knew how close you and I had become. I believe that Mike never wanted me to tell you everything I'm telling you now. He knew what I suspected, and he didn't want me to get in your ear."

"He knew what you suspected? Didn't want you in my ear about what? Him and my mother? About Khitab? About Tony Wells? What?"

Sean leaned back in the driver's seat of the jeep. He pulled out a piece of candy, unwrapped it and popped it in his mouth. "One day, Mike said something to me that didn't sit well with me. He said something about everybody getting what their hands called for, something about Karma catching up to disloyal niggas. Then he mentioned Ameen. Having been around Mike like I had, I knew how he thought. And I knew how dirty he really was. Something inside me made me say, 'He did it. Mike killed Ameen.' What made me think that, was the fact that I'd heard in the streets that Ameen was fucking Mike's wife, Patricia. The rumor was that Ameen had been fuckin' her for years…"

"Are you sure about this, big homie? This shit is starting to sound like a soap opera, Young and the Restless or some shit. First, you say that Mike was fuckin' my mother and Dontay's mother. Now, you're saying that my father was fucking Zin's mother. Come on, man, this shit…"

"I never saw your father fuck Mike's wife. I'm just telling you the rumors that were out back then, and what I suspected."

"You're talkin' in circles, old head. What you're telling me is that you thinking Mike Carter killed my father. And you think that because rumor had it that my father was fuckin' his wife and some karma shit he said to you, while mentioning my father. Is that the long and short of it?"

"Basically. He was the only one that could have got up on Ameen like that. He was a careful man. Ameen would never have let somebody get that close to him unless he knew the person, trusted him. Before I went to jail, I realized that. And

Mike knew I realized that because I said those very same words to Mike one day. He played coy and acted like he didn't hear me, but I knew he heard me. That's why I say that he wanted me out of the way. I knew too much. And if I told you everything I knew, that would turn you against him, and Mike didn't want that."

I thought about everything I'd been told and tried to digest it all. I couldn't. Mike Carter having an affair with my mother. Khitab being his son. My father fucking Zin's mother. Mike fucking Ms. Deloris, Dontay's mother. Mike paying someone to snitch on Sean to remove him from the chessboard of life. Mike Carter killing my father. I closed my eyes and pulled my gun. I screwed the new sound suppressor that Sean gave me onto the barrel of the Smith & Wesson 40 millimeter. I inhaled slowly and exhaled to try and calm the animal that lived in me. I side eyed Sean and for the briefest of moments, I thought about blowing his brains out.

"So, if Mike does make it out, if this affidavit gets him a new trial and he gets out, you gon kill him?"

"Mike Carter is a vicious snake, youngin'. He's an opportunist and a snake. Always beware of the snake with no hiss, they call you bruh, homie and friend. I don't fuck with him. Back in the day, I revered him. It was like I was under his spell or something. Once I went to prison, the spell lifted and I started to see him for what he really was. I will never fuck with Mike Carter again. And there's no way that the both of us can exist on the same streets. I can't trust him and he won't trust me. He knows it and I know it. So, if he makes it home, I'ma be there to welcome him with a smoking gun. It's either him or me, and it damn sure ain't gon be me."

"I feel you, Uck," I replied. "I feel you."

***

"There go Tony right there," Sean exclaimed as he opened the door and started out of the jeep.

"Where's the other nigga at? Rodney?" I asked as I opened the passenger side door.

"I don't know, but he can't be far behind Tony. Come on." We moved stealthily through the cars in the parking lot, headed for the entrance. I had my gun down by my waist. I was focused on Tony Fortune. Sean's eyes moved furtively to and fro.

"Where the fuck is this nigga?" I heard Sean say aloud. Then all hell broke loose. Gunshots rang out. I upped and find out Tony Fortune, who now had a gun in his hand, returning fire in my direction.

"You're too predictable, Sean," a voice called out, then laughed. I retreated towards the jeep and found Sean already there, crouching. He looked at me and smiled.

"They were ready for us, Uck. Rodney knew I'd come." Sean rose from this position and fired his gun in another direction. "Rodney's' over there by that pole, next to the row of cars. He got two guns blowing."

"And his man just ran that way after he fired on me," I told Sean. "What's the play now? It ain't often we're on the defense."

"Their gunshots woke the whole neighborhood. Let's bounce. Cops'll be all over this joint in a minute. Let's go."

Sean slid behind the wheel of the jeep and I crawled in the passenger seat. He pulled out of the space and raced towards the exit. I looked all around for a car or truck in pursuit of us but saw no one.

"We clear, bruh. No tail," I announced.

Sean busted out laughing, driving fast and laughing the whole way.

"Fuck is so funny," I asked.

"Rodney. Did you hear what he shouted out? Called me predictable. Ha. Ha. Ha."

***

Thirty Minutes later…
Outside of Planet Fitness
Clinton, MD.

"These niggas know about me, right? You did tell Rodney something about me, I know."

Sean sent a text on his phone, then looked up at me. "He… Rodney, knows that I got a partner named Quran. I told him that when we put together the hit on Baby E. He knows your name, but that's it. I'm sure that he knew your father, but I don't know if he'll make that connection. Rodney and Tony are dogs, youngin', just like us. They trained to go and know exactly what to do. So, we can't lay off at all. We gotta get them. We gotta hunt them every day, or we gon regret it. I know Tony is from either Lincoln Heights or 58th Street and Rodney's from Clay Terrace, so we gotta spin the bend a whole lot until we get both of 'em."

"What about everybody else?" I asked Sean.

"Everybody like who? Crud's sister and Ren Tyler? All my other old targets? I can get back to them. Rodney and Tony are priority numbers one and two. You?"

"All I got is one, KD, who I already got lined up. Ain't no witnesses pop up on Jihad yet, so that ain't a factor right now. Baby girl, Kendra, can wait until after we get Tony and Rodney."

Sean walked up and stuck his fist out. I bumped it with my own. "I gotta get home before Liv blows my phone up thinking I'm out with some other woman. I'ma hit you tomorrow, insha allah and we can link up. You good?"

"I'm good, Uck."

"Are you good?" Sean asked again. "I mean really good, in light of all the shit you learned about moms, pops, Mike and your lil brother?"

46

"I'm good, slim. Real live. Khitab might've been Mikes' kid, that's why he did what he did and I had to do what I did. It makes sense, if I believe that Mike gave Reese that brick to implicate you on that body. That was direct hot shit, if he did that. I ain't gon never hold no grudge against my mother for anything she may have done, or not done. I wasn't in her shoes back then. She was a good mother to me, and that's all that matters. My father is still who he always was in my heart and mind. If he preached one thing but did another, fuck it. Such is life sometimes. If he crossed muthafuckas, he had a reason to, so be it. Now, Mike, on the other hand, is the only person out of the bunch that's still alive. I feel you on the reasons you wanna crush him, and it don't make me no difference one way or another. That might be subject to change, because if I ponder on the fact that he might've killed my father for too long, you won't get the chance to kill him, not before I do. I'm out, big bruh. I'll holla tomorrow."

"Inshallah, Uck. Inshallah."

***

Zin answered the door, looking half asleep. She was dressed in a long t-shirt with Tweety Bird on it, her feet bare. She yawned twice before speaking. "I gotta give you a key, Quran, because I ain't gon be getting up in the wee hours of the morning to open the door for you. Come in."

Smiling, I entered Zin's condo and watched the shape of her ass bounce as she walked into the bedroom, after locking the door.

"And don't get no ideas because I'm tired as hell. If I do decide to give you some pussy, it'll have to be in the morning. Understood?"

I undressed quickly while nodding my head. "Understood."

Zin climbed in the bed and snuggled up onto her pillow. "Goodnight."

"Goodnight," I replied and spooned up against Zin's ass. I lifted the t-shirt until I could feel her soft skin. She wasn't wearing panties. My dick was hard on her ass. I reached out and rubbed Zin's ass cheeks before putting a finger inside her pussy. She stirred, but allowed my finger access and entrance. Zin's pussy got soaking wet in seconds. Growing bolder each minute, I positioned my dick between her cheeks and slid into her wetness.

"Quran, stop," Zin protested.

I ignored her pleas and did what I needed to do, made us both cum.

Chapter 7

Tomasina
Pope Funeral Home
District Heights, MD.
Saturday morning…

"Alone in a room/It's just me and you/I feel so lost/Cause I don't know what to do/Now what if I choose/The wrong thing to do/I'm so afraid, afraid of disappointing you/So I need to talk to you/And ask you for your guidance/Especially today, when my mind feels so cloudy/Guide me until I'm sure/I open up my heart/My hopes and dreams are fading fast/I'm all burned out and I don't think my strength's gonna last/So I'm crying out, crying out to you/Cause I know that you're the only one who's able to pull me through/So I know I need to talk to you…"

I couldn't control my tears from falling. Every time I wiped my eyes, they came right back. The woman on the dais singing the Yolanda Adams song had everybody crying and screaming. The mahogany wood casket that held one of my closest friends had just been closed. The viewing of Tosheka's body had been rough for me. I stood in the long, winding line that filed past the casket and couldn't believe how alive my girl looked. She appeared to only be sleeping, a sleeping beauty. Flowers and wreaths surrounded the casket. The pink and white dress that was on Tosheka was one of her favorites. A Christian Dior dress that Quran had purchased for her. My thoughts drifted as the preacher up front began to speak. They went back to the night that Tosheka was killed. We were on the phone together…

"I don't know what it is about that nigga. He's my kryptonite, Tom. I swear."

"Chile, please. Kryptonite. You felt the same way about Cat Eye Marcus when we were young. Just admit it, your crazy ass got a thing for pretty niggas with light eyes."

"And big dicks. Don't forget the dicks, bitch. I ain't gon lie, I loves me some fine niggas with nine inches or better, and lord knows both of them niggas fit the bill. Quran even more so, because that nigga holding a little over ten. I measured it while he was sleep one day. That shit was ten on the soft. And it's just something about him, Tom. His shit just hit different. That nigga shit hits a spot deep inside me that got me squirting and shit. My pussy don't do that for nobody but him. Touching my soul and shit. He just fuck the shit outta me. Got me walking bowlegged and shit. Hold on, girl, that's him on my other line. Nigga just left, he must wanna come back for another round, hold on." A couple minutes later, *"Let me hit you back, Tom. He left something in here. I'm about to run it outside to him."*

"A'ight, freaky ass. Hit me back."

Tosheka Cherelle Jenkins was preceded in death by her father, Charles Jr., and her brother, Shane, her maternal grandfather, Oliver Jenkins, and grandmother, Viola, her paternal grandparents, Charles Sr., and Mabel Norwood. Tosheka was born and raised in Southeast Washington, D.C. She attended Savoy Elementary, Douglas Jr. High and Balla High school. Tosheka was an avid volleyball player and member of the track team at the Barry Farms recreation center. She worked at several jobs throughout the city…"

***

"You going to the repast?" Bionca asked me.

"Naw, I gotta work this weekend," I replied as we filed out of the funeral home. "I'm sorry about all the losses you took recently, Bee, no bullshit. It can't be easy to maintain after all you and your family been through."

"I ain't gon lie and say that I'm good, Tom, because I'm not. But I gotta hold it together being the oldest surviving child. Losing two brothers to gun violence and my mother to a broken heart would break the average bitch, but I'm far from average, you know? I'm a ward Eight bitch. Raised in the projects, roaches and rats. All I know is struggle, heartache and pain."

"But it shouldn't be like that, though, girl. Nobody should have to go through the shit we got through. Either God don't exist, or he hates us. I'm convinced of that. Ain't no way no benevolent creator of the world gon sit back and just watch all this wild shit happening to us. As a little girl, I had to take a dope needle out of my father's arm, but he still OD'ed from a bad batch of dope. My mother got killed on High Street turning tricks for crack. My lil brother out here with more dicks in his mouth than me, hanging with a bunch of faggies. Talkin' about either you gotta check it or respect it. Shit fucked up. Look at what just happened to Tosh. Good girl, great heart, ain't never hurt nobody, never did shit wrong in her life, but fuck with the wrong niggas, and look what happened. One of these niggas out here gon shoot and kill that girl like that. Kill my muthafuckin' road dawg like that." My voice cracked and I almost broke down again, but I rebounded quickly, steadied my reserve. "I can't believe this shit," I said and wiped tears from my eyes. "My makeup fucked up, ain't it?"

Bionca smiled. "No more than mine is, Tom. No more than mine."

"I'm sorry, Bee, breaking down out here like this. Going off on God and all that shit. Don't pay me no mind, please. How are you holding up, girl? And don't give me the politically correct answer. Keep it gully with a real bitch. How are you, really?"

Tears welled up in Bionca's eyes and fell. "I'm fucked up, Tom. Real live. On the outside, I'm strong, but inside, I'm hollow. I'm tired of crying. I'm tired of hurting. I'm tired of saying that 'I'm good' when I'm not. I'm tired of saying goodbye. I can't sleep at all. I'm fucked up."

"Aaaww." I reached out and hugged Bionca. She broke down crying on my shoulder and I just let her cry. I held her tight and felt her pain.

Minutes later, Bionca recovered her composure and put her game face back on. "Damn, I needed that. I cried, but I haven't cried like that in a minute. I'm good now. Really. My brother Brion got cremated in a secret and private ceremony. So, that's out the way. And my mother's body is on the way to Sumter, South Carolina, where all my mother's family is. Brechelle went with her, and she's gonna stay there and live. Too many bad memories here. Brion's girlfriend is pregnant, so that's a blessing. He left behind a part of him."

"What are the police saying? Any leads on who killed either of your brothers? Do they think it was the same people? Are you in danger, girl?"

"I haven't talked to the police at all. My mother did, about Byron. Since she died, the police have reached out, I ain't talking to them. I believe in street justice, baby, good old fashion street justice."

"Street justice? Are you serious, Bee?"

"As a heart attack. I know who killed my brothers. The same nigga killed them both, and I ain't gon rest until I kill him."

"Bionca, girl, have you lost your mind? You ain't no fuckin' killer. Talkin' about' you ain't gon rest until you've kill somebody. I know you fucked up about Crud and Blast, but, oh, and Mama Love, but are you really gon be out here in these streets on your personal vendetta, kill niggas shit? I mean like, really?"

"I'm dead serious, Tom. you'd be surprised at the shit you can and will do if pushed hard enough. Killing is easy. Getting away with that killing is what's hard. But I plan on doing it anyway. You never wanted to kill the muthafucka that killed your brother back in the day?"

"On that note, I feel you a hundred percent. Look, just be careful out here, girl. Real talk. This shit is wicked out here," I said and smiled. "Street justice. I love it. Let me go. I'll be in touch, though, Bee, I promise." I hugged Bionca again.

"You take care of yourself, Tom. And hold on to the ones you love, you don't never know when they'll be taken from you," Bionca said, turned and left.

"Ain't that the truth," I muttered to myself as I walked to my car. Smiling to myself, I thought about how much alike Bionca and I were. We were on the same type of mission, and she just didn't know it.

Chapter 8

Bionca Clark
Temple Hills, MD

"How was it?"

"Sad as shit."

I followed Ren into her living room, sat on the couch and removed my heels. I put one foot in my lap and rubbed my toes.

Ren sat across from me on the loveseat with her laptop in her lap. She glanced over at me. "Nice heels. Love me some Red Bottoms. But you need to go get your feet done. Your shit looks crazy as hell. Polish all chipped off. Ratchet as hell."

"Girl, fuck my feet. I ain't bit more thinking about my feet than the men in the moon. Ain't nobody licking on these puppies, so they'll be alright til I get around to them. I know one thing, though, I'ma have corns and all that shit if I keep fucking with them pointed toe heels. Have you found anything else, yet?"

"Google search only turned up articles about his old case, the one he last had trial on in 1992. He killed some dude named Raymond Watson. I read all the newspaper articles from back then. All I could find out was that he has a daughter. One article said that she was a newborn when he lost in trial. So that makes her about twenty now. Couldn't find her name anywhere. I searched social media for any twenty-year-old woman's last name Branch and couldn't find none. Can't find nothing about no brothers or sisters, either. All I could find was that he was raised in Longdon Park but grew up in the Montera Avenue area. His father's name was Sean Branch, too. And the father, like the son, was a killer. He murder two people out of Maryland in Hyattsville, went to prison in Maryland and got stabbed to death at the prison he was in. Can't find nothing about his mother, or nobody else.

"What about Quran?"

"We already know where he hangs out at. Your girl that was killed told you that. His brother and his man all hang near Sheridan Road. Quran's never been to jail, it looks like. I can't find nothing on him. He doesn't do social media. There's no links to any name spelled Q-U-R-A-N. Are you sure he spells his name with a 'Q'?"

"Positive. Tosheka emphasized it. Said his name was spelled just like the Islamic book, the holy Quran."

"Well, it would help if we knew his last name. Did she ever tell you that?"

"Not that I can recall. I should've asked Tomasina if she knew anything about either one of them. That's what I should've did."

"Tomasina? Who's that?"

"One of my good girlfriends that I fuck with real heavy. Me, her and Tosheka go way back. We were cold blooded sluts back in the day, fucking in the gogo's and restaurant bathrooms, chasing all the hustlers. We were on some different shit back then. I ran into her today at the funeral. I never thought to ask her if she knew anything about Quran. I'll reach out to her tomorrow, try and see what she knows. Just keep looking. You'll uncover something sooner or later."

Ren put the laptop on the sofa and got up. She disappeared in one of the back rooms and then reappeared with a box in her hand.

"What's that?" I asked.

"A massager. A hot water, foot massager," Ren replied and pulled the massager out of the box. She plugged it into the wall nearest the couch I sat on. "I gotta fill it with water. And my special solution. After that, you gon put your feet in there for a while. When that's done, I'ma give you a pedicure. Just because we're grieving and planning murder, doesn't mean that you get to neglect yourself. What color polish do you want on your toes?"

I opened my eyes and really looked at Ren, noticed how truly beautiful she really was. Something stirred inside of me. Juices started to flow. I'd never been around Ren this much, ever, so she couldn't know about my affinity for women. "Uh, red. Red is always my go to color."

"Red it is, then. I'll be right back with everything to make the pedicure happen. I usually just do myself, so don't be expecting no salon experience up in here.

Ren was wearing Chanel slides and I couldn't help but notice how perfect her feet wore. Then she was gone. "Get your mind right." I cautioned myself. "She ain't for you. She's your dead brother's woman. Don't be awkward. And don't be transparent." Outwardly, I told myself all the right things, but inside, the inner voice spoke the truth.

"If she get to playing with your feet too good, try your hand."

"No. No. No," I said to myself and forced myself to think about something else. I thought about my desire for vengeance. I thought about killing Sean Branch.

Chapter 9
David Battle
Central Treatment facility (CTF)
1901 E St. S.E.

I slid Jihad's cell door open and walked into the cell. Jihad, dressed in uniform pants, a tank top and shower slides, was bent over the toilet, clearing it of water. He looked up at me as I walked in but continued what he was doing. "What the fuck was that on that lunch tray, slim?"

"Looked like some type of diced up lunch meat. I been over the jail almost 20 months and still haven't figured out what that shit is. I never eat that shit."

"Smart man."

"What's really good, Jay? I'm glad to see you, fucked up that you're in here, but glad to see you. I wanna know everything that y'all couldn't tell me over the phone, starting with Tabu and why the fuck he'd agree to fuck me around like that, ending with who the fuck killed Tosheka and why."

"After I get all of this water out of the toilet, so I can smoke, I'll tell you whatever you want to know. Roll some weed up while I do this."

I pulled out the small baggie of loud packs and rolling papers, then began to roll up. "You got honey or jelly?"

***

"To be honest with you, bruh, the only one that made sense to me was Tommy. You knew your cousin. He was a selfish, opportunistic muthafucka. I think he was already fuckin' with them people, slim. We read the paperwork, and he was too familiar with Gamble and 'nem. He must've caught a charge and started working. You saw the paperwork, right?"

"Yeah, I saw it. My lawyer brought me the papers. That shit fucked me up, slim. Bitch nigga cooked me to the grand jury like that. After all the shit we been through together, all the times I stopped niggas from getting on his ass, bailed him out of jams and broke bread with that nigga, he crossed me like it was nothing."

"If you cross me once, you'll cross me twice," Jihad said.

"I knew that my Aunt Betty would be fucked up, but slim had to go. Fuck him and the clothes they buried him in. He went against the code and paid the price."

Jihad laughed and passed the weed back to me. "That he did. That he did. We fucked him around something terrible, all face and neck shit. Same with Landa. Nobody could understand why she'd do what she did, though."

"I know why she did it," I told Jihad and finished the jay of weed, blowing the smoke down the cleaned out toilet bowl. Standing up, I dropped the last of the jay in the toilet and flushed it. The water returned to fill up the bowl quickly. Jihad got up off his knees and washed his hands in the sink. I did the same. "Me and Landa was fuckin' on the low. She caught feelings after seeing me with Tierra so much. She wanted me to change my life and be with her. I couldn't leave the streets alone. The day I crushed Manny, I was on Landa's porch arguing with her back and forth. Well, she was arguing, I was tryna fuck. That's where Tommy found me and told me that Manny was down the street. He knew that I was tryna see that nigga for what he did to Lil Marcus. When I walked back over to Landa, she knew what I was on."

"I heard about what Manny did to Marceles' lil brother. Everybody knows that that's your lil man. Don't do nothing stupid out there, Dave."

"That's the last thing she said to me before I stepped off and punished slim."

Jihad laughed out loud. "So, you think that Landa ratted you out because you wouldn't be her boyfriend?"

I nodded. "What other reason would she have to do that?"

"Get the fuck outta here with that lifetime movie shit."

Jihad's laughter was contagious. Laughing, I said, "Nigga, fuck you. My dick like that. Bitch couldn't have it so she didn't want nobody to have it."

"Nobody but a nigga out the feds who was on dick, huh?"

"Stop what you doing, slim. I'd cut my shit off before I give it to a faggie."

"Naw, though, real talk, bruh put her ass through a plate glass window. That forty fucked her life up. But the crazy part was how bruh tricked Mann and crushed him. After Landa's funeral, Mann was talking too reckless, wouldn't let it go. Every day, he talked about finding who killed his niece."

"Stupid ass nigga always talked too much."

"Bruh got right on his ass. Him and Tabu took him down Oak Park and flushed his ass. Threw him in the backseat, I mean, the trunk of a parked car and left his ass. Bruh told Tab that he really crushed Mann because he always tried to smoke all the weed."

Me and Jihad cracked up laughing at that.

Jihad's laughter stopped abruptly and he turned his head to the wall. He inhaled and exhaled a few times, then turned back to face me. "I can't tell you why my brother decided to do that shit, slim. He played the game with us and knew all the rules. Our father and Quran stressed the code to us, embedded in us. Why he agreed to tell on you is beyond me. Me or bruh couldn't figure it out. Right before he, before we found out, Tabu caught a gun charge and got locked up on

Southland Parkway. Park police pulled him over and found a gun in his car. He got held with a B1-A for a week because he was on probation."

"Probation? Fuck did Tab get on probation? For what charge?"

"He had caught an earlier gun charge and never told nobody. Me and bruh, none of us knew about it, not until he caught the second one. When he got out, five days later, I tried to talk to Tabu, but he brushed me off, made some feeble excuses about everything. He was my brother so, to me, he was above reproach, above suspicion of any real crime. I left his legal case alone. Bruh was so focused on Zin that he couldn't see past her pretty round ass. Then the paperwork showed up. The people disclosed it to Jen Wentz and 'nem. Zin got a hold of it and showed it to Quran. That was all she wrote after that. Bruh made the decision and carried out the execution. I ain't gon lie, slim, that shit fucked me up bad, real bad. Losing my lil brother was worse than when I lost my mother. I was only like seven or eight when I lost my father. I was too young to really understand that shit, him getting killed on our front porch like that. My mother dying of cancer fucked me up, but I was old enough to understand what happened. I'd watched her lose her hair, lose weight and really get sick. By the time she passed away, I was happy that her suffering was finally over. But Tab, Tabu's death fucked me around on a lot of levels. I ain't gon lie to you, slim, I'm still fucked up about that shit, mainly because I don't understand why he did it, why he agreed to rat when he knew that we kill rats. He and I killed rats together. Killing rats is the family creed. It's what we do. My father did it. All of his sons did it. Tabu knew that. So…"

"You didn't ask him before he died why he agreed to rat?"

Jihad shook his head. "Didn't get the chance to. Bruh got on his ass as soon as he read the grand jury statements implicating you in Manny's murder. He never gave me a chance to talk to Tab. I never saw him before it happened, after the paperwork confirmed his wickedness. I only saw him afterwards, after he was dead. Quran called me and told me what happened, where our brother was, where his body was. I went there and found him in the shape that bruh said he was in, way past dead. Shit broke my heart, slim. Seeing my lil brother hangin' from that pipe, eye popped out and bullet holes in his face. Still can't believe it. It's been almost 8 months and I still can't believe he's gone. Can't believe what he did."

"And he never said why he did it? Not even to Que before he was killed?"

Tears formed in Jihad's eyes and fell down his cheeks. He wiped them away. "Yeah. He told bruh that you were going to cross him."

"What?"

"You heard me. He told Quran that he ratted you out to keep you from crossing him. He said it several times, bruh said. That you were going to cross Quran."

The reality of those words hit me like a ton of cement fell on my head. How could Khitab have known? Who? When? "I'm glad that Que knew that that was bullshit. I'd never cross him. Never."

"He knows that," Jihad replied, got up and went to the sink. He ran the water and tossed it all over his face.

Khitab Bashir was dead and that fact visibly affected his brother Jihad, so it was time to move on from that subject. "What happened with you and Lil Bo?"

"My stupid ass was geekin' tryna flush this nigga name Baby E from Clay Terrance."

"Baby E? Eric Jones or Joyner or something like that. Getting a rack of money?"

"Yup. You hip to his wild ass?"

"Yeah. It's some good men over 1901 D Street that he cooking…"

"Was cooking. He's gone. We couldn't get him that night after the Bliss, but bruh caught him out Maryland somewhere.

Him and the nigga that shot me and Bo. Barbecued they asses. I'm fighting the joint at Benco Market. One of Baby E's men named Denico Autrey."

"I know slim. We was in YSC together. He got a brother in the feds named Vernon Autrey. They call him Big Vee. Damn. Denico killed Bo and shot you?"

Jihad nodded. "Killed my muthafuckin' man. Fucked me up."

"The whole hood's fucked up about that. Tierra told me…"

"Tierra? Nigga, you still fuckin' with Tierra's goofy ass?"

"Hey. That's my bitch, J. Don't catch these hands talkin' crazy about my bitch."

"A'ight, a'ight. I heard you were one of the sharpest niggas that ever boxed in Lorton. You got that."

"Last one. Tosheka. What the fuck happened to Tosh?"

Jihad leaned on the wall near the sink. He shook his head. "Long story, slim."

"We ain't got nothing but time, nigga. Talk."

***

"Why are you just calling me back? Lunch trays been served. You been on the phone with some other bitches, huh? Don't fuckin' play…"

"Tee, shut the fuck up," I spat into the phone. "I was in the cell with Jihad, choppin' it up about some street shit. We supposed to be locked down twenty-three hours a day, but the CO on duty fuck with me…"

"You got a CO bitch over there already?"

"Stop what you doing, Tee. You throwing me off with all this insecure shit. Do I do that shit to you? You out there stripping and fuckin' God knows who and I don't be on your line about none of that shit."

"You ain't on my line because you know me. This pussy ain't for everybody, unlike your ass. Community dick ass nigga…"

A call came through to the phone. I ignored the call. Seconds later, a text came in telling me that the caller was Quran. "Tee, Quran is calling me. I gotta take the call. I'ma hit you right back."

"A'ight. You better. Don't make me fuck you up, Dave."

"Yeah, whatever," I said and barged on Tierra. The call from Quran came back through. I answered the call. "What's up, big boy?"

"Ain't shit, slim. How you?"

"I'm good, slim, thanks to you. I really appreciate you, slim. Real talk."

"Slim, you already know how I do what I do. Enough said. What's up with lil bruh? He good?"

"Yeah, he gucci. Just left him. Had a session with him."

"That's what's up. You got the horn and the smoke I see. Did you get the package, too? The wet one?"

"Fuck, yeah," I exclaimed. "You did that muthafucka, slim. No bullshit. Babygirl is an animal. I'm gone off that joint. Whenever she comes through, I be all on the door goosing like shit. I'm a fuck around and be a jacker in a minute, a real fuckin' creep."

Quran laughed out loud, a raucous laugh that I hadn't heard in a while. "Naw, slim, don't do that. I'ma send them people's back your way in a minute. You know how long you gon be over there at CTF?"

"Naw, but I'm guessing until I heal up some more."

"A'ight. I'ma send some shit your way so that you can go back over the jail bowlegged. I got you, bruh. And just so you know, I got slim info, too."

"Who info you got?" I asked, confused.

"The dude that sent you over to the medical unit. Javon Jarrett. I'ma pay his folks a visit real soon."

"Say less, big boy. Say less."

"You already know what it is. You touch one of us, we all bleed. Be careful with the jack. Take the sim card out when you ain't using it. Get rid of it at the first sign of trouble. You feel me?"

"I feel you, homie. Say less."

"Good. Now, I gotta get back to my food and my woman. Love you, slim. I'm out."

Quran ended the call. I sat on the bed and thought about what Quran said about the dude who stabbed me. *'How in the hell did he find out the dude's name?'* I asked myself. But then I remembered that I had a cellphone, cigarettes, and weed in jail. And the fact that a beautiful female CO had fucked me. I smiled from ear to ear. Nothing about my situation surprised me. All things were possible through Quran Bashir.

Chapter 10
Zin
Oooh's and Aaah's
Restaurant on U Street
Northwest, D.C.

Those who fail to plan, plan to fail. But what if these best laid plans are suddenly short circuited by life's Qurants? The revelation that Quran didn't kill my mother was like the eight-ball falling in the corner pocket, and then the cue ball falling in after it. In the game of pool, you had to pull both balls out and shoot again after an opponent shot. On the second, you miss completely and lose the game. I sat at the table replaying several things Delores Samuels had told me, while eating. My father was solely responsible for my mother's demise. Michael Maurice Carter had destroyed my life and took my mother from me. Was the fact that life had taken him away enough punishment? Being in prison for the last seventeen years for a murder he didn't commit, was that penitence enough to balance the scales of justice?

I thought long and hard about that and decided that the answer was no. Prison for years was not enough to equal the penalty my mother had paid. Her price was she lost her life, not her freedom. My mother had not only lost her life and years living with the daughter she loved, she'd had to endure a brutal beating, rape, not to mention, the indignities associated with her body being tossed naked in the woods, tossed away like trash. My father, Dontay Samuels and

Quran. How was I supposed to feel about Quran now? Was I supposed to still hate him inside, while loving him outwardly? He was a fifteen-year-old teenager under the spell of a grown man, who ordered him to and fro. Was I supposed to still hold him accountable? That was the question that plagued me, the one that had the hardest answer to give.

As if on cue, Quran appeared in the room and headed my way. I looked at him, walking towards me, and couldn't take my eyes off of him. His swag was undeniable. He was like a cocksure cowboy, good with his gun and knew it. His whole aura was sexy. I was mesmerized and drunk with desire for him. A deep, dark, strong desire that I had never felt for any man before. I broke the spell of magnetism right before Quran sat down. I dug my fork into the sunny side up eggs sprinkled with cheddar cheese, then used the toast to soak up the egg yolk. I popped the toast into my mouth, wondering when I had ever craved half done eggs. It had to be the baby growing inside of me that wanted runny eggs, not me.

"Something I ate yesterday fucked my stomach up," Quran said and picked up his fork. He moved waffles around in the syrup before eating them. "Or was that too much information for you?"

"Too much information for me?" I repeated and laughed. "That you got bubble guts and had to take a shit in Oooh's and Aaah's bathroom? Boy, bye. I been in the bathroom while you shitted and fucked up my bathroom. I held your dick while you pissed before. And I know you remember the time you freed your dick in my ass, after I told you not to, and as a result of the pressure, shit got messy, literally. So I think we way past human nature being too much info. Besides, we are connected on every level, baby, so get used to it. You stuck with me, or shall I say stuck with *us*."

"Stuck with us? What's that supposed to mean?" Quran asked.

"Just what it says, stuck with us, me and the little life growing inside of me. I'm pregnant, Quran"

"Pregnant? Are you sure? When...?"

I studied Quran's face, his body language, for any signs of discomfort or anger. I saw none. Actually, he smiled that 1000-watt smile that I loved so much. "I'm sure. Found out yesterday from my doctor. That's why I'm eating these nasty ass egg yolk, runny eggs. The baby is making me eat that shit."

Quran stood up and came to me. He leaned down and hugged me tight. "Zin, baby, that's great news. Damn, baby, I can't believe it. I'm pregnant. I mean, you're pregnant."

"Quran, baby, please take it down," I said and looked around my arm. "You're embarrassing me. Sit down."

"Damn, my bad," Quran said and sat down. "Damn, damn, damn."

"Is that all you're gonna keep saying is damn?"

"Forgive me, baby girl, but I'm in shock, I think."

"Well, please, get out of shock."

"Okay, okay. I'm good now. I'm good?"

"Good. Because what did you think was gonna happen the way we be fucking and not using any protection? Wasn't using any since the very beginning.

"I'm hipped. I'm good with this, Zin. Straight up. I want this, need this. I've lost so much life and have taken so much life. I needed this to happen. I always wanted a little me, girl or boy. I don't know what else to say besides thank you. Thank you for all you mean to me, for all you've been to me. I'm a piece of shit, but you balance me, the right amount of estrogen to level out my testosterone. How far along, are you?"

"I'm not sure, yet. I'll have to go back to the doctor to find out. Can't be that for along because I'm not showing at all."

Quran reached under the table to feel my stomach. Then his hand invaded my skirt. He moved closer to me and let his fingers do the walking. Before long, they were inside my panties, probing, feeling, creating more wetness.

"Quran, stop."

"I can't, Zin. You know why? Because this is what I love about you, me finger fucking you in a crowded restaurant on a Saturday afternoon. You texting me to stop but you don't really want me to. I love everything about your bi-polar ass. You make anal sex sound dirty and disgusting, yet appealing. I wanna fuck you in your ass right now. You code switch with the best of 'em. Talking dirty and ghetto in one setting with a short skirt and fingers in your pussy and then you put on your business suits and heels and become a kick ass defense lawyer. I love that shit. My boxers are soaking wet with precum."

"You love that shit, huh, baby?" I said and put my hand under the table to rest on Quran's hand. "You wanna fuck me in my ass right now?"

Quran nodded, his eyes on mine.

"Show me how much you want it, too."

"Show you how?"

"Meet me in the ladies' room in five minutes."

I grabbed my raspberry iced tea and sipped it. I grabbed the fresh raspberry out of the glass by the stem and licked it, while Quran watched. Then I put it in my mouth. I got up from the table and sashayed across the room to the ladies room. Inside of the one and only stall, I removed my parties and used the wetness of my pussy to lube my tight ass. Minutes later, I heard the ladies room door open and close. I heard the lock click. The stall door opened and Quran was there. The look in his eyes was one of pure hunger. He pulled his jeans down as he entered the stall. His dick sprang loose like a freed animal.

"Let me suck it for a minute first," I told Quran and got on my knees. After sucking his dick for a minute or two, I stood up, turned, lifted my skirt and bent over the toilet. "Fuck my ass, Quran. Cum in my ass."

***

"It's starting to get nippy out here."

"Ain't nobody tell you to wear that lil ass skirt outside today."

"Bay, bye. You wasn't complaining in the restaurant when your hand was all up inside this lil ass skirt, or when it was hiked up over my ass in the bathroom stall."

Quran smiled. "Because my mind was on other shit. No pun intended."

I laughed at Quran's attempt at humor. "Boy, you dry as shit. But speaking of the bathroom stall, where are we walking to? My ass is sore as shit."

"Zin, don't tell me that you have never been to Tyson's Galleria?"

"I been to Tyson's 1, where Nordstrom's and Bloomingdale is, but never the Two. The Galleria was always out of my price range."

"Well, not anymore," Quran announced, as he grabbed my hand and led me into the mall.

***

After leaving the mall with bags on top of bags in each of our hands, I took Quran back to my place. I was horny as hell from the anal sex in public and ready to get my freak on. "Quran, I'ma go and take a shower, and when I come out, I'm tryna cum like twice. Can you handle that?

Quran smiled. "Just twice? I think I can do that for you, especially if you put on them garters and shit that you bought from that lingerie shop."

"Got you, brotha, I got you."

***

"Ooow..." I rubbed the soapy sponge between my butt cheeks and grimaced. My butt was really sore. "I'm a fuck around and get hemorrhoids fucking with Quran's big dick ass. Shaking my head, I couldn't even believe the woman I'd become in the last seven months. My life had changed drastically. It had to be fate that steered the course of my life to where it now was. Some type of cosmic force had put me and Quran on the same crash course to meet. I stood under the hot water, and convinced myself that everything that had happened so far, had been meant to happen. I'd been with Jermaine for six years and never felt as alive as I do now. After six years of unprotected sex with Jermaine, I'd never gotten pregnant, not even once. Seven months with Quran and here I was, carrying his child. There had to be an explanation for that and it had to be that Quran and I were meant to meet that day I ran into him on Dongles Place.

"Quran Bashir? How have you been?"
"Little Zinfandel Carter, it's been what? Ten years."
"Fifteen or so, and my name not Little Zinfandel anymore. Trust me, I'm all grown up."
"You all grown up, huh? Let me be the judge of that. Step out the car for a minute. You wasn't lying, baby girl. You are definitely all grown up"

From that day forward, I could never get him off my mind. I tried everything, to no avail. He was in my head. Always, I was with Jermaine sexually, and thinking about Quran. Then Quran kept showing up at different places where he knew I'd be. Him and his different colognes that I fell in love with. Then his brother Khitab got locked up and he called on me to represent him. That act was the beginning of it all. Next came dinner and getting reacquainted. After dinner, in a parking garage, things turned sexual. There and at the hotel later, suite 724, the things that happened in that suite were pornographic. For the first time in my life, I tasted cum, and even swallowed.

That's how things started. But sex wasn't what bonded me and Quran. That happened the night he killed his brother because he was a snitch, killed him and left him alone like he was nobody to him. If I was to leave Quran alone, it should have been then. But I couldn't. I was rushing head first into a tornado and didn't care how I ended up. I was addicted to everything him, everything Quran Bashir. And now I'm carrying his child.

"I'm pregnant by Quran," I said aloud, as if to wake myself from either a dream or a nightmare. Which was it?

I stepped from the shower and wrapped myself in a towel. I walked into the room to find Quran laid across my bed knocked out sleep. His light snores and handsome face made me smile. I was horny as hell, but sex would have to wait. While drying myself off, I heard Quran's cellphone vibrating. At first, I ignored it. But then it seemed to vibrate incessantly, getting up, I glanced at the phone. The screen read "Mike C. "How? Was the call? I picked up Quran's phone and swiped left to answer the call. My father's distinct voice said, "Hello? Que? YoungBoy? Hello?"

Quickly, I disconnected the call. I dropped the phone from my grasp as if it was suddenly poisonous. As I stared at it, it began to vibrate again. Again, the screen read "Mike C." I looked at Quran's sleeping figure, then back at the phone. How was my father able to call Quran without the computer prompt of the call being a federal prison call? The answer to my question came fast. The caller ID reading "Mike C" told the story. The number that my father called from was programmed in Q's phone. That meant the phone that my father called from was a personal one, a cellphone. My father had a cellphone in his cell, and he and Quran are in constant contact with one another. What could they possibly be discussing? How long have they been communicating with each other?

"I'm trying to understand something. Why didn't you tell me that you know my father? All this time we been fucking

71

around and you conveniently forget to mention that to me. Why?"

"I never thought it was that big a deal. Everybody who grew up in Berryfarms & Pork Chester and Sheridan Terrace knows your father. I assumed that you'd know that I knew him. That's why I never mentioned it."

"You assumed that I knew? How could I have known that?"

"Babygirl, slow your roll. You need to calm down. You coming all up in here ranting and raving 'bout nothing. What the fuck difference does it make if I know your father or not? What does that have to do with us? Did your father tell you something about me?"

What was Quran and my father hiding? Why keep their continued friendship a secret from me? My father was always lying to me, and so was Quran. Why? Did they both fear that the lawyer in me would ask too many questions? Or would their relationship, if known, reveal too many secrets?

I sat on the bed and rubbed lotion onto my skin, all the while wondering what my father's call to Quran could have been about. I wondered when was the last time he'd called me. Had to be at least a week or so, and all we talked about was the pending motion and the upcoming evidentiary hearing. Maybe he wanted to discuss the same thing with Quran. But if so, why? What did Quran have to do with Maryann Settles? He had to have come in contact with her over two years. Maryann was from Steriden Terrace, just like Owen was. Was he the person who had convinced her to come forward and free my father? I looked down into Quran's sleeping face. Suddenly, I had the urge to reach out and slap the shit out of him, for no other reason but making me have to wonder.

"I don't know your father personally."

You lying motherfucker. Every other word you spoke was a lie.

Chapter 11
Quran

When I next opened my eyes, it was dark outside. Zin laid next to me asleep, curled up in the fetal position. I lifted the blanket and saw that the only thing she wore was a platinum ankle bracelet on her ankle. Smiling to myself, II was about to wake her with a tongue in her soft ass, but my cell phone vibrated. I looked on the bed where I had left it, and it was gone. Light from the outside illuminated the room enough for me to clearly see. My phone vibrated. I followed the sound of the vibrating and discovered my phone on the floor. Zin must've moved it. I picked up the phone and saw that the caller was Sean.

"Assalaamu Alaikum."

"Waldikom assalaam. What's good with you?" Sean asked.

"I'm good, ock, was just sleeping, that's all. What's up with you?"

"Don't nothing come to a sleeper but a dream, and right now ain't the time to be dreaming. Niggas want our ass and we want theirs, so I'm ready to feast. You ready to eat?"

"Always," I replied and wiped sleep from my eyes.

"Good. You know where the 7-11 is on Division Avenue and Sherrif Road?"

"By Nook's Barbershop, 52nd and Sherif?"

"Exactly. Meet me there in like twenty minutes. I'm out," Sean said and ended the call.

I got up and went to take a quick shower. After that, I dressed in dark clothes, without waking Zin. Lastly, I put on black Nike ACG boots, grabbed my phone and a Moncler ski vest and put it on. I' kissed Zin on the lips and left.

***

From the 7-Eleven, I followed Sean to a small street off of Division Avenue, named Just Street. Sean exited the Jeep he was driving and popped the rear door. I walked over to the rear of the Jeep. Sean passed me a vest.

"It's the newest one out, lightweight and durable, capable of stopping a .762 and any other chopper bullet and laugh while doing it. Handguns ain't got shit coming with this bitch. She'll stop a four-fifty bullet and laugh while doing it. From now on, we wear these. Put it on."

I put on the vest, and after taking off my hoodie and ski vest, it didn't appear that I had anything on under my clothes. "Now what?"

"Now, we go and get Tony. He's gambling on 58th Street right now. Only a few blocks away from here. I got a man out there who's intentionally losing money to him. C'mon."

Once inside the Jeep, I asked Sean, "What about Rodney? Got a line on him yet?"

"Not yet, but I'm on his ass. You already know."

"Zin's pregnant."

"What?"

"You heard me. Zin's pregnant," I repeated to Sean.

Sean whistled. "Shit just got real, huh? Is she gonna keep it?"

"I think so. She ain't never said nothing about not keeping it."

"I guess that congratulations are in order. Having a kid can be a gift and a curse? Welcome to the curse."

"Gift and a curse? Explain that, slim."

"A gift because you did something that a lot of muthafuckas can't do. You fulfilled your delegation as a man. Your covenant to Allah to be fruitful and multiply."

I couldn't help but laugh. "Stop what you're doing, old head. That's some Bible Christian shit."

"You shittin' me. It's in the Quran, too."

"Where? What Surat?"

"I ain't sure, but it's in there. Having a kid, a child that looks like you, ain't no better gift for a man, especially for man like us, men who live by the gun and can be killed at any moment. If we die, we leave behind a piece of us that lives on, someone to know that you lived, that you were here. The curse comes in because, through that child, niggas can find a way to hurt you, to trap you, to kill you. I got a man, a good man, who I was in the joint with, named Ameen. He had two daughters that he loved with all his heart. Some young nigga just killed one of em, his oldest daughter. They killed her boyfriend first, then killed Ameen's daughter as she left the funeral. Sound familiar."

I nodded my head.

"If word gets out that you got a kid in these streets, you now have a certified weakness, Que. Get it?"

"I get it, okay."

"Good. I'm really happy for you and shorty, but never let the impending birth of your first seed dull your impulses. Never let it make you lower your shield. Always keep your edge, youngin. Always. It's great being a father, but never forget who you really are."

"Who? A Muslim?"

"No. A Killer."

As the Jeep drove slowly up 58th Street, I thought about everything Sean said. He was right. Having a child, children, made parents accessible. Vulnerable. Having three sons made Ameen Bashir vulnerable. Having Zin made Mike Carter vulnerable, just like having a child would also make me.

"You gon tell Mike Carter that he's about to be a grandfather?" Sean asked, breaking the silence in the truck.

"Why should I? If he makes it home, he ain't gon' live long enough to see the kid, right?"

Sean pulled the Jeep over on Blaine Street, from there we could see the large crap game in progress. "

"Good point, youngin," he said suddenly. "Good point."

***

"I can see Tony from here. He's kneeling in the circle. He's there shooting the dice right now," Sean said as we crouched in the bushes beside the building.

"So, how you wanna play this, big boy? Straight at Tony or act like we sticking the game up?"

Sean pulled out a nylon mask and put it over his head and face. "Everything about me is straight forward." Sean chambered a round into the ARP, to get it ready. "You ever heard the saying about the two bulls at the top of the mountain?"

"Two bulls on a mountain? Nah, why?"

"Because it's a good saying to know. Might love to teach it to your son one day."

"Or daughter."

"Yeah, or daughter. The young bull told the older bull, 'Let's run down there and fuck one of them cows down in the Valley.' The older bull responded, 'No, son, let's walk down there and fuck them all.' Make sense to you?"

I shook my head. "Naw, not really," I answered honestly.

Sean laughed out loud. "I'm going straight at Tony. If anybody get in the way, I'ma down 'em. You go around the other way. On my signal, look for my hand to drop, come out and watch my back. If anybody reach, crush their ass. You got a mask?"

My answer to Sean's question was to pull my hood up over my head.

"A'ight, go. Peek out from the other side when you get there."

I walked off into the night behind the building. I thought about Zin at the condo, still asleep. I thought about our baby growing inside her stomach. I thought about all those missed calls I'd had from Mike Carter. I thought about my life in an instant. I thought about all the killing and asked myself when I was gonna change my life. No answer came. I pulled both of my guns as I reached the side wall of the building. I peeked out from behind the building, until I could see Sean's masked face. Then I saw his signal. I ran into the night.

Chapter 12
Sean Branch

Anthony "Tony" Fortune was mixed with something other than Black. Like myself, he had a head full of thick curly hair and killer instincts. But unlike me, he was in no shape. Peeping the ambush, Tony took off running past me, as I fired the ARP. I got right on his ass as he headed toward Dix Street. He pulled a gun and fired behind him as he ran. I paid that shit no mind as I ran his ass down. Years of freedom, drinking, drugging and gambling had made Tony soft and slow. A couple feet behind him, I stopped, planted my feet and aired his ass out with the ARP. .223 bullets tattooed his body and dropped him. I walked up on him and finished him off. Just fast as I turned to go back the way I came, the Jeep pulled up with Quran behind the wheel.

"Let's go!" Quran shouted from the Jeep.

I ran to the truck and hopped in the passenger seat.

***

5200 block of Just Street
Northeast, D.C.

"Rodney probably knows by now about Tony. He's either gonna fall back or come after us hard." I told Quran as he leaned on his car. "I'ma ride through Clay Terrace and Lincoln Heights to see if I see him. What you about to do?"

"Go back to Zin's house and chill with her. Tomorrow, I got a few people to see. So, I'ma get some rest."

"People to see or people to kill?"

Quran smiled. "People that ain't gon make it into next week."

"Respect. Just be careful, youngin. Then I got to pick up Shontay and take her to Liv's joint to spend the night with us. Hit me tomorrow, Insha Allah."

"Insha allah. Assalamu Alaikum."

"Walaikum assalaam."

***

There were pockets of people outside on 53rd street, but none of them was Rodney. After Spinning the bend all over Clay Terrace, I gave up my hope of finding Rodney Shaw. Knowing how relentless I am and how dangerous I can be, it wasn't realistic for me to think that Rodney was outside, where I could pluck his feathers. I glanced at my watch and knew I had a little while before I had to pick up my daughter from work. I needed to toss the ARP, but I didn't want to do it just anywhere. I took Benning Road straight at to Bluden-Read and turned on to it. I took Bladensburg Road to New York Avenue, New York to Montana Ave. I recognize a few dudes congregating on the corner near Brentwood. Pulling over, I hit the horn. My partner, Rico Thomas' little brother, Rebo, walked over to the Jeep.

"Sean, what's up, big homie?" Rebo asked.

"Get in," I told him.

I drove through the neighborhood and headed for Langdon Park. You see that ARP under the seat you're in?

Rebo reached under the seat and pulled out the AR pistol. "Got damn, slim. This joint is a bad motherfucker."

"You like it, youngin?"

Rebo eyed the weapon and nodded his head.

"Take it. It's yours. It's hot, so be cautious with it, and don't tell nobody where you got it from."

"You already know how I get down, big homie."

"Where they got Rico at the feds?"

"He's in the FCI. Um… Petersburg."

"Where Ope O at?" I asked.

"I don't know. You gotta ask Raven."

"Listen, slim. I need you to look out for Moe Best for me. Whenever you see him, call me. Put my number in your phone."

Rebo pulled out an iPhone and put my number in. "Got you, big homie. When I see Moe Best call you. What's up though? He in violation? If so, I'll…"

"I'm good, youngin. Just get at me as soon as you see him stationary somewhere."

"Say no more. Got you. Damn, slim, this ARP a mean motherfucker. How many clips it hold?"

"Sixty, unless it's modified."

"Bad motherfucker," Rebo repeated, and rubbed the ARP.

I drove Rebo back to the spot where I picked him up from. "Cuff that joint and put it up."

"I'm on it."

"Give Miss Janice, Raven, and Bird my love."

"No doubt. One love, big homie."

"One love."

***

Shontay walked out of the Chipotle near Galleria PlayStation, still wearing her work uniform. In her hand were several plates, bags that were sure to contain food. Shontay opened the back passenger door and put the bags in the Jeep. Then she climbed into the front passenger seat. She leaned over and hugged me.

"Hey, Dad," Shontay said, then pulled at hair on her face. "Your beard is getting too long. Hairs and stuff getting all in my mouth when I hug you."

"Respect my beard, baby girl. It's a part of the religion."

"I know, I know." Shontay put her seat belt on." I gotta get a better job."

"Took the words right out of my mouth. This Chipotle is ghetto as shit. They got dope fiends and K2 heads hanging out, in and around this joint. One day somebody gonna say or do some wild shit to you and I'm gonna kill everybody in the neighborhood," I said as I pulled off onto 7th St.

Shontay laughed. "Dad, please chill out. You always doing too much?"

"Ain't doing shit, yet. And you need your own car. Got me all around these wild ass neighborhoods. It's full of trannies, faggies and…"

"Dad, please. Stop what you're doing."

"I'm dead serious."

"I know you are, and that's the problem," Shontay raved. "But I do need my own car, though. Then I could drive myself home every night."

"Sounds like you got a problem, then. Huh?"

"No, Dad, *we* got a problem. I'm your only daughter, I hope, and that's what fathers are for – to help their children in times of need. And this is my time of need."

I laughed. "You been working at fast food joints since you were fifteen years old. You're about to turn twenty, and you're broke as shit – that's a damn shame."

"Well, maybe if my father had been at home instead of in jail I wouldn't have had to start work so young. What do you have to say to that?"

"You had your mom and all of those niggas she was fuckin with over the years. You should've been straight."

"There you go, Dad, doing too much again."

"Naw, that's called *saying too much*, but I really meant it."

***

"Please, Sean, don't do this to me," Raquel screamed.

"Bitch, I dreamed about this day for almost 18 years."

Raquel Dunn, my daughter's mother lay in the trunk of the car, bound with rope. She struggled to free herself, but her attempts proved futile. I grabbed Raquel and lifted her out of the trunk. Her body hit the ground with a thud.

"Sean, stop this. Stop it. Please, don't kill me."

"Don't kill you?" I laughed to myself. "Oh, now it's don't kill you, huh? What happened to all that slick shit you talked over the phone, all them years ago? Huh? What happened to all the tough shit, Raq? All the gangster shit you talked? Remember when you told me to go and fuck my celly and suck his dick? Remember when you told me that I was gonna die in jail? You said you hoped somebody killed me in prison. Remember that one? Remember all the missed visiting dates, when I just wanted to see my daughter? You had that...a rack of different Niggas l around my daughter. Remember when you had Shontay calling one of them niggas Daddy? Remember that?"

"Sean, please, baby, I'm sorry. I'm sorry!"

"Ohh, now you sorry, huh?"

"Sean. I was. I was mad at you. I was hurt. I wasn't in my right mind back then. I never meant any of that shit I said to you. On my grandmother's grave, I didn't. You gotta believe me. Please, Sean. Please don't kill me."

"Don't beg, Raq. That shit ain't a great look. You gotta stand on all that shit you said it to me over there years. Be a woman and stand on your words. I told you, I promise you, that one day I was gonna come back home and make you eat your words. Well, today's that day, Raq, and you can. And know that it's not just you who's gonna die. Eric Kay. Moe Brooks, and all the rest of them niggas you fucked with are

going to die soon, too. So, you won't be alone in the grave tonight."

"Sean, I know. Noooo, don't do this."

Tiring of the back and forth, I pulled out the knife I purchased at the Asian market off of Florida Ave. in Northeast. Raquel, sensing that the end was near, started screaming and squirming against her restraints. I positioned myself behind her, But still over her. I grabbed her hair and pulled her head back. With my other hand, I viciously drew the knife across her neck, almost decapitating her. Blood poured from the deep laceration on her neck onto the ground. Raquel was dead in seconds. Her body slumped lifelessly forward. I turned her onto her back and rolled the knife through her, severing the fabric, with one' swipe. Then, like a butcher, I started at her breast and sliced straight down the middle of 'Raquel's pelvis. Her intestines spilled out. I stood over her and stabbed her in both eyes.

"Stupid bitch. You won't need eyes in hell because in life you were blind to the fact that you shouldn't cross a real, natural born killer."

After spitting on Raquel's body, I dragged her to the water and threw her into the river.

"Baby."

"Huh," I said, and turned to face Liv.

"What's up, baby? I don't know where your head be at sometimes. Did you hear anything I just said?" Olivia Santos asked.

"Yeah, you were saying something about Erykah Badu coming to Constitution Hall in the spring."

"Boy, that was twenty minutes ago."

I looked around the living room. "Where did Shontay go?"

"She was tired, decided to go shower, and then hit the sack. Are you ok?"

"Yeah, I'm good. I was just thinking about something she said to me in the car earlier, when I picked her up."

"Something I need to know about?"

Shaking my head, I said. "No. Wasn't nothing important, it just made me think about something in the past. I think I need a shower myself. You wanna join me?"

"Don't mind if I do. Come on, let's go."

***

The next morning...

"Dad, you love Virginia, don't you?" Shontay asked. "Where are you taking me to now? We could have gotten breakfast from somewhere in the city. Tony's on Grand Hope Road would have been great."

"You can take the girl out of the hood, but you never get the hood out of the girl. Just chill out, like you always tell me. We're gonna get breakfast."

"It's after noon, so it's more like brunch," 'Liv added.

"Well, brunch, then. I got a stop to make. After that, we can eat wherever you want."

Minutes later, I pulled the car into Alex's lot in Springfield, Virginia. Alex walked out to greet me an soon as I exited the car.

"Assalaam Alaikum, ocki," Alex said.

"Walaikum Assalam," I replied.

"Your Porsche is ready, and so is the other vehicle you requested. Shall I have my people go get them?"

I nodded. "Yeah, do that for me."

"Did you bring the money for the…"

Turning and walking back to the Mercedes, I popped the trunk and removed a bag. Inside the bag was fifty thousand cash, courtesy of Kenneth Sparrow. I walked back to Alex and gave him the bag of money. "It's all there. I'll do the paperwork later. Get the cars."

Alex spoke in rapid Arabic to two men, who had walked out the office. Both men left quickly. Ten minutes later, two cars appeared and stopped near the Benz. One was my

Porsche the other a candy apple red Infinity M Series sedan. Both cars were fitted with sixty-day paper tags. The two men exited the cars and gave the keys to Alex. Alex, in turn, walked over and handed the keys to me.

I tapped the roof of the Benz to get Shontay's attention. She climbed from the Benz's backseat with her phone in hand.

"Yeah Dad?" Shontay asked, as she looked up from the phone.

I handed her the keys to the Infinity. "Here you go, baby girl. Hope you like it."

Shontay turned to face the Infinity. She screamed, then covered her mouth. Tears came to her eyes. "Are you serious, Dad? This is mine?"

"It's yours, baby girl. You deserve it. Bought and paid for."

Shontay rushed me and hugged me tight. Her tears stained my coat.

***

On the way to D.C., a call came through to my phone. It was Liv.

"What's up, baby?"

"I love what you did for Shontay, baby. That was nice."

"I went to jail when she was seventeen months old. I owe her that and lot more."

"Well, I was so touched by her tears and your gift to her that now I feel like I owe you something."

"Is that right?"

"Yeah, that's right, and I'ma pay up as soon as I get you home later on."

"I'ma hold you to that."

"Is she still behind you in her car?"

"Yes. Do me a favor. Call her and tell her we're going to Tony's. I gotta call Quran."

"Aight, baby, love you," Liv responded and ended the call.

I dialed 'Quran's cell phone. He answered on the second ring.

"As salaam Alakum, What's up, old head?"

"You. What's good with you, youngin?"

"Ain't shit. I'm about to see a dog about a cat, feel me? "

"By all means. Be safe and holla at me later."

"I will, ok, later."

Tossing the phone into the passenger seat, I thought again about the day I killed Shontay's mother.

Chapter 13
Zin
Whole Food Grocery
H Street Corridor
Northeast, D.C.

"I'm thinking about switching my diet?" I informed my aunt Linda whose grocery cart was filed up already and we hadn't been in the grocery store for fifteen minutes, yet. "To a more plant based one."

Linda Carter dismissed me with a wave of her perfectly manicured had. "Chile, please, ain't nobody getting healthier off that shit. Them big companies engineered all that plant-based shit to attract vegetarians to their products. Partnering with fast food chains to offer plant-based Whoppers and shit. Don't f don't fall for the okey-doke, girlfriend. Besides, red meat and poultry look like it has done your body good to me. Thick and pretty as your ass is, glowing and shit, and if it ain't broken, don't fix it, a wise old black man always said."

I laughed at Aunt Linda. "Wise old black man, huh? Where he at now?"

Aunt Linda opened the refrigerator's glass case and removed frozen vegetables. "Dead, I assume, but he was wise. Why all the talk about changin' diets?"

"Because I'm eating for two, Auntie. I'm pregnant."

"Yeah right, and I'm flying to the moon in a week."

"Bon voyage, then."

My aunt stopped in her tracks and looked me up and down. "Are you serious? You're really pregnant?"

I nodded my head. "Found out a couple days ago."

"So, when is the abortion date? I'll go with you."

"There is no abortion date, Auntie. I'm keeping the baby."

"But, Zin, why would you do that? Baby, your career is just getting started, really. Your private practice is taking off. Now is not the time to be having a baby?"

"Auntie, reverse our roles for a second. What if I were you thirty years ago, and you were me, and I told you what you're telling me now. Would you have listened?"

Linda Carter's eyes dropped. When she looked up they were watery. "I always wanted children, Zin, you know that. But it wasn't a part of God's plan."

"My point exactly, Auntie. This baby is part of God's plan, and I have no right to kill it. Would you have gotten an abortion had you gotten pregnant?"

My aunt wiped tears from her eyes, then came next to me and hugged me. After a long, warm embrace, she disengaged. "Over the lawyer, huh?"

"It's who I am, baby, deal with it?" I replied and smiled.

"I guess I have no choice, Zin. I'm happy for you. I want what you want. And you were right to check your dear old auntie. Talking mess, knowing good and got damn well that it's time for another addition to the Carter family. Oh my gawd, now I'm excited. I'm gonna spoil her to death."

"Her? Wait a minute, who said anything about this baby being a girl? "

"It will. Watch what I tell you," Aunt Linda said and pushed her cart. "And she'll be beautiful and healthy, and we'll call her Zindaya."

As I followed my aunt into the next aisle, I listened to her talk and all I could do was laugh. This woman was really crazy.

Jongro Korean BBQ
Wheaton, MD
An hour later…

Sitting across from my aunt inside the Korean restaurant, I watched an Asian man light a gas burning grill that was buried inside the table between us. Two larger cut ribeye steaks, with rives of fat running through their ruby red muscles, sat atop the metal grade. Not a speck of seasoning on either. Our server dropped the meats on the grate, turned the heat up high, and then left us to our own devices. The Korean barbecue spot was attached to the Westfield Wheaton mall. It was a place that my aunt often raved about.

"This place is the first outside of New York City. They have a second location planned for Annapolis, expected to open in May," Aunt Linda told me. Shallow metal bowls formed a semi-circle next to the grill. "This is pickled radishes, cabbage kimchi, seasoned bean sprouts, cucumbers and jalapeño pickles. And these side sauces are for the meats. Zin, chile, these are scrumptious. Wait until you dip steak into any one of them, you gonna love it."

"I sure hope so, Auntie. You know that I'm a simple girl. We could've went to the MLK deli and got sandwiches," I replied. "Or some carryout food."

"Zin, hush. This is not a 'half of steak with cheese and French fry' moment. We are celebrating the life of a Carter woman inception. That calls for expensive Korean barbecue, not General Tao chicken wings and fried rice. You gotta broaden your horizons, chile, for the baby, my grandniece. Wait, is it grandniece or great niece?"

"I have no clue," I said, and sipped water from my cup.

"You haven't said it but I'm assuming that the baby's father is Quran Bashir."

"Your assumption would be correct."

"Have you told your father about any of this?"

Shaking my head, I responded, "No, I haven't. Have you?"

Aunt Linda's expression on her face answered my question before her mouth could.

"You told him? About me and Quran?"

"Inadvertently, Zin. He was concerned about you. Said something about you acting strange on y'all last visit. Said you asked a lot of questions that threw him off. He wanted to know if you were okay. I told him that you seemed fine to me, and that you were looking for a new place."

"So, this call happened months ago? And you never told me?"

"Zin, listen, don't' turn this into an interrogation, or something that it's not. I had a conversation with your father, my brother, about you. How was I supposed to know that you don't' share anything about your personal life with him?"

"What do you mean? I do share."

"Well, I can't tell. He 'didn't know anything about your breakup with Jermaine and the fact that you had moved back in with me."

"You told my father about Jermaine and Jennifer Wentz, didn't you?"

A guilty look crossed Aunt Linda's face. Then one of the contrition. "He asked me what happened and I told him, yes. Damn, Zin, I didn't know that we were keeping secrets. Were we keeping secrets?"

I dropped my head and shook it. "No, auntie, we weren't keeping secrets. I just would have liked to have told my father my truth when I was ready to, not when you were."

"Zin, I'm sorry."

"Auntie, *Sorry* is a board game made by Milton Bradley, remember?"

"Well, it's true. And I guess that's when you told him about me and Quran?"

"Somewhere about right there, I guess. I was telling him how, to me, you were living your best life and that you were happy with a new man. That's when I think I said something about that fine ass grey eyed boy and your father picked up on it. He made me clarify who I meant, and I told him that you were dating Ameen Bashir's son, and that's it."

Hearing my aunt so casually mention Quran's father brought back snippets of the conversation I'd' had on Friday with Delores Samuels.

"How Ameen Bashir got to Patricia..."

"Ameen Bashir? Back then? Before my father?"

"Yes, Ameen came before Michael. He was every bit of eighteen years old and the most sought-after dude in the hood but he wanted Patricia."

"Okay, then, the cat is out the bag," I said acceptingly. "And before I ask you something else, tell me what my father's response was to your revelation about me and Quran."

"His response? He didn't' have one."

"He didn't say anything?"

"Nope, he changed the subject."

The Asian server returned to our table and pulled the steaks off the grated grill. He seasoned them and sat them on the two plates. One plate he sat in front of me, the other in front of Aunt Linda. He turned to a nearby cart and got other plates.

"Here's the Korean fried chicken you requested, the seafood pancake, your soy garlic chicken, the spicy pork bulgogi, and your favorite yum-yum sauce. I hadn't noticed how hungry I was until my stomach flipped at the sight of the food. I grabbed my knife and fork and cut into the steak. I popped a piece into my mouth and chewed it. Damn, this steak is good."

"I told you. Wait until you try the Korean fried chicken and the spicy pork."

"Uh, hold the pork, auntie. Quran would die if he even knew I was seated at a table where pork is on the plate."

"Quran, not here, chile. You haven't lived until you've tasted this pork."

"Thanks, but no thanks. I'll pass, auntie. But back to what we were saying. You told Michael Carter that his daughter was dating the son of his murdered best friend and he said nothing?"

"Not a syllable. I swear it."

"That's odd, considering that fact that him and Quran are friends and they've both tried to hide that from me."

Suddenly, my aunt's eyes were fixated on her food.

"The day that Quran came to your house to see me and I introduced the two of you, did you know then that Quran and my father were friends?"

Linda Carter forked Korean fried chicken into her mouth. "Did you hear what I said earlier about being interrogated? Usually, I'd stick to my guns, but since 'you're with child, I will oblige your sudden curiosity. I have been a workaholic all my life Zin, you know that. Being a workaholic keeps me out of other folk's business and I prefer it like that. My brothers, Kevin and Kirk, were different from Mike. I was never really close to them. Kevin died in prison, and Kirk was killed because he snitched on someone in a murder case. Mike was always heavily in the streets, and he did his best to shield his only sister from that life. I appreciated that. Still do. Did I know that he had, or has a relationship with Ameen Bashir's son? I have always heard things, Zin, rumors, nothing I could confirm. Why? Because I'm what?"

"A workaholic, by choice."

"Right, there were rumors about Mike recruiting Ameen Bashir's son to do the work that their father did for him. The streets talked of the young boy killer with light grey eyed. Efficient, ruthless, dangerous just like his father once was. I have always heard the rumor, Zin. So how do I answer your question to your satisfaction? Did I know they were friends? No. Connected together? Yes. Still connected? Definitely not. Why do you ask, though? Why is any of that important?"

"It's important because they made it important, by not disclosing their friendship, or connection as you call it. It seems suspicious. When I ask my father certain things, he lies to my face. Quran does the same thing. Quran lied about even knowing my father. Now why would he do that? I keep asking myself."

"Have you asked Quran that question?"

"No."

"Why not?"

"Because, he's only going to lie to me. Yesterday, I saw a call come through on Quran's phone. The number was programmed in and the initials for the contact were MC. I answered the call, and guess who it was?"

"Your father."

I nodded. "This isn't an integration, but did you know that my father has a cellphone in prison?"

"Zin," Aunt Linda said exasperated. "Where are you going with this?"

"Auntie, did you know it? Yes or no?"

"I knew that Mike had— *has* a cellphone in jail. Yes. But I still don't understand why that matters."

"It matters because he's my father. I'm out here fighting for his freedom and he didn't think it was a good idea to let me in on the fact that he could talk to me on a phone other than the jail phone that is always monitored or recorded? What the fuck kind of shit is that, Auntie."

"Has your hormonal shift from that pregnancy caused you to lose our fucking mind, honeybun? Who the fuck do you think you're talking to like that? Cursing and shit. I have no clue as to why Mike didn't tell you about his cellphone. Hell, I thought you knew. I don't know why he's lying about his connection, or whatever you call it, to Ameen's son."

"Do you know a woman named Delores Samuels?

"Delores Samuels? Yes, I know her. Her mother raised your mother after your grandmother died. Her family is from Sayles Place. She's older than me, but we all came up in Sheridan Terrace. Why?"

"Because I met her recently and had a long talk with her."

"About what?" Aunt Linda asked.

"About the past."

"Whatever that junkie bitch told you is a lie. Mike is in jail for killing her son and she's still fucked up about it."

"My father didn't kill her son Dontay. She knows that."

"Oh, she's read the affidavit from Maryann Settles?"

"Nope, she hasn't. She doesn't know anything about the affidavit. She told me who killed her son, and who witnesses watched kill her son, and it wasn't Dad."

Linda Carter calmly pushed her plate aside and in a low moaning voice, she said, "Zin, you are starting to piss me the fuck off. I don't' know what Delores' crackhead ass told you, or what you think you know but…"

Seething inside, outwardly, I smiled. I went into my purse and pulled out my mother's letter. I passed it to my aunt.

My aunt unfolded the papers and read them. Silently, I ate the rest of the steak and some of the soy chicken.

The next sound I heard was as if the air had been let out of a tire. My aunt's body sagged with the weight of knowing that I knew. "Where, where did you get this?"

"It was inside one of the two boxes that I had in storage, one of the boxes that contained my mother's things."

"This can't be. Zin, you can't possibly believe…"

"Which part, auntie?"

"What?"

"Which part can't I believe? The part about my mother having an affair with Ameen Bashir? The part about my father catching them in the act one night, and him killing Ameen Bashir because of it? The part where my mother predicts her own death? Or the part where she accuses Quran, Dontay and my father of being the people who were going to kill her?"

"My brother, your father, didn't kill your mother," Auntie Linda hissed in a low voice across the table. She folded the letter and passed it back to me. "Mike didn't do what she suspected he would do."

"If not, who did, auntie?"

"Maybe you should be asking your baby daddy that question."

"I will, in due time. Did you know about the affair?"

"Between Patricia and Ameen Bashir?" Auntie Linda said, and I nodded. "Everybody in the neighborhood knew about it. Everybody except Mike."

"So, that part is true. Did you know that my father killed Ameen?"

"Speculation and rumors, never proven."

"But, you did know about it, though?"

"Am I on trial, here?"

"Of course not."

"Well, stop acting like it then. Sometimes the past needs to stay just that— the past. I don't want to talk about any of this. Today was supposed to be a great day, with us spending quality time together. Let's not spoil it further. Are you still up for shopping and a movie?"

"Yes, auntie, I am. Sorry for almost spoiling the day."

"*Sorry is aboard game made by Milton Bradley,*" Aunt Linda smiled. "How do you like the Korean fried chicken?"

Chapter 14
Quran

"I'm ready to see you. You ready for me?"

"I stay ready, pretty boy."

"That's what's up. I apologize for the delay. I couldn't get into you yesterday, like I said. Had some personal shit I needed to deal with. I got the fifty for you, though."

Kendra Dyson laughed on the other end of the phone. "Right game, wrong lane, Pretty Boy. You need sixty of you want twenty of 'em. I told you before, no exceptions. "

"Had to try it out. When and where?"

"Public place. Come alone. "

"When and where?"

"I won't be alone, though. There'll be two cars. I'll be in one, and the pounds in another. You'll give me the money, and I'll make sure it's sixty and good money…"

"*Good money?* There's a such thing as *bad* money?"

"Of course there is. You know how many niggas out here passing counterfeit bills, and making fake bundles of cash? If you want to deal with me, it's a process. Every time. I gotta safeguard myself from thugs, especially drop-dead gorgeous ones, like you. Once I see that the money is good, my girl in the second car will give you the weed."

"That's cool but how do *I* get a safeguard? What if you take my money and I can't get the weed? Or I don't like what you give be me? What guarantee do I have that everything will everything?"

"None. You came to me, remember? You gotta trust me. It's the only way that this will work. So, what's it gonna be?"

"I'm in. And again, I ask when and where?"

"One hour. Outside Union Station, where the bus station is."

"Bus station? What?"

"Where the Greyhound buses come to the depot from."

"Oh, right. I got you."

"Good, one hour, Union Station, bus depot."

"I'll be there."

***

In the life I live, one always has to expect the unexpected. Real life game plans sometime call for game time decisions. The meeting I made wasn't that smart, but taking KD off the chessboard of life was critical and imperative. I was parked at the arranged meeting spot minutes after getting off the phone with KD. The area wasn't as crowded as I assumed it would be. There were a few cars that loitered about, but not enough to make me abort the mission.

The majority of the people waiting on Greyhound buses probably waited inside of the Union Station. Although, the sun shone bright in the sky. The covering over the bus depot gave the crew a lot of shade. And it was chilly as hell outside, so the number of people to witness what I was about to do were few as well. Getting out the car, I pulled the Moncler beanie down over my head completely. My attire was the same as always: black pants, hood, ski vest and Nike boots. I walked over to the entrance/exit to the bus depot area. I leaned on the concrete beam and waited for Kendra "KD" Dyson to appear. She hadn't told me what car she'd be in, but it didn't matter. As long as the windows weren't tinted, I'd be able to spot her.

Just as the cold started to seep into my clothes and chill me inside, two vehicles pulled into the area, a Cadillac CTV-

S coupe and a Jaguar SVU. There were two women in the Cadillac and one driving the jag truck. The two vehicles sat side by side, near the curb, at the entrance to Union Station, from the station. KD was in the Cadillac on the passenger side. I pulled Ruger 45with the suppresser from my waist and cuffed it by my leg as I walked towards the car. The phone in my pocket vibrated and I knew that the caller was KD. My heart beat quicker as I got closer to the Cadillac. Impatience overtook me, so I jogged the last few feet to the car. Kendra Dyson's face registered shock as I appeared and popped the Ruger. I opened fire immediately. I could hear a scream as I got closer to the car. The window had been completely blown out by bullets. I wanted to make sur that KD was dead. The person driving that Jag truck pulled off loudly. After I was satisfied that Kendra Dyson was dead, I walked away.

***

"You can go ahead and scratch off the last one," I told Mike Carter.

"That's good news, Que. Keep up the good work. I got another job."

"Aw, big guy. I'm cool right now. Gotta chill for a minute. I been lucky for a long time. Kinda feel like that ain't gonna be the case if I keep poking the bear. I'ma chill out for a while and focus on helping Jay get out of jail. I got a few other things I need to handle, too."

"Say less, youngin. Say less. Just holla when you ready to get back to work. The money for that hot bitch will be there today. Check it and send me a text to confirm you got it. It's always good to take time off. Take as long as you need, but don't' stay away forever. The good men need you. Feel me?"

I listened to Mike Carter talk, but I couldn't hear him. My thoughts were on everything that Sean told me. Images of

Mike fucking my mother came to mind. Images of him shooting my father on our porch popped up. The lies he told me to get me to kill Tony Wells lingered as well.

I thought about Mike getting rid of Sean because he didn't' want Sean to pull my coattail about all of his manipulation and deception. I thought about the desire I had to kill him that grew inside of me as two days went by. I thought about Sean's motives and commitment to killing Mike. I thought about his legal situation. I thought about the fact that Mike Carter would know that he was about to be a grandfather soon. "What's up with your legal situation, old head? Any word on how that's coming along?"

"My daughter and lawyer are all over it. It's promising. We're still waiting on the judge to decide if and when I can get an evidence hearing. That's what I'm waiting on."

"Hopefully, something good happens for you. You been in there long enough."

"Tell it to the judge, again. Tell it to the judge. I'ma go ahead and put that money in play. Holla at me and keep me posted about Jay and Dove."

"I will. Be safe, old head."

"You, too, youngin."

Ending the call with Mike Carter, I got out the car and dowsed starter fluid all over the seats, steering wheel and center console. Pulling out a lighter, I set the Cadillac XTS a blaze. As I walked down the deserted street near the old Potomac jobs corps, I unscrewed the suppressor from the Ruger and threw it as far as I could. I put the Ruger in my pocket. the trek back to Sheridan Terrace was a long one, but I was up for the task. I needed to exercise. I zipped up the ski vest all the way to the neck and let the cold and the thoughts in my head become my companion.

***

151 Howard Road SE

The spot on Howard Road had a different feel to it without my brother in it. His crew of soldiers appeared lost without Jihad and Bo. I dapped up all the lil homies before going into the building. I wanted to provide them with positive words, but I was devoid of all positivity at the moment. In the spot, I undressed and hopped in the shower. Letting the steaming hot water massage my head, body, and soul, I dropped to my knees under the stream of hot water. Then I sat all the way down in the tub. Bringing my knees up a little, I laid my head back and tried my best not to drown myself.

***

"Que, I miss you. I need to see you, baby."

"Stop what you doing, Kiki. You got a whole husband. Besides you stood me up the last time we planned something. Then I had plans. Damn that was a only a couple days ago. I'm – lunching like shit. I ain't fucking with you go fuck your husband."

"Can't fuck him, Que. The feds ain't New York. There ain't no conjugal visits where wives get to fuck their husbands. All he can do is feel on my ass when we take pictures. I need a real man with a real good dick to fulfill my needs."

"There's plenty of niggas out here who fit that bill, baby girl."

"That may be, but there ain't a lot of 'em with the body you got. All the pretty hair and them damn eyes. Shit crazy how hypnotizing them grey eyes are. When you look into my eyes while 'you're on top of me, I swear to God, you be touching my soul. Body, hair, eyes, dick and your swag make five things that keep bitches addicted to niggas like you. I been working on a TV series and trying to get a script approved by them people I flew to LA to see last year. I been working hard as shit, but I need a release, A good release. I need you, Quran."

"I thought you were still mad at me for what I did with hubby."

"We talked about that already, Que. I already told you that I'm over that shit, and so is he. Nigga been in jail so long that the shit done fucked him up. After he got over the fact that I lied to him about me not fucking with nobody, what he heard turned him on. He's a grown man that's smart as shit. I told you that he writes books, too, right?"

"No, but that's good to know."

"Yeah, he writes books, too, and we work together on projects. But anyway, like I was saying, that nigga remembers that shit he heard. Told me that he used it to beat his dick in his cell. Got me on the phone calling out your name as I play with my pussy."

"Get the fuck outta here," I said and laughed out loud.

"I ain't laughing, Que, I'm dead ass. This nigga got my ass in here licking and sucking on my fingers, while moaning and acting like I'm sucking his dick. Got me putting dildos in my ass, while begging you to cum in my ass. Did I really do that? Beg you to cum in my ass that day? "

Laying on the couch in the spot dressed in only basketball shorts and a tank top, I felt my dick getting hard. Thinking about the last time I had fucked Kiki's ass got me brick. "Yeah, you sorta did. I mean, I asked you could I fuck your ass and you went nuts. Said something to the effect of, 'Yes, please fuck my ass?" Then I asked you could I cum in that ass and you begged me to do that. So yeah, you did kinda beg me to fuck and cum in that fat ass."

"Mmm, mmm, mmm," Kiki muttered. "Damn, I wish you were right here, right now. Boy, I swear I'd let you wear this fat ass out. Cum all in it two times. Fuck. I want to fuck you so bad, Que. My pussy wet as shit just thinking about it."

"You, too? My dick wet as shit with precum all over the head of it."

"Stop it, Que."

"No bullshit. I got it in my hand right now. It been in my hand for a few minute now. Ever since you said that Slim be having you call out my name."

"FaceTime me, Que," Kiki begged.

"Can't," I replied.

"Why not? Why can't you?"

"Don't have a iPhone."

"Damn, Que, fuck."

"What?"

"Wanna see that dick."

"Come to D.C.."

"When?"

"Whenever you get a chance. You were supposed to been came."

"I was coming, then shit got hectic. I'ma come though."

"When?"

"Today is Sunday, right? Um, I can't come now, as bad as I want to. It's gone have to be next weekend, either Saturday or Sunday. That's cool? "

"Next weekend? Saturday or Sunday? Yeah, that's cool. I'll be here waiting to get my hands on your sexy, big lip ass. You got me in here playing with my dick. Damn. You got two niggas in the world thinking about fucking you and jacking off. You a bad, bad bitch."

"Watch your mouth, nigga. You can only call me bitch if your dick is in my mouth, pussy, or ass," Kiki said salaciously.

"My bad, baby. My bad."

"Damn, I'ma ride the shit outta that dick."

"I want you to."

"Show you all kind of new positions."

"Can't wait."

"A'ight, Que, let me get back to what I was doing. I'ma call you and confirm my plans to fly in on Thursday or Friday, okay?"

"Bet. I want you to sit on my face and cum on my lips."

"Shit. Now I gotta go take a shower. Bye, Que."

Letting myself go, I dialed Halina Ndugu's number, but again got no answer. Wanting to relieve the sexual tension I now felt, I called Zin.

"Hey, baby. What's up?" Zin said.

"You. What you doing?"

"Still out with my Aunt Linda. Why?"

"Just miss you, that's all. "

"Aaaww! Miss you, too. I'ma call you when I get home."

"A'ight, bet. Love you."

"I love you, too."

I was just about to toss the phone and take a nap when a call came through. It was Tomasina.

"What's up, Tom?"

"Ain't shit. Got your text with the new phone number in it. Just wanted to call and acknowledge."

"Tom, where you at, right now? Work?"

"Uhh un, at home."

"I'ma text you an address. Pull up," I instructed. "I need to holla at you."

"A'ight. Send the text, then I'm on my way."

***

"Whose spot is this, Que?" Tomasina asked as soon as she walked through the door. "Don't be having me in any of your bitches' spots while they ain't home."

"Shut the fuck up, Tom," I told her.

"Why do I have to shut up, Que?"

Tomasina was dressed in warm clothes for comfort. Her Ugg boots matched the color of her coat. Her jeans hugged her every curve. The lip gloss on her lips appealed to every inch of my dick. I grabbed Tomasina's hand and led her to the couch.

"Because you talking too much. I told you I needed to holla at you. I didn't call you here to holla at me." I pushed Tomasina down on the couch.

"Well, what do you need to talk to me about? Pushing me and shit."

I moved my shorts to the side and freed my dick. "About this," I said and put myself into Tomasina's mouth.

Twenty minutes later…

"I got something for you, too," Tomasina said as she put her Ugg boots back on. She reached into her purse and got a piece of paper. She passed that piece of paper to me.

I read the information on the paper and smiled. "That's why I fuck with you, Tom. You knew exactly what I needed without me even asking. How did you get it?"

"I told you I know people. I got a nigga that's a C & P over D.C. jail. Nigga been tryna fuck for years. But I won't give him none. Anyway, he remembered that I called and asked about that dude that stabbed David Battle."

"A random C & P nigga? Can you trust him, Tom?" I asked as I rolled a jay of OG. I put the paper on the coffee table.

"Of course, I can. I wouldn't put nobody in my shit that I couldn't trust."

"A'ight, go ahead. Finish what you were saying."

"Dominck, the C & P guy, called today and told me that the dude who stabbed David, Javon Jarret, got stabbed yesterday himself. According to him, some dude named Anthony Williams, who was locked own in south one for getting caught with a cell phone, slipped out of his cuffs going to rec and attacked Jarret the same way Jarrett did David, while handcuffed and shackled. Jarrett's wounds are superficial. I just went on and got the info and the paper I just gave you."

"Damn, I appreciate that, Tom. No bullshit."

"Don't trip, I got you. I fuck with you, Que. No bullshit. I respect what you do for me and what you did for Tasheka.

And now I owe the C & P guy some pussy, so you know I got to really fuck with you."

I smiled as I lit the blunt. After inhaling the smoke a few times, I said, "And I already know how much you fuck with a nigga. You just showed me that when you let me finally get that ass."

"Please, don't remind me."

I laughed at Tomasina.

She grimaced, "Fuck you laughing at? That shit hurt. Ain't a damn thing funny. I don't be giving niggas no backdoor like that. Your smooth talking ass. I'm still trying out figure out how I went from sucking dick to being ass up, face down, you in my ass. Shit crazy."

I laughed again. "I think it was the weed."

"I'm about to leave, Que. You gon make me mad. Keep laughing and shit."

"A'ight, a'ight. I'ma stop laughing. Promise. I got some money for you, but it ain't here. I need you to fuck with Dove again for me."

"Unh unh, Que. That was a one and done."

"Please, Tom. One more time. Slim is gone off your pretty ass. Cut him outta the street one more time for me and I got you. Heavy. I promise.

"A'ight, nigga, damn. You sexy when you begging. Makes me wanna suck that dick again, since I didn't get to finish."

"You didn't get to finish?" I asked Tomasina.

"You know I didn't."

"Go get a washcloth out the bathroom closet. Soap it up and wash my dick off. You can finish now, if you want to. The bathroom is straight to the back on the left."

Tomasina got up and headed for the bathroom.

Chapter 15

Susan Rosenthal
United States Attorney's Office
5554 St. Northwest

"Was Kendra Dyson your CI or Greg's?"

"Neither. She's with Ian."

"*Was* with Ian, you mean."

Putting my laptop aside, I gave Ari Winston the attention that he was looking for. Aristotle Winston was a good-looking guy and a great prosecutor, but he was a conniving, sneaky son of a bitch, and he though nobody recognized it.

"What do you mean '*was*,' Ari?"

"Exactly what the word infers, Sue—*was*. Kendra Dyson got herself killed yesterday in the lot of a bus depot at Union Station? Don't you watch the news?"

"Sometimes, but I mostly stay clear of it. It's depressing."

"I second that, but I think it's good to get a heads up on the breaking news."

"Kendra Dyson was a drug dealer before she was allegedly raped and shot by guys on the L Street case from 1998. Only after her arrest and a pending indictment for distribution of said drugs that she come forward and give us information on Thomas Fields and Bernard Johnson. Grey groomed her and turned her over to Ian McKinley, who happened to tell me that Kendra, while operating as a paid informant, was back distributing narcotics. Her getting killed in the parking lot at Union Station does not qualify as breaking news to me, so excuse me if I'm not moved to tears because of Kendra 'Dyson's demise."

"Sometimes you can be a heartless bitch, Susan."

"Blame it on the job, Ari. The murderers, the drug deals going bad, the cold-hearted nature of the human beings that I prosecute and send to prison for dealing has made me this way. And whether you know it or not, Aristotle, you are just like me."

Ari Winston's scowl turned into a fast smile. "Agreed. And well said, Sue."

"What's the word on the Jayden Beaver's case?"

"Nothing new. We start trial next week, unless there's another delay by the defense. What's going on with your case load?"

"No excitement on this end. Janelle Johnson's probably going to the cops. But him being on parole might impede that. He'll be subject to the parole violation number on the top of the time he cops for the two new cases. Then there's the Cinquan Blakney case that's still in limbo. Let me see… I have opposition motions to file in the Nehemiah Hampton and Tyrone Clipper 23-110, post-conviction case. The Lafayette Dotson and Raymond Smith appeal. Maurice Hoffmann's 2255 pro sè and twelve other state cases. Plus, fifteen new federal cases. I'm swamped and going through PMS. What would you like to hear about next?"

"I think that's my cue to leave. Talk to you later, Sue."

Once my office door was shut, I turned my computer back on to face me. As soon as I did, a knock on the door caused me to look up. "Come in."

Ann Sloan walked into the room. "Susan, I need some advice. We got the Antonio Felder trial coming up in May. My star witness is Luther Fuller."

"Khadafi, the serial killer, is your star witness?" I asked.

Sloan nodded. "Believe it or not, he is right now. He's being held at the CTF on the 4th floor in the witness program there. I promised Khadafi that I would get his murder case in Maryland thrown out, but I'm running into snags. I'm afraid, he won't go through with his promise to testify against Antonio Felder."

"Antonio Felder? Why does that name sound so familiar?"

"Because in 2000 a man was killed on Congress Street in Congress Heights, a man named Quincy Walters. Antonio Felder was arrested and charged with that murder. His friend Eric Fraser testified against him in 2001 at trial. Antonio Felder was sentenced to 50 years in prison. A constitutional error in his trial and ineffective assistance of his trial consent got the case overturned and the charges dismissed in 2012. In 2007, while in federal prison, at a penitentiary in Beaumont, TX, Antonio Felder and Luther Fuller killed Keith Barnett."

"Keith Barnett, another name that sounds familiar," I mentioned.

"Should sound familiar. You and I prosecuted James Carpenter in 1998. I think it was on the double homicide that happened on Galveston St. The two twin brothers got killed. Keith Barnett was Carpenter's co-defendant that turned states against him. Barnett helped us to get Carpenter sixty years. In prison, Luther Fuller, motherfucking Kadafi, and James Copper became close friends. They ended up at the same federal prison. the federal system, Luther ... uh ... Khadafi ends up in Texas at USP Beaumont and sometime later Keith Barnett shows up on the compound. Khadafi and Antonio Felder killed Keith Barnett and dismembered his body. From what I'm told, Antonio Felder admitted to the murder of Barnett to let Khadafi go home. Well, we both know all of the shit Khadafi did when he got home, both times. Well, in 2012, they both were back on the streets of D.C."

"But what about the prison murder? Felder wasn't charged?"

"He was charged with Keith Barnett's murder. Antonio Phillip went to trial in Texas and got acquitted on all charges. Didn't you just say that fella admitted killing Barnett?"

"Yeah, but Rudy Sabino flew in Texas and defended Felder."

"Our Rudolph Sabino? The defense attorney here in D.C.?"

Sloan nodded her head. "The one and only. He got the confession thrown out and then sparked our counterparts in Texas. Felder walked away Scot-free. Then Sabino got his conviction thrown out here in D.C. That's why all the names I'm mentioning to you sound familiar."

"Okay, so now that I'm caught up, what's your dilemma?"

"Last year in February, Tyjuan Glover was killed as he walked of the 'Circle' on F Street in Simple City. His girlfriend witnessed the murder. We believe that the person who killed Tyjuan Glover ambushed and killed the girlfriend in a car at a gas station after she left Tyjuan's funeral. Well, that girlfriend was sixteen-year-old Kenya Dickerson. Antonio Felder's daughter. Do you remember when seven people were killed on Alabama Ave. In Southeast last year."

"Of course I do."

Well, those seven murders were committed by one man—Antonio Felder After that, three people were killed in a house on Burns Place about three blocks from where the seven murders happened. The victims were Linda Holloway, her son Curtis Holloway and his girlfriend Larcel Davis. Curtis Holloway was already driving the getaway car the day his cousin Terrell Holloway allegedly killed Kenya Dickerson.

We knew that the triple homicide on Burns Place was connected to the seven on Alabama Ave. But couldn't prove it. Then a woman who was involved in the case turned up dead. Tashia Parker. Was being sought for questioning at the time of her death. She was the girlfriend of Terrell Holloway. Then the six people gunned down on a basketball court in the same neighborhood where the seven people were killed weeks earlier. A man who was killed in the convenience store was the father of one of the main players in the neighborhood. His death also connected to Antonio Fedler and Luther Fuller. Finally, two bodies found days later ended the reign of terror. The bodies of Fellano Jasper and Terrell Holloway were found on Firth Sterling near. Berry Farms. There was a detective who investigated the entire case."

"Maurice Tolliver. I remember Moe Tolliver very well, worked with him on several cases I prosecuted since I got to this office. Died last year after a shootout with Kadhafi in Maryland."

"Right, but the medical examiner ruled that Maurice Tolliver passed away as a result of a blood borne infection that may not have come from the bullets he took in the shootout. The state of Maryland couldn't convict Khadafi of his murder. He was going to walk after a few years for assault on an inmate at the jail in Upper Marlboro, but he didn't know that. I convinced him that he would be charged with Tolliver's murder in Prince George County and on kidnapping and murder charges here in D.C. It took some time, but he finally broke. Confessed his soul. Implicated Antonio Felder in all the murders, and even closed a few cold case murders that he committed."

"Sounds like great news to me. So, what's the conundrum?"

"The agreement I made with Khadafi. The officials in Maryland want to renege on the promises they gave me. District Attorney Delores Monroe has been demoted to ADA and the man who's taking her place— Thomas Dexter— is unwilling to drop all the charges against Khadafi in reference to the Maurice Tolliver case. I have an ethical duty to tell Khadafi about the wrinkle in PG but if I do that what if he clams up and stops cooperating. Antonio Felder has invoked his speedy trial privilege and his trial date is set for May. That's three months from now. I need Khadafi's cooperation to convict Antionio Felder and close the books on sixteen murders that he committed alone. Not to mention the ones that Khadafi confessed to. So, what do I do? How do I salvage this? "

Ann Sloan was a beautiful woman in all of her Midwestern splendor. Her auburn-colored hair accented her innocent face and dark, pouty lips. Her smile could disarm a bandit. I looked at Anne Sloan and saw her through Greg Gamble's eyes. Ann was married to Coleman Sloan, a noted neurosurgeon at George Washington Hospital, and a tenured professor at its University. But she was involved in an affair with the detective who was investigating cases with her. Detective Corey Winslow. And didn't know that anyone knew about her late-night rendezvous with the handsome black detective. She had no clue that I knew. I had been in the office on a few occasions when the two of them locked themselves behind closed doors and had sex. Loudly at times. But who was I to judge her? I, myself, was in a decade long situation with a man that was not my husband. She liked Black dick. I crave Latino dick. We were both white women who love to suck dick outside of our race.

"Ann, the solution to your problem is simple, be quiet."

"I beg your pardon?" Ann said with a vexed look on her face.

"You heard me correctly. I said to *be quiet*. Meaning don't say shit to Khadafi. Who cares about your ethical obligations when you're coddling a psychopath? Nobody. Say nothing to Khadafi about the Maryland dilemma until after Antonio Felder's trial. It's called plausible deniability. You can't tell the client what you don't know. Get it?"

Sloan's expression turned from irritated to a smile—a mischievous one. "*Susan Rosenthal,*" said Ann. "How dare you turn into Greg-fucking-Gamble on me?"

Before I could respond, someone knocked on my office door.

"Come in," I called out.

Greg Gumbel, the devil himself, walked into the office. "Have you heard about Joseph Morris?" Greg asked.

"Who?" Ann and I said simultaneously.

"JoJo Morris. One of the most profound snitches to ever come through these doors. Apparently he was shot and killed on Friday. He was scheduled to testify against the Venable brothers. Tone Black and Sleepy. The two brothers are the nephews of James and Marquis Venable another two pieces of shit that I want to put away forever. This obviously sets us back in that case."

"Was Kendra Dyson working on any of your cases?" And asked Greg. "Because if she was, your day is about to be real shitty, boss man."

"Kendra Dawson, KD. No, she's with Ian."

"Not anymore. She was murdered yesterday near Union Station."

Greg smiled. "It was inevitable. No one could control Kendra. Not me. Not Ian. No one at First District. She was a live wire. Used us when it benefited her. "I'm not surprised to hear that someone killed her. Susan, you and I need to talk."

"Well, I guess that's my name I hear being called on the other side of the door. Susan, I'll see you later. You too, Greg. Bye." Ann Sloan departed the room.

"I'm starting to feel kind of important. You are the third visitor I've had in my office in the last thirty minutes. What's up, Greg?"

"My deposition."

"What deposition?" I asked, confused.

"I just talked to the clerk inside Judge Hamilton's courtroom."

"Is this about Michael Carter's 23-110 motion?"

"Who else would I need to be deposed for?"

"When you said Judge Hamilton, you confused me. I thought Judge Benson was handling the motion."

"You must not check your emails, Susan. I emailed you a week ago to tell you that Judge Benson is retiring in a few weeks, and he passed the case over to Hamilton.

"Beatrice Hamilton or Theodore Hamilton?"

"Neither. It's in front of *Bruce* Hamilton."

"No shit! *Not Cut 'em loose* Bruce!"

"Yes, Cut 'em loose Bruce Hamilton, and according to the clerk, he's going to schedule an evidentiary hearing for early next month."

"Early March? Why so soon?" I asked.

"That, I don't know. But he's going to announce the decision and the date this week. I need you to depose me."

"Greg, my name might come up again. Do you think it's wise to pick me for the deposition?"

"It has to be you, Susan. Who else can I trust?"

"I hear you, Greg, but it can't be me."

"You're right."

"And you already know why it can't be me."

Greg Gamble capitulated quickly. He turned to leave the office. "I can get Arie to do it."

"Sounds good to me. Or you could get Ian McNeely."

Once Greg was gone, I made a call to a friend. Margie Roth answered on the second ring.

"Susan, I've been meaning to call you."

"No need. I'm calling you. You have everything I gave you about the situation that's about to unfold, correct?"

"Correct."

"We'll give it a few days, Marge and run with it. Heavy rotation. Around the clock."

"I'm all over it. Susan's all over it."

Chapter 16
Greg Gamble

Play a fool to catch a fool. I remember the words that my father always said to me when I was a kid. Susan Rosenthal really believed that she had the upper hand in the situation that I now forced. Smiling to myself, I closed my office door and sat down. My cell phone vibrated and a call came through. The caller was Saul Levine. "Hello."

"Go ahead and say I told you so," Sal said.

"Whatever are you talking about, Sal?"

"Just got the call from Marge Rother. She has a story about you paying some waitress to frame a guy named Michael Carter in 1995. She has witnessed vouchers and an affidavit form and a woman named…"

"Maryann Settles."

"So, you know all about the story and you know that. Meg Ralph would be the one to leak it. How?"

"Because in The Land of Oz, I'm the Great and Powerful Wizard. I knew this was coming and who would initiate it? Thanks for the heads up Sal. Go ahead and run the story, but you'll be the first to get to break a few stories of mine How does juicy tidbits about my number two at the office Susan Rosenthal, Carlos Trinidad and your very own Marjorie Roth sound?

"Like food to a starving man," replied Sal.

"Good. Just do what it is. That you do. Sal and you'll have your breaking news. All in good time, agreed."

"Agreed. Call me when you're ready, Greg."

"Will do. Bye."

***

"So, what are you going to do about it?" Martin asked.

I sip my drink and reclined in the Lazy Boy recliner in Martin's living room. "Do about what, Martin?"

"About this upcoming attack on you? About these lies."

"They're not lies, Martin."

The look on Martin's face was priceless. "They're not?"

"No. I'm guilty. Everything that they will say I did, I did all of it."

"But why? Why would you—"

"In the beginning, it all made sense. Until it didn't. When I was young, going into the US Attorney's office, I was arrogant. I was headstrong. I was… Courageous, and I was full of vengeance."

"Vengeance. Vengeance for who?

"There are a lot of things about me that you don't know, Martin, and that's the way I wanted it. Hold out the cards close to your chest. That's always been my model. But now I think it's time to unload some of the dirt. I've been carrying around for decades. Unlike some people… well, maybe even most people like us. I wasn't born gay. I wasn't… I didn't choose this life. It chose me. I was molested for 10 years by one of my uncles— Donovan Gamble. Until one day my brother Lynell walked in on what was happening. He was a few years older than me. I was 12 and he was 15. My brother pulled a gun and ordered my uncle to the basement of our house. He made him kneel in front of him. Then he made my uncle do to him what he forced me to do since I was a small child. My brother didn't show no emotion. He received no pleasure. He told my uncle that he wanted him to feel what I felt for years. Then, without provocation, he killed him.

115

"My brother and I carried that body from the from the basement and put them in the shed in the backyard. That night we moved the body to the woods near our home and left it there. That night bonded me and my brother like the blood in our veins could not. The only person who would've told about the murder was my sister Cindy. After that incident, I struggled with my sexuality. I tried to pull the attraction to men out of me. I dealt strictly with women. I tried to overcompensate because of the other things in my head. My brother sent women at me left and right and I knocked them all down. Gave them all the pleasure they deserved. I've performed just as I should have, but I was the only one who knew the truth. That I was ruined, man. Women didn't interest me the way men did. I knew it. But no one else did or could ever know.

"I threw all of my attention in academics and watched Law and Order on TV. Watching the shows and then seeing *A Time To Kill* as a teenager made me want to be a lawyer. Getting into college was easy for me. I earned a scholarship and a full ride. Getting into law school was hard. Being able to pay for law school was going to be even harder. But lo and behold, my older brother stepped in and paid almost $200,000 for my tuition. A lawyer friend of his made the transition appear legitimate, but the money was dirty money. He knew it and I knew it. I love my brother more than I loved oxygen, Martin. He meant the world to me. He was my savior, my protector, my hero. Then while at the school, I got a call that my brother was dead. Killed in a beauty salon that his girlfriend operated by a kid. A kid walked into the salon, walked into a back room and took my brother from me. I was obsessed with two things after that. Becoming a prosecutor and finding out what happened to my brother. A lot of resources, time, money and sex with men that I loathed netted me the answers that I sought. The man responsible for my brother's death was—"

"Michael Carter."

"Correct. Further due diligence afforded me the knowledge that the man, the kid who pulled the trigger, fired the bullets that killed my brother was none other than a notorious killer named Sean Branch. I was a lot of things back then, but I wasn't a killer. As bad as I wanted to find both Sean Branch and Michael Carter and kill them both, I couldn't. It just wasn't in me to kill. So, I waited and waited for the right time and apparently to get my revenge once I was inside the US Attorney's office, and on the fast track to success, the opportunity came first to get Sean Branch. A man named Maurice Payne got arrested in Northeast. In a neighborhood where I knew Sean Branch to hang out in. I went to see Maurice and learned that he was a witness to a murder committed by Michael Carter. But when he told me that Sean Branch was also at the scene of the murder, I decided to exact my revenge on Sean, first.

"I offered to drop the drug charges against Maurice if he implicated Sean Branch for the murder. He wouldn't take the bait. That was not enough to make him put his life in jeopardy. He needed something more, he said. He needed money. Lots of money. I gave him the next best thing—drugs. I removed the kilo of cocaine from the evidence locker at my office. The cocaine was about to be presented at the trial of one of Carlos Trinidad's associates. He was arrested with 50 kilos of pure cocaine. To me, 49 was the same as 50. So, I updated the property forms and evidence logs to reflect 49 kilos instead of 50. I gave the kilo of cocaine to Maurice for testifying against Sean Branch on the murder he didn't commit. I got Sean convicted and sent him to prison. Next came the tragic murder of my sister Cindy. She was going down Wade Road in Southeast while leaving an apartment there. Her killer was identified as a teenager who looked very young…"

"But it couldn't have been Sean Branch. You sent him to prison, all right?"

"I never said that her killer was Sean Branch. He was older then and, yes, he was in prison. But the irony of the situation didn't escape me. Both my brother and sister were killed by teenagers who looked like kids. After a brief investigation, my theories were confirmed. The same person was responsible for Cindy's death. His modus operandi was to use teenagers who look like kids."

"Michael Carter again."

I finished my drink and set the empty glass down on the coffee table next to the recliner. I nodded my head. "Correct. But this time, the team who killed Cindy was the son of a well-known D.C. assassin. A man named Ameen Bashir. Evidently, the apple didn't fall far from the tree because after the father's death in 1991, the son began to kill in his place. That son's name is Quran Bashir. In 1995, Quran walked onto a porch in the Sheridan Terrace neighborhood in Southeast and killed his friend. Dontay Samuels. Then he walked away and got into his car with Michael Carter. Soon after, I caught my next break. Just like in the Sean Branch case, a woman got arrested on Talbert Street. Her address was 2522 Sheridan Road. One house away from where Dontay Samuels was killed. I didn't believe in coincidence back then. Maryann Settles falling into my lap was by design. It was fate. The big guy upstairs was answering my prayers, finally. I coerced— Maryann— into implicating Michael Carter—"

"With drugs again?"

"No. With money. Witness vouchers. Paid her about a hundred grand over the course of a year and some change. I secured a conviction against the man who had killed my brother. I sent him to prison for 40 years for a murder he didn't commit. That was my revenge."

"But your best laid plans are now beginning to unravel. You never factored into the vengeance that one of them or both..."

"Maurice Payne is dead; killed months ago."

"You never thought that this woman… Maryann Settles, would have an attack of conscience and come forward to expose you."

"Nope. Never thought in a million years. I also paid a man named Thomas Turner to implicate Michael Carter, too."

"Did he come forward as well?"

"No, he's dead. Died of a drug overdose in Portsmouth, Virginia two years ago. I had Olson check on it for me."

"And Susan Rosenthal is about to expose— well, help to expose— you for the whole world to see?"

I nodded. "Yep. The dirty cunt has an audacity to turn against me."

"But why? Why would she do that to you?"

"For two reasons. One, to save herself because she's the one who orchestrated the voucher payments to Maryann Settles. And two, because with me out of the way, by default she becomes the next US Attorney. Or so she thinks."

"Or so she thinks?"

"That's what I said. Susan Rosenthal will never so much as smell the seat of power. She's playing checkers while I'm playing chess."

"I have one more question before we go to dinner."

"Ask it."

"There's one person left that you didn't mention. The one person that you haven't extracted revenge from. What about him?"

"Oh, his time is coming, and when I finish with Quran Bashir, he won't know what hit him."

Chapter 17
Greg Gamble

In the parking lot across from D.C. General, a food truck there had the best jerk chicken salad in the city. Already at the food truck with Bruce Culbreth, the deputy director of the D.C. Department of Corrections, I'd park my car closer to the D.C. Jail than the D.C. General and got out to take a walk.

"Eat here often?" I said as I approached the food truck.

Without looking at me, Bruce ordered me the jerk chicken salad. He laid a thumb drive on the counter of the food truck near the array of displayed chips and other snacks. "Food is pretty good. You should try the jerk chicken salad."

I moved in close to Bruce and put the hand over the thumb drive. "I think I will."

"Give the salad to him," Bruce told the food truck worker, then walked back towards the D.C. jail.

Quickly, I pocketed the thumb drive. A minute or so later, the food truck worker passed me the salad inside a plastic container. "Can I have three Ranch dressings packs, please? And a Lipton's Brisk iced tea. Thank you. I'm also paying for the gentleman's lunch who ordered me the salad."

***

United States Attorney's Office
555 4th St. Northwest.

You already know what happened. Bruh read the work about the witnesses and it was all work call after that. He wasn't gonna let you go down like that. The shit fucked us up, though. And to be honest with you, bruh, the only one that made sense to me was Tommy. You know your cousin; he was a selfish, opportunist motherfucker. I think he was already fuckin' with them people, slim. We read the paperwork and he was too familiar with Gamble and 'nem. He must have caught a charge and started working. You saw the paperwork, right?

"Yeah, I saw it. My lawyer brought me the papers. That shit fucked me up, slim. Bitch nigga cooked me to the grand jury like that. After all the shit we've been through?

Using a mouse on the laptop, I stopped the recording. It was the third time since getting the thumb drive that I listened to the conversation between Jihad Bashir and David Battle. Smiling to myself I tried to figure out the best way to use the recordings. I couldn't reopen the case against David in the murder of Solomon Robinson. Nor could I make a case against Jahid and Quran Bashir about the murders of Yolanda Stevens, Thomas Caldwell, or Khitab Bashir. The recording device that had been placed inside the CTF's medical unit wasn't legally put there, making anything said inside the cell inadmissable in court. It did confirm my suspicions about David Battle having the witnesses in his case killed, and who had killed them. On the recording, Jahid Bashir bragged about how efficient he'd been in Thomas Caldwell's killing. And he kept saying the word "bruh". Being familiar with street vernacular and other slang, I knew that Bruh was his way of referencing his brother Quran. He bragged about Yolanda Stevens' body being knocked through a glass window from the force of the bullets fired into her body. I fast-forwarded the recording a little. There was something that I needed to hear again.

"...The crazy part was how bruh tricked Mann and crushed him. After Landa's funeral, Mann was talking

reckless; wouldn't let it go. Every day, he talked about finding who killed his niece."

"Stupid ass nigga. Always talked too much."

"Bruh got right on his ass. Him and Taboo took him down Oak Park and flushed his ass. Threw him in the back seat... I mean the trunk of a parked car and left his ass. Bruh told Tab that he really crushed Mann because he always tried to smoke all the weed."

(Laughter)

"I can't tell you why my brother decided to do that shit, slim."

I typed the words *Yolanda Stephens* into my computer, then typed *Mann*. In parentheses I put her uncle killed after her funeral by Quran Bashir. There's something else that caught my attention...

"...To me he was above reproach. Above suspicious of any real crime. I left his legal case alone. Bruh was so focused on Zin that he couldn't see past her pretty, round ass. Then the paperwork showed up. the people disclosed it to Jen Wentz and 'nem, Zin got ahold of it and showed it to Quran. That was all she wrote after that. Bruh made the decision and carried out the execution."

I learned two things from the recorded conversation. Zinfandel Carter was involved in an intimate relationship with Quran, and that she was the person responsible for Khitab Bashir's death, having shown Quran the grand jury statements that Khatib made. I also confirmed another suspicion; Quran Bashir had killed his own brother for violating the code of silence—the omerta 444The next words I heard wouldn't be admissible in court, but Detective Bob Mathis would definitely need to hear them.

"What happened with you and Lil Bo?"

"My stupid ass was geeking, trying to flush this nigga named Baby E from Clay Terrence—"

"Baby E? Eric Jones Joyner? Or something like that. Getting a rack of money?"

"Yup. You hip to his wild ass?"

"Yeah, it's some good men over on 1901 D Street that he was cooking—"

"Was cooking? He's gone. We couldn't get him that night after the Bliss. But Bruh caught him at Maryland somewhere. Him and the nigga that shot me in Bo. Barbequed their asses. I'm fighting the joint at Benco Market. One of Baby E's men named Denico Autrey..."

Eric "Baby E" Jonah had recently been shot and killed at the Woodmere Town Center in Largo. Him, two other men and a woman. Joyner was familiar to me because he provided pertinent information on three men about the killing of Amari Jenkins on the grounds of Saint Luke's Catholic Church. I'd heard about his death but never thought that Quran Bashir was involved. I typed all the info I needed onto my laptop. There was one last part of the recording that I needed to hear again...

"Last one. Tosheka. What the fuck happened to Tosh?"

"Ever since bruh been fucking with Zin, he curbed Tosheka. I mean all the way curbed her. No going back, no sneaky head, nothing."

"Does Mike Carter know that Quran fucking with his daughter?"

"Fuck no. Her or Quran ain't said shit to him about that."

"A'ight, I was just curious. Finish what you were saying."

"Since bruh curbed her, she been all over me; real live on my dick."

"Stop what you're doing, slim Tosh- ain't fucking with you." (Laughter.)

"By Allah, I ain't lying. Wallah, she was on me. I started hitting that joint, and bruh caught me one day..."

"Man, stop it. Stop that shit. You trying to say that Quran killed Tosheka?"

"(Unintelligible.) But not because she was fucking with me. He tried to say that he flushed her because she was dangerous to him, potentially."

"Dangerous to him? Potentially? How?"

"Because she saw him and Sean Branch at a funeral for a dude named Crud, minutes before his brother was killed after the funeral."

"But why would she—"

"It's his... connection to Sean. Sean Branch been out here killing like shit since he been home. Cutting niggas heads off..."

"That shit was all over the news months ago."

"Sean killed the dude Crud and Bruh killed a nigga named Whistle. After Sean cut the dude's head off, they tried to set the whole house on fire or something, but it didn't go up. The dude Crud had a brother. Him and a broad tried to flush Sean but missed, Sean and Bruh went Crud's funeral and caught the brother there. Sean crushed him. Bruh just drove. Tosheka knew the family. She was there at the funeral. She saw Que and Sean there and put two and two together. Later that day, she called Bruh and asked to meet. He went to her spot out Maryland and crushed her. Told me that she had unknowingly become a witnessed to the case and he couldn't lead witnesses, but I really think he did it because she was fucking with me. Why? Because zin Carter was there when he killed a muthafuckas. Why didn't she become a fucking danger to him? She was a witness, too..."

Crud, Whistle, Tosheka, and Zinfandel Carter were accessories to murder! In a blur, my fingers flew over the keys of the laptop. I had a lot of research to do. Then a lot of politicking would come next. I picked up the phone to call Bruce Culbreath.

"Yeah, Greg," Bruce answered.

"How did you know it was me?" I asked.

"It's called caller ID, buddy."

"Right. Silly me. Hey, so you know that Jihad Bashir has a cell phone in his cell at CTF, right?"

"I listened to the recordings. I'm aware of it. He has drugs, too, from the sound of things. Doesn't surprise me. Correctional officers are unpaid. They bring in contraband to supplement their meager income. I'm sending a shakedown team—"

"No, Bruce, that's why I called. No shakedown team."

"What? Greg, I can't let Bashir keep the phone once I..."

"Bruce, listen to me. Nobody knows about any of that but you and me. Us and the CO who gave him the phone. If you blitz his cell to find the phone, he'll know that we are on to him, and I don't need that. I need him comfortable and talking, so leave the phone for now. I'm also willing to bet that David Battle has a phone, too. I need to get a similar device put into his cell, too. Can you do that for me?"

"You're asking for too much now, buddy. We've been friends since college, but now you're infringing on my kindness, Greg. I let you into my jail to talk to David Battle while he was in the infirmary after he stabbed Warren Stevenson. I called in a big favor and had my tech guy put a recording device in an inmate's cell at CTF. Now you want me to replicate the illegal act? Not gonna happen, buddy. You're just going to have to suffice with what you have with Jihad Bashir. End of story."

"End of story, huh? Well, let me tell you *a story*." I went into the locked drawer of my desk and retrieved a file. I opened it. "Seven years ago, when you were just a captain, you worked with a woman named Sierra Sanders, who was a lieutenant. Sierra Sanders went to the 6th District Police Department and filed a report with two detectives. Detectives Robicheaux and Pointer, where she detailed the sexual assault by her supervisor at work. An arrest warrant was drafted. My office was contacted about the validity of the criminal charges. I had the name of the person being accused of sexual assault. I took the case and buried it. Three

IF YOU CROSS ME ONCE 4 | ANTHONY FIELDS

years ago you were Major then. A different woman, Crystal Jordan, a newly-hired correctional officer contacted a friend of hers named Dalia Craven, an Assistant U.S. Attorney, and told her about her superior officer at the D.C. jail who had committed forcible sodomy on her. Ms. Jordan also had several other women at the jail who were prepared to accuse a certain superior of various sexual crimes. Dalia Craven brought the case to me. I convinced Ms. Craven to forget about the case. Incentivized her to do it. There is no statue of limitation on—"

"Okay, I get your point," Bruce acquiesced. "I'll have my guy put the device in Battle's cell. But after this, no more favors, Greg. None."

"Let me know when it's done, Bruce. Thanks."

Chapter 18
Zin
Jonathan Zucker's Office
30th and M Street

"Mr. and Mrs. Settles, please come in and get comfortable." Jon greeted the couple as they walked into his office. "Mr. Settles—"

"Call me Christopher," Mr. Settles said.

"Thank you, Chris," Jon replied, and directed traffic. "I'm gonna need you to sit over here in this seat by the wall, out of the view of the camera. This deposition will be recorded. Mrs. Settles—"

"Maryann. Please, call me Maryann."

"Okay, Maryann. I'm going to need you at the table in the chair facing the camera. If for any reason you'd like to stop recording or take a break, please just say it. This young lady here is—"

"Zinfandel Carter," Maryann Settles offered. "I know who she is. I've seen her enough times on TV and I remember her as a little girl. You attended your father's trial every day; didn't you, Ms. Carter?"

I nodded my head. "My aunt Linda thought it would be a good idea for the jury to see me. Maybe have some sympathy for the nine-year-old little girl's father."

"Ms. Carter." Maryann Settles walked up to me. "Please forgive me for what I did to your father. To lose your mother to a senseless act of violence had to be traumatizing to you.

Then to lose your father to prison had to have made the situation worse." Tears formed in Maryann's eyes. "I know who your father was in the neighborhood, and I know that he didn't kill Dontay Samuels, but I was so strung out on drugs back then. Crack, powder, coke, heroin— I used it all. I did a lot of things that I'm not proud of, but the worst thing I did, by far, was to testify against an innocent man and send him to prison, I ruined your life even further…"

Tears threatened to fall from my eyes. The woman's apology was heartfelt but years too late and unnecessary. "You didn't ruin my life, Maryann. The person who killed my mother did. I've read your affidavit a hundred times. Both of them. And I understand exactly why you did what you did and I understand way you've come forward now. I'm a defense attorney, and being in that courtroom as a kid changed my life in a good way. Made me want to be a part of the system and not a prosecutor. I sit in front of defendants with stories like yours almost every day and every one of them would have taken the deal that Greg Gamble and Susan Rosenthal offered you. So, please, no more apologies. Everything in life happens for a reason and at it's due time. I honestly believe that had you not done what you did, my father would have died in the streets; a victim of something his own hand brought about.

"I'm still young, Maryann, but I'm not naïve. I know all about what my father was a part of back in the day, and I've told myself that hopefully prison has changed him. He may have been innocent in Dante's death, but I know that he was guilty in others. I believe that God has a way of balancing the scales of justice in a way He sees fit, and I believe that is what happened *then* and that is what's happening *now*."

"Thank you again," Maryann stated. "For forgiving me and understanding. Okay, Mr. Zucker, now what's next?" Maryanne took the chair she was directed to and sat down.

"I'm going to stand over here and ask you a lot of questions about what happened in 1996. Are you ready?"

"I'm ready," Maryann said and removed her coat.

"Comfy?"

"I'm good."

"Thirsty?"

"No, I'm good. Let's get this over with."

Jon remote-started the camera that sat on the tripod near the table. "Today is February the 4th, 2014. The time is 1:17 PM. This deposition is being recorded with the permission of Mrs. Maryanne Settles who is seated at the table wearing multicolored hospital scrubs and a dark colored t-shirt beneath the top. My name is Jonathan Zucker, criminal defense attorney for Michael Maurice Carter. This deposition is taking place in my office on 30th and M Street Northwest in Georgetown, Washington, D.C. Missus Settles, are you here on your own free will?"

"Yes, I am."

"Have you been threatened to be here?"

"No."

"Have you been paid to be here?"

"No. I have not."

"Do you swear under the penalty of perjury that everything you say will be the truth."

"I do."

"Okay, please state your name and date of birth for the record, please."

"Maryanne Louise Settles. Date of Birth 4/17/1962."

"So, you are 51 years old. And what is your occupation?"

"I'm a licensed nurse practitioner."

"Let me direct your attention to January 17th, 1996. Do you remember that day? What happened that day?"

"I do. I was arrested on that day for prostitution with intent to distribute heroin after being caught with thirteen dime bags of blow that I was selling to get bags of my own personal use. I was arrested on Talbert Street where it intersects with the 2400 block of Martin Luther King Junior Avenue. I was transferred to the 7th District Police Station.

From there I was taken to CCB Central Cellblock. The next morning, I was taken to the court building, and while waiting to talk to the attorney, my name was called. I was taken to a room somewhere inside the building. That's where I met Greg Gamble. He was just a regular prosecutor back then..."

Chapter 19
The News

"A staff member who works for the Senator William Rand was stabbed Saturday evening by an inmate released from prison a day earlier in an apparent random attack on a busy commercial street in Northeast Washington. The staffer suffered life-threatening injuries but was considered stable while awaiting surgery to address a punctured lung, internal bleeding and a brain injury. Senator Rand works on an oversight committee that deals with Homeland Security issues. He released this statement today..."

"This past weekend, a member of my staff was brutally attacked in broad daylight in Washington D.C.. I ask you to join Donna and me in praying for a speedy recovery and thanking first responders, hospital staff and the police for their diligent actions."

"The incident occurred at 5:15 PM in the 1300 block of H Street Northeast after the staffer and his friend left a nearby restaurant. According to charging documents, the staffer told police in an interview from the hospital that he didn't know the man who stabbed him or why he was attacked. Police on Saturday arrested 42-year-Old Glenn Nill of Southeast D.C. and charged him with assault with intent to kill. Mr. Nill was released from prison a day before the attack, according to Federal Bureau of Prisons inmate locator. Nill was convicted in 2002 for pandering, kidnapping and other charges. He spent the next 11 and a half years in prison. On Saturday, law enforcement identified Nill as the attacker by using a cell phone found at the scene and calling a woman who turned out to be Nill's sister. After his arrest, Nill told police that he heard a voice telling him to attack someone.

"The attack came days before the House Oversight Committee's planned hearing Wednesday on crime and public safety in the Nation's Capital, which I expect to focus broadly on D.C.'s approach to reducing violent crime. Chairman Jon Christianson blames the radical Left Wing Politics that he believes have led to the crime and crisis in D.C.. As of Tuesday, homicides in D.C. are up 19% compared to 2012. Property crime is up by 27%, while other violent crimes have remained steady compared to the same period from last year.

"In other news today, City Under Siege, Fox News 5 has been told that a woman has come forward accusing United States Attorney Gregory Gamble of serious improprieties. Social say that the unknown woman was a witness in a 1996 triple trial against a D.C. man being tried for murder. The woman alleges that she was given several lump sum payments and had her charges dismissed in exchange for her perjured testimony. The allegations have cast a dark shadow over the city's US Attorney's Office. More about the trial and potential scandal as more information unfolds.

"One person is dead and two people were wounded today in Prince George's County. The shootings happened about 12:40 AM in the 2500 block of Chillum Road near Queens Chapel Road and the Maryland, D.C. line. When police arrived, they found three people with gunshot wounds. They were all taken to an area hospital and one person was pronounced dead. Police have quickly identified the victims a Antwan Lindsay of Landover, who was a security guard at the nightclub. The two others are in stable conditions. PG police said..."

Chapter 20

Michael Carter
USP. CANAAN
Waymart, Pennsylvania

"My homie Gutta Almighty told me to holla at you when I got here."

I took the razor blade and cut into the onion and proceeded to slice and dice it. I did the same with the green pepper before responding to the short dude with long dreads standing at the table in my unit. "What's your name, youngin?"

"Supreme."

"Supreme is your nickname, but your government name is Terrell Armstead, right?"

"Yeah, but how—"

"Listen to me, youngin. I'm gonna be straight up with you. I don't really like fucking with niggas with pimping cases. I'm an old-timer street nigga, and I can't understand all that pimp shit. I got a daughter that I love with all my heart, and if I found out that she was selling pussy for a pimp, I'd kill 'em both. All that human trafficking and having the word *minor* in y'all's paperwork; That shit throws me off on some *chomo* shit…"

"Whoa, hold up, Mr. Carter," Supreme stated.

"Mr. Carter was my father. Call me Mike."

"Aight, yo. I mean, Mike, I did have one bitch that was seventeen and I didn't know it, but the counts, in regards to her, I beat so my paperwork doesn't have that minor of shit in it no more. But I get where you coming from and I respect it either way if you ain't trying to fuck with me."

"Never said that I wasn't gonna fuck with you, youngin. Gutta hit me and told me about your situation— all of it. I fuck with Gutta, and you his lil homie from his city. So, I'ma definitely fuck with you. Besides, I hate the fact that a nigga from D.C. got you jammed up like that. What part of Baltimore you from?"

"Over East."

"Alright, that's what's up. What's the dude's name from D.C. that cooked you?"

"Zeke. His government name is Isaih Green. He's from 14th and Fairmont."

Saving the name in my memory bank, I dumped 2 packs of imitation crab meat into the plastic bowl. Then I added baby shrimps, clams, oysters, mackerel and Kepper Snacks. "Zeke from Fairmont, huh?"

"Yeah. The wild nigga sold me a rack of guns for the low. Then he gon' take his stupid ass to the gun show in Virginia and tried to purchase a rack of big guns. The ATF got on his line, followed him to D.C. and caught him with some shit. Instead of taking the pinch and doing his time, the bitch nigga told on everybody that he sold guns to. I got the gun case and the pimpin' case, but Zeke started everything."

"How's that?"

"Because my dumb ass was supposed to meet Zeke in Greenbelt to cop some more guns, but I couldn't make it. I sent two of my bitches to meet him and cop the guns. When the ATF cracked the bitches, they told on me about the pimping shit. Gutta told me the play. I got thirty bands—"

"Say less, youngin. Say less."

***

"That muthafuckin' seafood pasta salad you be making be like that, slim. Remind me of how Grandma used to make it," Lil Man stated as he took a finger and swiped the rim of the bowl and licked his finger. "That shit be taking me out there— street shit. I swear to God. Bad muthafucka."

I laughed at Lil Man's description of my pasta dish as I punished my bowl of pasta

Lil Man shook a peach drink up in his half gallon plastic jug and drank almost half of it. He walked to the cell door and peeped out the glass. "Both pigs are in the office too, big boy, so you can rock out whenever you ready."

"Aight, slim, that's what's up. I'ma finish this food first before I make my calls."

"Bet. While you do that, I gotta ask you something that's been on my mind, slim."

"What's up, homie? Talk to me."

"Remember a couple weeks ago when we were talking about all the niggas with bones on 'em about some hot shit? And we were saying what's hot and what's not?"

"Of course, I remember. Why? What's up?"

"Because there's two niggas that I fuck with that niggas been dragging through the mud on some hot shit, and I forgot to mention them before you laid down to take a nap."

I finished off the seafood pasta, set my empty bow down and said, "Alright, I'm up now. I'm full but alert. Shoot."

"My man named OG. He from Savannah Terrace. He got a codefendant named Tony Rone. In 2008, OG was in Pollock with me. He came to my unit with tears in his eyes. He asked me who I know in Lee County that could put the knife in his codefendant for him. He said that his codefendant, Tony Rone, was in Lee County telling niggas he was hot. I couldn't help him on that one. So, it passed. Cool. Fast forward to about three years ago I was in Hazelton when Tony Rone got there from Thomson. He worked the codre Thompsons until he got into a fight. They sent him to Hazelton. Now, keep in mind that OG is my man."

"Which OG? There's two of them."

"I'm hip, but one of 'em is from Uptown – Six Forty, I believe. He just came back on a body for killing a nigga that put a *hot* bone on him years ago. Not him. My OG is Ronald Randolph, who also went out and came back in on a body. Lunchin' ass nigga smoked a broad that did the bid with him. Aight, Check this out though. I run into Tony Rone in Hazelton and confront him about the bone he put out there about OG. Here's what happened: Tony Rone went and got some paperwork; his appeal transcripts In the case, most of the evidence was stronger against Tony Rone due in part to the fact that he threatened his baby mother one day and told her, 'I just put three bullets in Carlos' head; don't make me put the other three in yours.' The baby mother was on the phone with her girlfriend who heard what Tony said. She contacted the people and told the cops what she heard Tony Rone say. The people got on Tony Rone line and raided the baby mother's spot. She told the people that Tony had a gun under the fridge. The people got the gun and it turns out to be the murder weapon. Tony Rone goes in on the beef. Other muthafuckas start talking. Along the way, OG gets picked up on the case, too. They go to trail and lose. On appeal, OG's lawyers do a good job of arguing OG should have never been found guilty at trial. His 40-year sentence gets overturned, but Tony Rone's didn't. Instead of another trial, the government offered OG a cop to ten years served. OG took the cop, but here's the thing: Tony Rone was still fighting his appeal. Something OG said when he took the cop was wild, but I need to know if you think it's hot or not."

"What did he say?" I asked Lil Man.

"When he went in front of the judge to take the cop, the judge asked him, 'On September 3rd, 1998, did you and Phillip Stewart kill Carlos Thompson?' And OG answered yes."

I thought about what Lil Man had just said. The situation his man was in was a wicked situation to be in.

"OG never made any statements in the case before the appeal. He never did no hot shit in jail or otherwise. When Tony Rone showed me the paperwork where OG said that to the judge it fucked me up."

"If his words to the judge fucked you up, then you already know the answer to your own question.

"But see, you gotta know OG before you judge the situation. Slim is a gangster. He's a man's man who gon' give it out however you want it. Hands, knives, guns, whatever. Cold-blooded assassin out there."

"So was Poppy and Omar."

"I'm hip, but you can't put OG in the category with them. They wicked on a whole other level. I kind of look at OG joint as a mistake. He should've gotten his lawyer to craft out a cop where Tony Rone's name wouldn't be mentioned..."

"Or he could have just told the judge no. Me and Phillip Stewart didn't kill Carlos Thompson. I did alone. He was already at the "take a cop' phase of his appeal. He could've just took the beef. What was they gon' do?"

"Yeah, I get that, homes. But realistically, who gon' do that and risk jeopardizing the freedom they're about to get after 10 years in the bing? I think OG was just geekin' too get home and wasn't really thinking about the adverse effect it could have on his codefendant. Did OG go home? Wait, you said he did, right? And come back in."

Lil Man nodded. "Yeah. He went out in 2010. I think he had a bowlegged year or two to do after he took the cop on another beef."

"So, what does Tony Rone say?"

"He told me that he never called OG hot. The man that read his paperwork did, because they had OG plea in his appeal. He says OG is his brother and he would never call him hot. But he feels that OG's answer to the judge while taking the cop did kind of hurt him."

"Well, there you have it, slim. I can see both sides of it. I couldn't argue with either side. The dude, Tony Rone, was already found guilty of the murder, so it ain't like OG got him convicted. I would have never said what he said to the judge, but I can see your view that slim just blundered and his words were not intended to harm Tony. He just wanted to cop and get out. I get it. But I can also get what dudes are feeling when they call him hot. That's one of them ones where I'd stay out of it."

"Respect. Respect. A'ight, I got a man named Tookie—"

"Swamp brother?"

"Naw, not Allen Lawrence. That nigga anything My Tookie from Uptown. He got a brother named Mort and a little brother named Deon. Anyway, Tookie was ever the jail and the people came to see him. They wanted him to wear a wire and set a dude up for them. He agreed and went out. But once he got on the street, he never met up with the feds. He ran on 'em; never set anyone up or nothing."

"So, what's the problem then?"

"You got people saying that he's still hot because he agreed to do it. They saying that he must've told the feds something they liked, because they freed him from jail to get the dude. They saying that in order to take the deal he had to have said something. What you think?"

"That's another head-scratcher, slim. I can see the arguments made from both sides. I guess that's gon' come down to who's saying it and whether they like slim or not. I can't say either way."

"Damn, you were a big help."

I laughed and got up from the bunk. "Sorry, homie, you asked for my opinion and I gave it to you." I went to the sink and washed out my bowl.

***

As soon as I turned on the cell phone on, the voicemail alert chimed. I listened to all of the voicemails and then checked my incoming text messages. One text in particular made me pause. Immediately, I dialed my sister's phone. Her message was a week old.

"You've got a problem," Linda said as soon as she picked up. "More like *problems*. Plural."

"What problems are you talking about?" I asked.

"Your daughter is your problems. She knows that you have a cell phone and kept it from her."

"What? How the hell does she know that? You told her?"

"Now why the fuck would I do that? It wasn't me. She was with Ameen's son."

"Quran?"

"Yes, and that's your other problem. Well, another one of them. Zin know that you and that boy are friends and are in contact with each other."

"But, how?"

"I told your ass that she's been seeing that boy for months now. They were together recently when you called. The boy has you programmed in his phone as MC. While he was sleeping, Zin saw the call come in, got suspicious and answered the call. She heard you and recognized yo' voice."

"Fuck! I remember that day I called Quran."

"You called Quran? Why didn't you ever tell me that you are still in contact with that boy?"

"That boy is a man, Lin, and I've always been in contact with him. I didn't know that I needed to brief you on that."

"Well, it's not a good look from your daughter's prospective because she say that you and Quran have both lied about knowing the other. It's all bad, Mike. You lied to that girl about the cell phone, and you lied about knowing Quran. The trust between you and your daughter is irretrievably broken. And that ain't all; she thinks you killed her mother."

I almost dropped the cell phone from my hand. "*What? Why would she think some stupid ass shit like that?*"

"It's in the letter."

"The letter? What letter? Lin, what the fuck are you talking about? You throwing me off like shit. I ain't never wrote no letter."

"I never said anything about you writing no letter, dumbass. The letter I'm talking about wasn't written by you. You keep cutting me off and shit. Let me finish a fucking sentence, will you? The letter was written by her mother."

"Patricia?"

"What other mother she got, Mike?"

"No way."

"*Yes, way!* The letter was in one of the boxes that had Patricia stuff in it. The ones that Zin has had in storage for years. She went through the boxes and found a letter that her mother wrote before she died. I saw the letter and read it."

"What the fuck does it say, Lin?"

"Look, nigga, all the fucking cursing at me is about to make me hang up on you and say fuck you."

"Aight, aight. My bad, Lin. No more cursing. You read this letter. What does it say?"

"I didn't memorize it. I don't remember all of it, but it said something about you treating her different. She believed you were there that night and saw her with Ameen. She thinks you killed him—"

"Killed who? Ameen?"

"Yes, and she mentioned that you brought Ameen's son to y'all's house, and he reminded her of Ameen. Something about Quran and the friend Dontay killing people for you and she believed that you were going to kill her and probably get Quran and Dontay to do it. That's the gist of it."

I smacked my forehead. "Man, what the fuck?"

"And big brother, that ain't all. I saved the best part for last."

"Best part? And none of what you just said…"

"Your daughter is pregnant, by the gray-eyed boy Quran."

"This can't be happening."

"It's happening. I don't know how far along she is, but she's keeping the baby."

"This can't be real. I must be dreaming."

"You're not dreaming, Mike. And before I forget, don't ask me how this happened, butut it did. Zin linked up with Delores Samuels. According to Zin, Dolores, gave her the complete rundown of her whole family history, starting with her grandmother moving to D.C. from Mississippi. Zin called her Aunt Dolores and they're going to visit grave sites at Harmony in the upcoming weeks. So now you know everything I know. I'd hate to be in your shoes right now, brother. But you're a survivor. Always was, always will be. Figure things out. Talk to your daughter. We'll talk later. Love you. Bye."

The line on the other end died, just like the relationship with Zin was about to. Silently I prayed that didn't happen.

Chapter 21
Michael Carter

Karma was a bitch called life that threw temper tantrums when she was just supposed to shut the fuck up and fall back. I laid in my bunk listening to my celly snore and fart simultaneously. If you can't beat them, join them. I ended up a little gassy in myself because seafood pasta will do that. I thought about what my sister told me on the phone. I lost the trust of my daughter. The sad part of it is all was that she was probably right. I asked myself why I never told Zin that I had the cell phone and why I never called her on it. The answer came to me quickly.

You never told her about the phone because she'd ask too many questions about how you'd gotten it and what you needed it for. You never told her about the business you created and operated from your jail cell, all the hits you called, and the money you've made. The less Zin knew, the better.

My anger started to boil. Quran was out of pocket and he knew it. That's why he lied to me when we spoke and he never mentioned anything about Zin. My daughter wasn't for him and he knew it. He knew how overprotective I was about my only daughter. He was supposed to protect her, not fuck her. The stab wounds of betrayal punctured my heart. It was no surprise to me that Quran had betrayed me. Betrayal was in his blood. The gene had been passed down to him from his father.

But you betrayed Ameen, too. You had an affair with his wife and birthed a son with her. A son that Ameen thought was his. Betrayal is betrayal, no matter who dishes it first.

A smile crossed my face as I thought about Khadijah Bashir and all the freaky things I've done with and to her. I whispered, *God bless the dead*, to myself as I remembered her. How Khadijah had come to me upset about Ameen's promiscuity and how I took advantage of her vulnerabilities. I thought about the day when she called to tell me that she was pregnant and that the child was mine. No one could ever know, she said. That was a secret that would have to die with us both. At first, I didn't believe Khadijah, but when the baby was born, I knew it was true. There were no extra curly hair or gray eyes as all the other sons of Ameen had. The baby boy had Carter eyes. Karma is a woman scorned that is supposed to accept her failures but can't.

My daughter was pregnant and the father was Quran Bashir. How had the cards in my hand been dealt so viciously. My entire life was a never-ending labyrinth that wouldn't allow me or betrayal to leave the maze. Ameen had loved and sexed Patricia before and after me. I had sexed wife and impregnated her. My son had two older brothers, Quran and Jihad. One brother I raised after I killed his father. Then life threw me a curveball. I ended up in prison for killing Dontay Samuels, a murder that Quran committed. After I'm in jail, Quran kills his brother, my son, Khalid, and falls in love with my daughter w ho's forbidden to him. Now my daughter is eventually going to give birth to a gray-eyed child that will always remind me of the man I killed. My friend, my heart, my biggest betrayer— Ameen Bashir. The circle of life was a muthafucka. Karma is a vindictive bitch that caught her man – fate – cheating and vowed to get him back. I couldn't believe the way things had turned out. In my wildest dreams, I never imagined a future like this. I asked myself why I didn't reveal to Quran that I knew about him and Zin. That answer also came quickly.

You never said anything to Quran because you want to keep him asleep, but there will come a time when you'll wake him up, and that's right before he dies.

I turned my thoughts to the letter that Zin had. A letter Patricia had written before she was killed. Dirty bitch couldn't just die and be gone. She had to leave something behind. Her truth. From the grave, she was still fucking me over. I thought about what Linda said was in the letter read. I thought about the truth of it all, except the part about Quran and Dontay being her killers. That part, Patricia had gotten wrong. I would be her killer. I became her killer. I killed her.

"One death wasn't good enough for you, bitch," I mumbled.

Things had certainly spiraled out of control, and I had to find a way to regain control. I had to find a way to get the train back on track, at least until I got home. The next thing I knew, sleep found me and took me to another place.

***

Three Days Later...

"Carter, pack your shit and take everything to R and D." The counselor knocked on the cell door early in the morning and said.

Getting up out of the bed, I walked to the door. "R and D, pack up? Where am I going?" I asked.

"All I know is that the unit says 'US Marshals D.C.'. Pack it up."

Lil Man woke from his slumber. "Mike. What's up, slim? What they talking about?"

"The evidentiary hearing came through. I'm on my way back up to the jail."

"That's bigger than baseball, slim."

"I already know, homie. I already know."

***

After I packed out, things moved at a whirlwind pace. The US Marshals showed up in Cannan the next day to drive me to D.C.. The trip took a little under four hours and was scenic. When I saw the sign that said, *Welcome to Washington, D.C.* I almost cried.

Chapter 22
Zin

"Hello, Miss Carter. You represent Robert Barton, right?"

"I do," I replied to the mature white woman who sought me out as soon as I walked into the conference room at the Wilson Building in downtown D.C.. "And you must be Pamela Bailey."

"Please. Call me Pam. Everybody else does. Has Robert told you all about our organization?"

I nodded. "He has, and so has my other client, Denzel McCauley. *More Than Our Crime* sounds like a great platform to get the word out about the injustice our family members face in the criminal justice system. It's much needed."

"Thank you. We thought so. That's why we founded it. You have a family member incarcerated too, I'm told."

"Yes, my father."

"Was he incarcerated before 2001?"

"Yes, ma'am. He went to prison in 1995."

"Well, this forum affects him as well. Come on, let's go in."

***

"Parole boards often keep offenders in the dark. So, too, do the practices of the United States Parole Commission, which was jurisdiction over people convicted in the

District," Avis Buchanan said to the room. She adjusted her microphone at the podium. "These problems cannot be ignored. *Must not be ignored* In any discussion about incarceration, and it's disproportionate effect on poor, over-policed minority communities The Commission, a federal agency with broad discretion and limited accountability, has local jurisdiction because of the 1997 National Capital Revitalization Act. That act separated the D.C. government from certain criminal justice institutions and functions. It abolished the D.C. Parole Board and transferred authority over D.C. parolees to the Commission. It abolished indeterminate sentences followed by parole and replaced them with determinate sentences followed by periods of supervised release. It also closed the locally run prison facilities and transferred jurisdiction of all D.C. premises to the Federal Bureau of Prisons..."

I took a moment to look around at some of the people gathered in the room. Most were community leaders, activists and former prisoners who acted as violence interrupters in local neighborhoods. I spotted the Mayor of D.C. and the Deputy Mayor. I recognized Congresswoman Delanore Holmes-Norton. Also in attendance was none other than the US Attorney for D.C., Greg Gamble himself. Our eyes met and held each other's stare. Then subtly, a smile appeared on his face. He winked at me. The blood in my veins began to boil. *Fuck you, motherfucker.*

"Most D.C. prisoners serve their sentences at various BOP facilities throughout the country. They face unique challenges. They have limited, if any, access to family, limited if any contact with defense attorneys specializing in parole affairs and limited access to recently programming specific to the District. These formidable obstacles make it more difficult to achieve release at parole hearings. It is well past the time to move beyond overly punitive mindsets, unfair processes and inaccurate assessment tools. Whether it is the Commission or another entity that continues to hold power over people convicted in D.C., the rules and practices surrounding parole and parole-revocation should be a vital part of a broader dialogue about the urgent need for criminal justice reform."

Pam Bailey stood and replaced Avis Buchanan at the lectern. "Hello. My name is Pam Bailey. and along with two incarcerated lifetime D.C. residents, Robert Barton and Denzell McCauley, I started the More Than Our Crimes organization to give a voice to the voiceless men and women who've been forgotten by a lot of the people in this room. When D.C. Mayor Yvette Bowers asked Congresswoman Holmes-Norton for legislations, wresting central of D.C.'s parole system from the federal government, naming it critical in the path of statehood, she estimated that the city would need two years to prepare. That was January 2012. But today, D.C. remains in virtually the same position. No agreement on the path forward for a new parole system. Even after agreeing to pay a company at least $765,000 to work on it and another criminal justice matter. Last Wednesday, the city told Congress in a closed-door meeting that it would need at least another two years to get it done. This delay means that the city will miss an opportunity to secure more local autonomy under a Democratic controlled Congress. The D.C Public Defender Service, which represents people in parole hearings before the U.S. Parole Commission, said the District should put the D.C. Superior Court exclusively in charge of parole decisions. D.C's. U.S. Attorney Greg Gamble has echoed that belief. He's here today to speak to you as well..."

When it was time for Greg Gamble to speak, it was my cue to exit the building.

***

Surfside Taco Stand
Dupont Circle

"Thank you for meeting me for lunch, Aunt Dolores."

"Baby, trust me, it's a pleasure to be here with you. I told you I wanted this; prayed for this. Being with you reminds me of the time I spent with Patricia. Your mannerisms, your eyes, your regal grace is all her. I'm looking forward to us going to Harmony Cemetery so that I can take you to everybody's burial site. So make sure that you wear sensible shoes that day. No heels."

"Got you. Are you ready to order?"

The windchill wasn't bad, but it was cold out. Even with the sun high in the sky, Dolores Samuels was dressed casually in jeans, a winter coat, Doc Martin boots, a fashionable scarf in her ever-present hijab. "I sure am. I've heard a lot about this spot, but never had the chance to eat here. I've been staring at the posted menu. I think I'll have the Bonaire chicken burrito. It's stuffed with sauteed chicken breasts, pico de gallo, lime crema, yellow rice and pepper jack cheese."

"Sounds good, but I think this baby inside me once the Nevis shrimp tacos. The menu says it's stuffed with shrimp, rice, salsa, crema and guacamole. I don't really like guacamole, but I think the baby does."

Dolores laughed. "Then you have to promise me that no matter what happens, you'll stay in touch with me and let me be a part of the baby's life. Promise me that."

"Easy promise to make. But why would you say *no matter what happens*?"

"Let's order the food first, then I'll explain."

At the stand's counter, I ordered the food for me and Dolores and paid for both meals. I grabbed Dolores' hand and led her to a nearby table with chairs that were set up outdoors. "Talk to me."

"I don't know. I'm just being precautious. You said that your father may be getting out and we do know each other from the past, but…"

"But? But, what?"

"After your mother's death, after Dontay told me about what happened to Patricia, I hated Mike Carter. Hell, I still do. And there's no way that I can be around him without hating him and not hiding it. I want to be around you and this baby, but I can't do Michael Carter in no form or fashion. I wanna love you and the baby. I don't know what type of influence your father has on you—"

"Aunt Dolores, we have a lot of catching up to do, a lot to learn about each other, and I welcome that. But I must tell you that I am my mother's daughter first and foremost. I am not completely convinced that he killed my mother. No disrespect to you or Dontay God bless the dead and what he told you, but I have to figure things out. But make no mistake about it, Auntie, I am a grown ass— excuse my language— woman and nobody can influence me in any way. Good or bad. So, our friendship, our relationship is gonna be, regardless of who's in or out of the picture. I promise you that. From my mouther to God's ears."

Dolores' eyes watered, but she wiped away the tears. "Okay, I had a moment. I'm back. Sorry."

"No apologies or worries. And just so you'll know, my father's back in the city. He's at the D.C. jail right now. He has an evidentiary hearing scheduled for two weeks from today."

"You think the system will free him?"

"I think so. All signs and case low support him being freed, and the US. Attorney Greg Gamble being ousted at Triple Nickel. I can't say when he'll be released, but I believe he will be. Depends on the judge."

"Have you talked to him? Told him about me?"

The two taco stand workers called out our numbers. "Hold tight, let me get our food." I grabbed the two trays of food and went back to the table. Despite the weather, it was comfortable being with Dolores. I handed her her food and drink. Picking up one of the shrimp tacos, I bit into it and savored the exquisite taste. "Oh my God this is good."

"Mine, too. I sure hope ain't no pork seasoning in none of this."

I laughed at Dolores. She reminded me of Quran. "Shouldn't be. They can be sued for not disclosing that ingredient. As for your question, no, I haven't talked to my father since we met and talked, so I didn't tell him about us, but I'm quite sure my aunt did."

"Who, Linda?"

I nodded.

"You told Linda about us meeting and talking?"

"I did. Unfortunately."

"When something was amiss, your mother had that some look about her. What did Linda say?"

I bit into my taco and chewed. "She called you a junkie."

"Honey, I've been called worse by better people. I already told you that I went through a rough spell where I was strung out on drugs, powdered coke, Crack, woodah blunts, pills and even sometimes a little heroin. I did that *unapologetically me*. That's my albatross that hangs around my neck. It started after I learned that Donnie was cheating, and it lasted for years. Chile, I was out there. I was terrible out in them streets. Especially after Dontaye died. I was in everything but a hearse. I did things in those days that are against the law in all 50 states *and* the District. I don't deny any of what I did or of who I was. I've been called bitch, slut whore, crackhead, dope fiend, a trick, a smoker, a base head, a clucker, a pipe head, a whole lot of other stuff that I forgot. I never shied away from ridicule; from judgment. Those negativities help to build my incomparable spirit. I am 10 years sober and loving it. So, nothing Linda Carter calls me offends me. And I could tell you a few things about your aunt too, now, but I won't. People who live in a glass house can't throw stones. But I digress. Knowing Linda, if you told her about me, she definitely told Mike. I don't care though. Just wanted to know if you told him about us."

"I really respect everything you just said, for real, and you'll probably come up later when I see my father."

"You going to visit him at the jail?"

"Not at the jail. In-person. Visits over the jail are on the TV-screen."

"Well, good luck with that."

***

D.C. General parking lot
D Street Southwest
Unsure of what the balance held/ I touched my belly overwhelmed /by what I had chosen to perform/ but then an angel came one day./Told me to kneel down and pray./For unto me a Man child would be born/Woe this crazy circumstance. I knew his life deserved a chance/But everybody told me to be smart./ "Look at your career," they said. / "Lauren, baby, use your head."/ But instead I chose to use my heart./Now the joy of my world lives in Zion...

I could feel Lauryn Hill's words inside my soul as I sat in the car waiting to go inside the old hospital. D.C. Jail utilized the reception area of the closed hospital as the area where people came to sit in front of a screen and visit inmates at the jail. Getting out of the car, I made the short walk to the entrance to the reception area. After checking in, I was directed to one of about twenty screens.

"At exactly 6:30 the screen will come to life with your inmate on it. Enjoy your visit," the correctional officer said, and walked away. Just as he disappeared behind a door, my father's face appeared on the screen. Michael Carter smiled his Kool-Aid smile at me.

I didn't smile back. "Hey, Dad, how are you doing? You good?"

"Hey, baby girl, I couldn't be better. I'm glad you scheduled the visit."

"Yeah, me too. We really need to talk, Dad."

"Well, let's talk then, baby girl."

"I guess the first thing you need to know is that I'm pregnant."

Chapter 23
Michael Carter
Southwest Two
Housing Unit, (D.C. Jail)

Thirty minutes flew by and what seemed like seconds I laid in my bunk after the visit with Zin was over and thought about our conversation. She told me about the pregnancy, about Quran and how they met, knowing that I knew about most of that. She never mentioned her mother's letter that she found. She never asked me anything about my culpability in her mother's death. She never asked me about my relationship with Quran, why it existed or for how long. We ended the visit by discussing my case. In most conversations, it's not always what a person says that's the most telling. It's inside of what they *didn't* say. Knowing my daughter like I did, her pain lay in the things that she wanted to say but didn't, and I understood why. Did I come away from the visit feeling that our trust, or her trust in me was inevitably broken? No. Did I sense her reservation? Yes. I guess the real issue between us would have to wait until they could be discussed in person.

The door of my cell slid open suddenly. I stood up to see why it opened. When I got to the door, I saw a man with a bed roll approaching the cell. I stepped out. He looked at me and I looked at him. A moment of silence passed as he got to the cell. The man dropped his bed roll onto the floor. It was a moment of truth. A smile slowly crossed my face. The same smile crossed the man's face as we embraced.

"Bucky Fields! What's up, slim?"

"Mike Carter! How you, bruh?"

I reached down and picked up Buck's bed roll, and together we walked into the cell.

***

"I like the beard, slim. All gray joint. Almost didn't recognize you."

"I been on my deen, so I let the joint grow out. But I like it because it helps me to trick niggas. Especially the young niggas. They see the gray and think stuff sweet. Calling a nigga Unc and OG and all that goofy stuff. They think a good man done got old, and because of that they jump out there."

"I hear you still putting hands on shit."

"All the mutha-loving time."

I laughed at my old friend. "Still don't curse at all, huh?"

"A lot about me has changed, but mostly I'm still the same. Don't drink, smoke, do no drugs, don't curse. And I ain't messing with no faggies or pulling my penis out on no female staff. That makes me still the same, despite all the whispers."

"The whispers, huh? That's crazy that you mentioned that, and that I'm here and you're here, because me and my celly was just talkin' about you and that bone niggas is whispering."

Buck's disposition Notably changed to one of aggression and defense. "Is that right? And y'all said what?"

"Damn, homie, calm down. We on your side," I cajoled "The men all know that shit is some bullshit."

"Who is your celly? You still in Canaan?"

"Yeah, I'm still in that wild ass joint. You know the cop got crushed out there in February of last year. Them crackers been on some cold-blooded bullshit ever since, but I know how to maneuver around them. My celly is Lil Man."

"What Little Man? Henry James?"

I nodded.

"What's up with that lunchin ass nigga? He good?"

"He good. ADX got that nigga burnt out. But other than that, he cool, tryna get back on that IRAA law the city just passed."

"That's what up."

"He was talking to me about the men that niggas is putting bones on right now and back in the day and your name came up."

"Homie, the name of the game today is character assassination. That's the new *I don't like somebody*. Niggas hate me and I get it, because I've been busting my knife, putting hands and feet on niggas for almost four decades. Since Cedar and Oak Hill. Niggas can't control me. They can't take me, and I'm not a follower. I don't have any visible weaknesses. None! I hate jackers, rats and faggots. Oh, and cowards. I've always been firm in my stance about a lot of stuff that niggas love – wild shit. So, I'm not surprised that so-called men have believed and spread a bone about me that ain't true. Character assassination is all they can do to me, but they do it outside of my presence, and that's smart. It shows intelligence, but where is the intelligence when they condemn a good man with no proof?"

I nodded. "Preach."

Buck laughed a long and resounding laugh that reverberated throughout the small cell.

"Stop that bull-jive, slim."

Smiling, I told him, "Naw, big boy, I'm feeling you one hundred percent. I ain't tryna be funny."

The smile faded and the passion returned to Buck's face, and his voice. "That bone stuff been eating at my soul, slim. I ain't never had my name associated with no slander like that. I'm messed up inside my core. I keep telling these niggas the same thing over and over about how the bone started..."

"I heard about it."

"Naw, slim, you gotta really hear me. The nigga on the beef with me, Lonell Tucker. I thought he was working with them people when I first came in. I called to the streets and voiced that to some dudes. Word got to him that I was calling him a rat. The people bought him and some other dudes in later, and made us codefendants. At trial. Lonnell was out of the box. I got on the stand and tried to deny everything that rat Crud said. The sucka Lonnell told everybody that I was up there trying to put the beef on the dude Will that owned the barbershop. He lied. The coward nigga was on get back because of what I said about him earlier in the case, when he came over here to the jail after we lost a trial, he convinced a rack of young niggas and punks that I told on the stand. All these young niggas know is the Bucky Fields that write books. They don't know the Bucky Fields that's going to nail them to the ground for repeating that slander. This stuff crazy, slim. A good man shouldn't have to defend himself against lies. The burden is on the dudes who spread the lies to prove it."

"You right, slim. no bullshit."

"My man Nut hit me from Pollock. You remember Nut?"

"Angelo Daniels from Eastgate?"

Buck nodded. "Yeah. Slim hit me in the letter and said, 'Bruh, stop explaining yourself to niggas. You keep explaining your situation in the books. Fuck them niggas. The men who matter know what's up. Stop explaining yourself to them nobody niggas."

"Wise words from a great man."

"Tone said the same thing using different words. So did Nehemiah, LA, KK, Duck Sauce, and my codefendant named Lacy. I hear them all, slim, loud and clear. But what they don't understand is this: Niggas is slandering *me*, not them! It's easy to say *slim don't pay that stuff. no mind* when it ain't you.

"True. Very true."

"I got a platform with the books everywhere. Niggas everywhere, real live, love my books. They reading 'em all over the country, slim, so I gotta tell the men who've heard the bulljive, what the real deal is. Gotta let him know that I never broke, never told, and that the dingaling eating nigga, Lonnell Tucker, used my defense at the trial to get back at me for calling him a rat. I agree with the men that a rack of these niggas are nobodies, but I still gotta safeguard myself by spreading the word that the bone ain't true. Why? Because I'ma kill about my name, slim. I'ma die about my integrity and honor. So that makes me afraid..."

"Afraid? Afraid of what?"

"Afraid that I'ma kill one of these stupid niggas. Real live, and I don't wanna do that, slim. I got one more killing in me left and I'm gonna save it for somebody that need it the most like Crud."

"Byron Clark."

Buck nodded.

"He dead already".

"You sure, slim?"

"Positive."

"Damn! I didn't know that. Alhamdulillah. You gotta fill me in on that later. But like I was saying, I'm saving my last kill. I'm not trying to waste it on just anybody. This prison stuff is for lesser niggas than you and me. I'm tryna to get out of here the right way. I ain't tryna be trapped in here for the rest of my life. That's why I talk about it so much and write about it. I'm trying to get the bone cleared up before I gotta kill one of these niggas" Buck said and unrolled his bed roll.

As he started to make up his bed, I saw the knife he pulled out of the sheets. "Got damn, big boy, you strapped already."

Buck picked up the homemade weapon and tucked it in the waistband of his uniform pants. "You already know. I cut this joint out of the desk in the intake block. Gotta have it. I ain't playing with none of these young niggas in this jail. What are you back here on?"

"A Rule 33 and the 23-110 motion. The fag nigga Greg Gamble paid a witness to lie in my trial and the witness recanted and exposed him…"

***

Early the Next Morning…

"I already told you that I'm not taking any new clients, right?" Jon Zucker asked me.

"Yeah, you told me that."

"Well, it's true. After I resolve the cases that I have, I'm out of here. Thinking about taking an extended vacation to Europe; spend some of the money I've made over the years. I consider this my last hoorah, so I'm serious about sticking it to Gamble. Here is your copy of Maryann Settles' deposition. Read it, but understand that she's even better in person. A perfect witness. Better than when she testified against you years ago. She's articulate, believable, and convinced that she needs to atone for what she did to you. She even apologized to Zin for taking you away from her all these years. Her charisma and personality doesn't translate on paper, but it shines in person. She's going to do great, even under the threat of perjury, which Gamble's office can't pursue because they coerced her to lie. She's going to wear her work outfit to court. Her hospital scrubs will project her as a person who helps people, almost like a first responder. That looks good to a judge, especially this one. Bruce Hamilton is a program judge. His nickname around the courthouse is 'Cut 'Em Loose' Bruce," Jon said and laughed.

Jon Zucker's laughter was infectious. I laughed too.

"We couldn't have drawn a better judge, Mike. Maryann Settles is contrite. She's adamant about why she just decided to come forward after all these years and her explanation is viable, believable, and relatable. I'm looking forward to this hearing, Mike, and seeing Gamble's face as he's being grilled on the stand. I can't wait to tear into his ass. It's going to be like a Mongoose on the snake, and without Thomas Turner, there's no way the government can ever attempt to retry you. Cut 'Em Loose rules in your favor, you walk right out the double doors. No going back to Canaan. Nothing. Instant freedom. Guaranteed."

"I love the sound of that, Jon. Straight up," I said.

"Is there anything else we need to clear before I go?"

"Naw, I think we've covered everything.

"On that note, I'll take my exit. Stay out the way while you're here. This jail is weigh station for fuckups. Stay clear of any bullshit because they're charging people for everything they do here now. Got that?.

I stood up and shook Jon Zucker's hand. "Got you, big guy. I got you."

***

In the day room in the units at the D.C. jail there were 4 cafeteria style tables. There was a left side and the right side of the unit. Cells 1 through 40 were on the left side, and cells 41 through 80 was on the right side. Every cell held inmates, and the unit was basically full, but only one side came out for recreation at a time. The left came out in the AM, the right side during the PM, and then the next day it would rotate. My side was out for rec. Bucky Fields and I sat at the far end of one of the tables playing Scrabble.

"I'm challenging that, slim. Gimme the dictionary," I called out as I looked at the word that Buck put down. "What the fuck is *wirra*?" I grabbed the Scrabble dictionary and looked the word up. *To my dismay*. It was true. I looked up at Buck who busted out laughing.

"Put my seventeen points down and it's my go again," Buck said.

As I was writing down the score, the conversation down the table caught my attention. I looked down and saw four young dudes talking. One was stocky with a fresh haircut and the other three varied in size and shade of brown, but they all had long dreads.

"A lot of them urban novels be chump as shit That's why I stopped ordering them joints at the feds. You get them joints and read 'em and they be garbage. I be mad as shit about that," Haircut said.

One of the dudes with dreads replied, "I feel you, slim, but all them joints be something to read. I like the joints with a rack of fuckin' in 'em. A nigga be needing them joints while he in, they be taking a nigga out there."

A light skinned, skinny dude with tattoos on his face and dreads had claimed to be a rapper. Every time we came out for rec, he rapped in a circle. He didn't sound that good to me. "My girl like them joints. She be downloading them joints to her iPad, reading 'nem at work. She gone off them *Angel* joints the homie from D.C. wrote."

Haircut added, "Them joints is wicked but they ain't fucking with them Ultimate, Sacrifice joints. Them joints too like that. I can't wait to read part four when it come out."

The fourth dude at the table was tall his dreads were pulled up into a bun and the side of his head was shaved. He said, "Yeah, them joints cool, but I ain't fucking with them joints no more."

"Why not?" Haircut asked.

"Because the nigga that wrote them joints hot as shit."

I grimaced and looked up from the Scrabble letters. Silently, I prayed that Buck hadn't heard what I heard, but my prayers weren't answered. Buck glanced to his right at the person speaking. Shaved heads was 12 feet deep in his spiel about the homie Bucky Fields being a rat. Buck looked up at me; his eyes held mine.

He shook his head as he reached beneath the table. "See what I mean, slim?" That was all Buck said as he rose from the table, knife in his hand.

The dude who had been talking never saw what was coming. Buck reached out and grabbed the dude by his dreads and started stabbing him. I got up from the table and headed to my cell. As I walked down the stairs, all I heard was the CO yelling into his radio.

Then a voice came over the intercom:

"All available, Southwest Two. All available, Southwest Two!"

Chapter 24
Greg Gamble

"Mr. Gamble, Detective Robert Mathis is here to see you. He has four other gentlemen with him as well, all with law enforcement," my secretary said over the intercom.

"Okay, Tera, give me about five minutes and then send them in, please."

"Sure thing, Mr. Gamble."

I read the e-mail on the computer again, then I got on the phone and made a call."

"Hello. Appellate Division. Jacoby Meyers speaking."

"Jacoby, it's me. Greg Gamble. Where is Christopher Spade?"

"In his office, sir."

"Connect me to him, please."

"Yes, sir."

Elevator music played for a minute or so, then Chris Spade came on the line. "Hi, Greg. What can I do for you?"

"You've been assigned the Attorney Fields 2255 motion, right?"

"Uh, yes, sir. I have it right here. I've been working on the government's reply."

"No need, Chris. We won't oppose the motion. Fields can walk on the claims made in his motion."

"What? No, sir. Are you sure? I believe we can argue that his trial attorney wasn't ineffective based on—"

"Did you hear what I said, Chris?"

"I did, sir, but—"

"No buts, Chris; don't oppose it. Fields stabbed a guy at the D.C. jail yesterday, and that guy is barely clinging to life. He can walk on the conspiracy case. We're going after him now for attempted murder. And if the victim dies, that will be murder one. He's been in prison almost six years on the drug case. Let him walk. We'll get him on the new case. Am I clear?"

"Crystal clear, sir. I'll do as you say."

"Good, Chris. Talk to you later. Bye, bye," I said as the call ended. I went to my office door and opened it. I could see the men waiting for me. Three were black and two were white. I motioned for them all to come into my office. "My office is spacious enough to accommodate everyone," I said as I leaned against my desk. All five men present stood in front of a chair. "Bob, would you please introduce me to these gentlemen?"

Detective Robert Mathis took the floor. "This, everyone, is Greg Gamble, United States Attorney for the District of Columbia. Greg, this guy to my left is Detective Jacob Newsome with the Prince George Police Department. He's investigating, along with his fellow detectives, the murders of Eric 'Baby' Joyner, Derrick Hill, Leonard 'Silk' Johnson and Antriece Fortune. Next to him is Detective Xavier Vincent. He's the lead detective on the Tosheka Jennings murder in Oxon Hill, Maryland. He's also with the Prince George Police Department. The next gentleman is Detective Nate Hackett, a detective with the MPD assigned to the homicide squad at 6th District. He's investigating the murder of Brian Clark, who was killed in the rear of Stewart's Funeral Home after his brother Byron's funeral. Lastly, but surely not least, is Detective Phillip Krouse whom you already know is assigned to the Benco Market murders of Denice Autry and Bolé Ndugu."

I went down the line and shook hands with all the men in the room. Once that was done, I said, "Gentlemen, I asked

Bob to contact you all for a reason. As a public servant like yourselves, I've come across information that might help a little in all of your cases. Please, sit down and get comfortable. I have a recording that I would like you all to hear. After you've heard the recording, I will answer any questions that you might have."

***

"This is sort of like a confession, right?" Nate Hackett asked first.

"No, it's a recording," I answered.

"But doesn't that make the guy talking like a witness against himself and the guy he keeps calling Bruh?" This from Jacob Newson.

"No, it doesn't, because he doesn't know he's being recorded."

"Okay, he's saying it to a C.I. That's even better. The C.I. becomes a witness," Jacob Newson continued.

"This basically closes our cases, right? We just arrest this guy and make him confess and then implicate his accomplices," Xavier Vincent chimed in.

"We already have one of these guys arrested. The man on that recording, doing all of the talking is Jahid Bashir," Phillip Krouse said.

"And the man asking the questions is David Battle, a man who's been in jail for about 20 months. I believe both of these men are in jail, being held at the Central Treatment Facility in Southeast. I cannot tell you where or how I came to be in possession of this recording, but it's real..."

"Can anything said on it be proved?" Hackett asked.

"Yes," Bob Mathis replied. "One thing that's definitely factual is when Jahid Bashir speaks of the murders of a guy named Mann, he says that the guy was killed and left in the trunk of a car near Oak Park. We don't know exactly when the murder took place, but Jihad Bashir said that it happened after Landa's— that's Yolanda Stevens, a witness against the guy he's talking to, David Battle, after her funeral. Yolanda Stevens was killed seven months ago at a Safeway on Alabama Avenue in Southeast. So that means that Mann, who we've identified as 40-year-old Maurice Todd, Yolanda Stevens' uncle, had to be killed after that. We went to every street in Oak Park and canvassed the area- for any cars that looked to be abandoned or not in use. We used a cadaver dog to sniff these cars that we determined to fit our description. Nothing. Then we remembered that cars considered to be abandoned or ticketed with no action rendered are towed to our spacious facility where we auction them off at We took cadaver dogs there and hit on a new model black 4-door Buick Lucerne. In the trunk of the Buick were human remains. The forensics and DNA tests are not in yet, but we're confident that the remains found are Maurice Todd. His family reported him missing twice last year."

"Detective, I called this meeting in pursuit of justice not to waste your time, but like I said earlier, this recording is real, and unfortunately, Detective Newsome, David Battle is not a confidential informant. Far from it. And from what I understand – and I know this personally – Jahid Bashir will never be a witness against himself or against the man who he constantly refers to as Bruh, which is his brother, Quran Brashir. But not to be deterred, these recordings help you. Detective Nelson, you're investigating two men now. You have no leads, I assume? Well, now you do. Scour your crime scene again. Go over everything your crime scene people collected. View video footage. You're looking for anything that connects Sean Branch in Quran Bashir to those murders at Woodmore Town Center. You'll be provided with everything that our system has on both men. That goes for you too, Detective Vincent. You are investigating the murders of Tosheka Jennings. You heard Jahid Bashir yourself. He doesn't know that he's being recorded, so I believe he's being truthful. You heard what he says..."

"Can I have a copy of the recordings?" Detective Vincent asked.

"Absolutely not. But what you can do is hear that recording whenever you need to. I'll make it available to every officer in this room whenever necessary. You know the details surrounding your cases, now you have a name, face, fingerprints, etcetera, to go with that. Jahidir says on the recording that *he* – meaning Quran Bashir – and David Battle confirms when he asks 'Quran killed the Tosheka?' Flushed her, because she was dangerous to him. I think Quran Bashir is your man. Did you recover the victim's cell phone?"

"We did. It was in her pants pocket."

"I'm willing to bet that a call or text came in from Quran Bashir the night of her murder. Do what it is that you do in Prince George's County and I'm confident that you can put a case together against Bashir. Bob, have you found out anything new about Crud's and Whistle' murders on 3rd Street now that you have a new lead?" I then asked.

Shaking his head, Bob replied, "Nothing. There was no video footage we could retrieve from any other houses on the block. And as you know there was a fire, so a lot of evidence was destroyed. No witnesses, nothing. Just your recording."

"Okay, just keep at it. Detective Cross, you and I have spoken at length about the Benco Market murders. We had Bashir arrested for these murders. But I need everything you can find to get him indicted. You have eight months remaining. You just heard him tell all of us they were trying to kill Baby E that night. Find me something that I can use to persuade a grand jury to indict him. That's a start. Once we indict, we'll build a good enough case to convict him in court. Lastly, Detective Hackett, Sean Branch killed your victim. It's your job to prove that. If what Jihad says is true – for some reason, Sean Branch killed Byron 'Crud' Clark and then went to Stuarts Funeral Home and killed his brother Brian – hopefully the information I've provided helps all you guys with your cases." I grabbed business cards off of my desk and passed them out to the detectives. "Feel free to call me whenever you guys need to."

***

"I have someone downstairs that you want to see," Bob said after all the other detectives had left.

"Someone that I wanted to see? Who?"

"Maurice 'Moe' Best."

"You said that he can tell us something new about Sean Branch, right?"

 Bob nodded.

"He's downstairs in this building?"

"No, he's outside down the street by the Metro Station. He just texted my phone."

"Well, tell him to come on up."

***

"Listen to me. Sean Branch is back at it. And when I say back at it, I mean *really* back at it. He's been home, what, for four months? Five? I'm telling y'all some good shit. Sean done killed like 20 motherfuckers that I know of. Let me run it down for y'all, because really, y'all missing a good game. Tracy and Eric Kay. Leon. Clea, his brother, Andre killed one of Shawn's men back in the day. Leon told on them R Street dudes in the early 90s. Rick Bailey and his cousin Frank. He killed his baby mother Raquel. They found her floating in the river. Sean smoked her ass — believed that! Kenneth Sparrow got his head cut off. Sean killed him. That dude over Southwest that got his head cut off — Sean Branch. It's three other niggas missing out here. They just upped and disappeared. Frank Johnson, Maurice Brooks and Stephen Hartwell. Sean told somebody he killed and buried them. Where, I don't know. The homie Reese told on Sean. Sean smoked him as soon as he got out. You know the house on Longfellow Street? Last month someone went in the Hope Village halfway house and killed Pig that told on Raf. Fice and Mad Dog. Sean killed him, trust me. And that same day the police found the homie Eric Ford dead in his Camaro. Who do y'all think did that? Sean. That's like 18 motherfuckers I just told y'all about. Do the police work and watch what I tell you. All the shit gon' lead to Sean Branch doing all the killing."

Bob Mathis wrote down everything that Moe Best said.

"Did you get all of that, Bob?"

"Of course, I did. And I'm going to investigate every word of it."

"Let me ask you this, Moe. You don't mind me calling you Moe, do you?"

"You're the head in charge here. Call me whatever you like."

"Okay, Moe. What's in this for you? Usually, the guys who provide this much information are in prison trying to get out. But you're already out. You're free. What's your motive for telling us all of this?"

"I'm doing it for three reasons, Mr. Gamble. One, because I want to do my part in helping to make the streets safer. Two, because I hate Sean fake ass. And, three, because I'm trying to help my nephew out on his case. He don't know that I'm doing this; can never know; but he's fighting serious case and I need to get him a super sweet cop."

"What's your nephew's name?" I asked.

"Kenneth Gray. He's my brother Kenny's son."

I wrote down the name *Kenneth Gray* on the notepad on my desk and wrote *God plea deal* beside it. "I can do that for you, Moe. He's locked up at the jail?"

Moe Best nodded.

"I'll take care of it myself. Just keep the information coming, okay?"

"Got you. Say no more."

169

Once Moe Best and Detective Mathis left my office, I sit behind the desk and thought about Sean Branch. The man who killed my brother Lonnell. "I'm going to get you Sean Branch. Even if I have to die doing it," I vowed.

***

"How in the hell did the media get ahold of a copy of the motion that Maryann Settles gave Jonathan Zucker?" Ari Weinstein asked as he sat across from my desk.

"The answer to that could take at least an hour, but the long and the short of it is basically what I told you before. There are forces at hand that want to tarnish my legacy here at Triple Nickel. And one of those people is Susan Rosenthal. Susan knows that I know about her and Carlos Trinidad. I told you that. Remember what I told you about contacting any Martin? And to answer your question, I can prove it, but I'm sure that Susan gave the media the affidavit."

"The local news is mentioning the case every day. It's going to pick up steam, Greg."

"I already know that, Ari. Have I been talking to myself when I conversate with you? Susan is going to make sure that it gains steam, but I got a trick for her ass, buddy. Just you wait."

Chapter 25

Susan Rosenthal
United States District Court
333 Constitution Avenue
Washington, D.C.

"Your honor, from the late 1980s until the 2000s, Kevin Grayson and Randolph Moore ran a prominent drug trafficking business in Washington D.C. The drug ring distributed significant amounts of powder and crack cocaine throughout many neighborhoods in the city. Members of the organization also committed serious acts of violence including at least twenty-seven murders and several attempted murders. Some of those acts of violence were committed to expand and to protect the organization's drug trafficking business. Others were committed to extract revenge on those who harmed members of the organization. And in later years, members of the organization began committing murders for hire. As a participant in the organization the defendant purchased large quantities of crack cocaine from Kevin Grayson and distributed it to buyers all over the greater-Washington area. Like many of his co-conspirators, the defendant engaged in violent acts to protect the organization. In late 1999, shortly after Grayson's arrest, the defendant and another co-conspirator named Frank Howard saw a man walking nearby. They recognized the man as Charles Schubert. Charles Schubert was rumored to be a witness in the then-pending criminal case against

Grayson. The defendant told Howard that he wanted to kill Schubert to gain favor with organization's leader Grayson. To do that, the defendant followed Charles Schubert into an alley and shot him twice with a 38-caliber revolver. The defendant returned to Howard and told him that he had killed Schubert. Charles Schubert survived the shooting, but a bullet severed his spinal cord, leaving him paralyzed.

"In 2000, a grand jury returned a 131-count superseding indictment charging 16 members of Kevin Grayson's and Randolph Moore's drug ring. The superseding indictment charged members of the group with conspiracy to distribute cocaine and cocaine base. 32 counts of first-degree murder, assault with intent to murder, tampering with a witness or informant by killing and other violent drug-related crimes. The defendant was not included in the first group. Instead, he was indicted separately in 2002 for six offenses related to his involvement in the organization. The grand jury charged the defendant with conspiracy to distribute and possession with intent to distribute 50 grams or more of cocaine base, conspiracy to participate in a racketeering influence corrupt organization, assault with intent to murder, attempted murder in aid of racketeering, tampering with a witness or informant and using a firearm during commission of a drug trafficking crime. The indictment alleged that the conduct giving rise to the first two counts occurred between 1995 and late 2000. And the conduct giving rise to counts three through six occurred on November 16th, 1999. After the defendant was indicted, the court granted the government's motion to join the defendant's case with the pending matters against the other 16 co-conspirators. The group was divided into two groups for trial. The defendant joined five of his codefendants in the second trial which began in 2003. After an 8-month trial, the jury found the defendant guilty of all counts. The court sentenced the defendant to 4 concurrent terms of life imprisonment. The defendant is now before the court for a motion to reduce or modify his sentence. The government opposes a reduction in sentence for the defendant, as outlined in the government's opposition motion..."

"Your honor, may I approach the bench?" Dwayne Crawley asked.

"You may approach the bench, counselor. You come too, Mrs. Rosenthal," the judge said.

"Your honor, I would like to amend the motion to include pertinent information that the court needs to hear. I would like to submit…"

"Your honor, I would oppose any amendments to the timely filed motion."

"Your honor," Dwayne Crawley continued, "the defendant Keith McGill is under a very real, very imminent death sentence..."

"Mr. McGill is not under any death sentence, Counselor Crawley. What in heaven's name are you talking about?" Judge Mays bellowed.

"Not a court ordered death sentence, your honor, but a more serious one to be carried out on site in any facility in the Federal Bureau of Prisons. Documents were unearthed and disseminated to known and unknown criminals throughout the prison system. Those documents revealed that Keith B McGill testified in 1988 trial of a man named Howard Smith. It was an attempted murder case. And now that the information is floating around all the prisons, Keith McGill's life is in grave danger. Bureau of Prison officials have intercepted letters – called kites – where very dangerous men want Keith McGill dead. His co-defendants are outraged that they were duped by Keith, being that he never disclosed his cooperation with the government in 1988. Kevin Grayson has considerable influence amongst inmates from Washington D.C. and there are D.C. inmates in every prison in the FBOP. There is no way to assure Keith McGill's safety. So, we humbly asked this court to modify the defendant's sentence for that reason alone with all the other reasons we've put in the rule 35 motion, your honor."

"Your honor with all due respect to Mr. Crawley, this would set a bad precedent. We can't modify every defendant's sentence just because their life is in danger while in prison. We can't ignore the grave danger Keith McGill's release from prison would place on the community..."

***

Later that day, at her house…

"Mark's leaving and moving the company to Massachusetts," Grant said after ending a call on his cell phone. Abandoning a democratic state for one that leans more republican.

I was reviewing some notes, only half listening to my husband. "What Mark would that be, honey?"

"Mark Smith, the CEO of Smith and Wesson. The grandson who inherited the company from his grandfather who founded it. He's fed up with politics of Washington."

"What's stoked his ire?"

"Smith and Wesson has become the largest gun manufacturing company in America. The lion's share of their profits came from the sales of the AR-15 styled rifles. Lawmakers here are considering a bill to ban the AR-15 style rifles from being sold to civilians. The proposed legislative will cripple Smith and Wesson. And Mark's not the only CEO who's hightailing it to the republican states like Tennessee, where they are enticed by tax breaks and promises of cheaper labor. But the main reason for this exodus is the democratic push for stricter gun laws in blue leaning states."

"We need stricter gun laws, Grant. Being an Assistant US attorney, I get to see what people like Mark Smith doesn't. I get to see the results left behind by those AR-15s that Smith and Wesson peddle to civilians. These type weapons t often end up in the hands of violent criminals. Mark Smith doesn't get to see the carnage and destruction the AR-15s leave behind. The innocent bystanders get ripped apart, literally—and the children who are dying on our streets because of them. We are a civilized society. We are not soldiers on a battlefield. We do not live in war torn countries like Afghanistan and Ukraine. What is the need for civilians to possess AR-15s other than the fact that the Second Amendment gives them the right to bear them?

"I agree, Susan. You're preaching to the choir. But I'm a lobbyist. Companies like Smith and Wesson and the NRA pay me a lot of money to circumvent partisan politics to keep their revenue flowing. In good conscience or bad, our bills have to be paid. I'm just the messenger. Don't kill me."

I slipped my feet back into my heels and walked over to my husband. I leaned in and kissed his face. "I'd never kill you, honey. No matter what message you brought. I need to go out for a while. I got to retrieve some stuff from the office. I need to prepare for a big case tomorrow. If you need me I'll be at Triple Nickel."

"Okay dear, drive safe," Grant said before answering a call on his cell phone.

I grabbed my briefcase and after putting on my coat, I walked outside to my car, wondering if Grant had a mistress out there somewhere. Deep inside, I hope that he did.

***

"The US attorney's office is vigorously pursuing all avenues that will directly lead to the arrest of all persons connected to the Trinidad Crime Organization. We plan to file charges against these people in hopes that our investigation of the individuals will lead us to indicting and eventually convicting the leader of the organization, Carlos

Trinidad." I turned to face the most handsome Hispanic men I had ever seen.

Carlos Trinidad smiled at me.

"How does this sound?" I asked.

"That was marvelous, baby. Come here and let me show you how much I liked it."

Carlos Trinidad loved attention. Craved it. He loved for me to create and put out fake sound bites about how many officers were pursuing his organization, knowing that I'd do everything humanly possible to thwart any efforts to bring him and his associates down. I stepped out of my skirt, then removed my blazer and blouse. All the while, I danced for him. Seductively, assimilating myself on a pole inside the strip club, I could see Carlos's erection rise in his pants. Suddenly, he crossed the room. Carlos reached down and picked up my pantyhose. With one strong pull he ripped the other hose into two pieces. Then he kissed me forcefully.

Carlos led me to his bed and laid me down. He tied both of my wrist to the wooden headboard. His head disappeared between my legs. Carlos nibbled gently on my clit. Then, he put his tongue inside me and drove me crazy.

"Oh, Carlos… yes… just like that! Don't stop!" I loved the way my Latin lover ate my pussy. There was no one better than him. Briefly, I thought about my husband at home. Grant Rosenthal didn't know how to properly eat a woman's pussy. So, I never let him try after a couple of horrible times. I loved my husband with all my heart, but I craved loving from another man. A man who wasn't my husband. My eyes looked down and locked on the top of Carlos Trinidad's head. His unruly, dark curls adding to his sexy. Oot off all the women in the world, one of the country's most powerful drug kingpins wanted me. He could have had any woman he wanted. He had billions of dollars and all the trappings of a very wealthy bachelor. But yet, he loved me. He craved me. With that thought in mind, I orgasmed all over Carlos's face.

***

"Susan, do you remember a woman that I did business with years ago that was arrested on several high-profile murders? Her name was Angel."

I nodded. "Kareemah El-Amin. Of course I do. I got rid of the DNA evidence we had on her for you. How could I forget?"

"Well apparently, Angel doesn't appreciate what I did for her because she's back in the streets and playing ball for a different team. I never released her from her contract. I need you to get your informants in the streets to verify if I'm right or wrong about her. I need to be 100% sure of what I'm saying before I take action. Can you do that for me?"

"Of course I can. Anything for you, baby. Is that all?" I replied.

"No, one more thing. I'm hearing that there is talk about murder investigations being initiated against Quran Bashir. His father, Ameen, was a friend of mine. When those investigations reach your office, dead them. Just like you've always done."

***

I drove home from Carlos's palatial estate trying to figure out how he knew about the recent investigations into Quran Bashir's possible murder spree. I had only found out about it a day ago myself. Then, I wondered why Carlos wanted to protect the man so bad. I understood that Quran Bashir's deceased father had been a friend, but why all the assistance years after Ameen Bashir's death? I thought about all the things that Greg Gamble had told me about the Bashir family. Then I wondered what Greg Gamble would say if he knew that I was the person responsible for stonewalling all the investigations into Quran Bashir. He had no idea that he had a powerful ally on his side. He had no idea that Carlos Trinidad was his guardian angel, and according to Carlos, he was not to know until the time was right.

Chapter 26

Jihad Bashir
Central Treatment Facility
1901 E. Street S.E.

"Zo just caught a body at the Feds," a dude in the cage said.

"I heard about that. Happened at Pollock," another dude replied.

"What Zo is that?" someone asked.

"Zo that's on the case with Whoadie from the Farms. They went in on that Berry Farms conspiracy," the dude who spoke first replied.

"I heard that he was fucked up," another voice entered the conversation.

"Niggas been saying that shit but ain't nobody seen no work on slim."

"*You shitting me!* It's out there. The dude Mal from Park Chester put it on the Gram. He the one promoting that shit."

"Mal? How the fuck Jamal Thompson from up the Nut gon call a nigga hot? Niggas been saying that shit about him for years. He was supposed to be on the joint with Whoadie and nem. How he ducked that joint?"

"He ducked the Park Chester conspiracy too. The joint with Holroy brother, Foots and Oatmeal and nem. And he still out there doing him. I wonder who the fuck he know?"

"Whoever he know, I wish I knew em."

Everybody in the holding cage laughed.

179

I smiled to myself as I listened to the crowd of inmates in the cage continue to talk about different niggas in the street. Some I knew. Some I didn't. I thought about what they said about the homie Mal from Park Chester and really smiled. Whoever had said the stuff about what was said about Mal for years was right, but what really tickled me was that everybody who had called Mal hot to his face was now dead. He'd killed them all. The bench that I laid on with my arm covering my eyes was getting too uncomfortable. My back ached the worst, but my entire body was in pain. The gunshot wound and the surgical cuts healed nicely, but inside, I still felt pain.

"Bashir?" a female CO called out.

"Right here," I said as I sat up.

The CO stepped to the cage and opened the door. "Step out, Bashir. Your lawyer is ready to see you."

***

"How are you doing, Jihad?" Charles Daum asked after we were both seated at the table.

"I'm good, Mr. Daum. What's the word," I replied. "Anything new?"

"Not at all. To be honest with you, I think the US attorney's office is grasping at straws. I think that they have overcharged you. Getting a panel grand jury to indict you on First Degree Murder is a big stretch with the paper-thin evidence they have. Even the secondary charge of Second-Degree Murder under the theory that you shooting a gun caused the death of your friend, Bolé Ndugu is a stretch from here to the Washington Monument. Without the top two charges you can't be indicted on any of the gun charges and the negation of the primary and secondary murder charges negates all gun counts. I've been over the discovery in your case five times since being appointed council. In my professional opinion, I don't see an indictment coming. All they have is a video from Bliss Nightclub that appears to show you and another man whom they say is Bolé Ndugu leaving the club minutes after four men that they believe we're also at the Benco Market. One of the four men being the decedent of Denise Autry. Detectives from MPD pieced together a narrative that they believe will get you indicted. They have your statement."

"I was on medication and completely out of it."

"I agree. And you weren't mirandized, so the statement is inadmissible in court, but can be used at the grand jury proceedings. You told the detective that you were shot near Bliss and there's nothing to support that. That's neither good nor bad. As of today, there's still no sign of any Buick, no gun that can be linked to you and no video footage of you exiting a vehicle near Benco Market. The footage of the shootout in the parking lot is not good quality. I think that I can make a solid case that the person firing a gun in the video is not you but the most important piece of evidence that they do have is compelling. The bullet fragments taken out of you match the ones taken out of Ndugu. There is no way to get around that. That evidence essentially puts you at the scene of the Benco shootout unless I can convince a jury that you and Ndugu were shot at Bliss like you said. But then again that's no good. It opens up too many doors." Charles Daum, started talking and staring off into space. If we dispute the video footage, how do we explain you being shot by the same gun that killed Ndugu?"

Before I could say a word, Charles Daum answered his own question.

"We have to argue that you were shot somewhere else. Either way, it's still early. We'll figure it out if and when you're indicted. With no guns to match those bullet fragments to... No gun was found on Denico Autrey either. There are more questions than answers on both sides. Which reminds me, the government's theory is that you took Bolé Ndugu's gun before fleeing the scene. They say the video shows you bending down over his body. After that you limped away. They also have your brother's statement."

"My brother's statement?"

"Yeah. They questioned him at the hospital. He said – and I quote – that he picked you up at or near Bliss where you'd been shot. He drove you to UMC and dropped you off. They attempted to question him further but he refused to answer any more questions. It's not a bad statement. If we need him, do you think he'll testify?"

"Fuck no," I explained emphatically. "I'm surprised he even said shit. So, exclude him from any strategy you put together."

"Maybe that's for the best anyway. Wouldn't want him up there and then we get blindsided by what they're investigating him for."

"Wait, what did you just say? Who's investigating who?"

"The government. Metropolitan Police Department. They're investigating your brother for several murders. My investigator is in Duluth with law enforcement. He was once on the force."

"How long have you known about this?"

"About what? Your brother?"

"Yeah."

"I just found out yesterday when I mentioned to Sal, my investigator about possibly having to find Quran Bashir because he might be a good witness. Why?"

"No reason. I was just curious."

"Okay, back to you. The best thing that's in our favor is that there is no witnesses to place you at the scene or to say you did anything. Getting a conviction with just grainy video footage and bullet fragments is a longshot and Greg Gamble's office knows that. The three men who police allege was with Denico Autrey the night at Benco Market were all recently killed as they left a restaurant in Largo. If I was a betting man, I'd wager and say that these murders are probably the murders that law enforcement want to pin on your brother Quran." Charles Daum pulled a piece of paper out of his briefcase. "Those men were Eric Joyner, Derrick Hill, and Leonard Johnson. Do you know either one of them?"

"Naw. Never heard of them."

"Did you know Denico Autrey?"

"Naw."

"Jihad, listen to me. I am here for you. The courts appointed me, but I am not a public defender and I'm not here to sell you out. I am one of the biggest names in criminal defense circles in town. I have my own law firm, Daum and Associates. I take a certain amount of cases from the courts pro bono because I'm obligated to. I've been in the game for twenty-three years and I've defended hundreds of people who were fighting murder charges. I've seen guilty men get acquitted and innocent men get found guilty. My win ratio versus my losses is higher, trust me. I'm pretty good at what I do. But I can't defend you nor can I help you unless I know everything there is to know about the case. We have an attorney/client privilege that bonds me to an oath, a code of ethics. Nothing you ever tell me will go further than the room we're sitting in. You have to trust me and I have to be able to trust you or this union between us will not work. When I'm fully equipped with all the ammo, I'm a bad mutherfucka, Jihad. In court, I can paint pictures like Leonardo Da Vinci but again I have to know everything that you know. If you don't want to tell me everything you know about this case, then I suggest you retain a new attorney So what's it gonna be? We level with one another or not?"

I thought about everything he'd just said. "Aight, you're right. What do you need to know…"

***

Back in the cell…

During the day between the hours of eight AM to four PM the medical unit could be visited by anyone. Doctors, nurses, administrators, lieutenants, captains, majors and religious staff members were always in and out of the MDU. I never pulled out the cellphone until nighttime unless it was a weekend but today was different, I needed to call Quran and tell him what Charles Daum said about him being under investigation. I wanted him to know that as soon as possible because time could be of the essence. I quickly pulled the phone from its hiding spot and inserted the SIM card. Once powered on, I quickly dialed Quran's cellphone. But there was no answer. So, I dialed it again.

"Come on, come on, bruh! Answer your phone!"

Chapter 27

Quran
The Embassy Suites Hotel
Pentagon City, VA

"I'm glad that you can make time for me, Q," Kiki said as soon as he removed his coat. "Your dick is so good that I had to double back for another round." Kiki stepped out of her Christian Louis Vuitton heels. "Last week, you put that dick on me and had my head all fucked up when I left D.C. I was at home working on a new book and could not concentrate for shit. Then, on top of that Juice kept calling me on some freak shit. He always wants me to act like I'm getting fucked by you and that didn't help me any. Kiki reached behind her and unzipped her skirt. The skirt fell down to her ankles. She stepped away from the skirt and then seductively unbuttoned the blouse she was wearing. Since my husband had me simulating sex with you, I figured I'd just come back to D.C. and really have sex with you."

I stood in the living room area of the suite and watched undress. When she was completely naked, I smiled. I had to appreciate her stance of wanting to always sex me. My eyes held Kiki's as she stood frozen in her lust and sex appeal. Her hair was cut short on one side and long on the other. Her face was devoid of makeup except for lip gloss that accented her luscious lips. Her toenails were glittery pink and76 matched her fingernails and lip gloss. The sparkling diamond anklet around her ankle had a length of gold that ran down her foot and attached itself to a toe ring on the second toe of her left foot. Kiki's breast sat up firmly on her chest, her nipples appeared to be solid dark chocolate against caramel skin. A single, gold link chain with agold heart pendant hung around her neck; attached to it a gold heart.

"Are you gonna take off your clothes? Or do you need me to help you?"

"Come and help me."

Kiki walked over and tore at my clothes, "Your wish is my command."

***

KiKi wiped corners of her mouth, then, swiped at the excess spit that had run down her chin. "Now that I got the first nut out of the way, I need you to focus Que."

"Focus on what?" I said from my position on the bed.

"These new positions that I want us to do together. The first one is called the Scissors.

"The Scissors? How the fuck?"

"It's easy, just follow my lead," KiKi replied and laid on the bed on her side. "Climb in between my legs but put your left leg under mine and your right leg over me."

I did as I was instructed.

"Yeah like that. Now put your dick inside me."

Again, I followed instructions.

"Oooo, see the way our bodies are aligned? My legs over and under you? We look like a pair of scissors. Damn… Q… The penetration is crazy. It's in me so deep! Damn!"

***

"The next position is called Pretzel Dip. It's similar to the one we were just in. I'ma turn back on my right side. You kneel and straddle my right leg. I'ma curl my left leg around your left side. You'll be able to get deeper penetration as if we're doing doggy, but you still can see my face while you're in there. Go ahead and put your dick back in me. Use your hands to rub my clit… Yes… like that!"

***

Twenty minutes later...

KiKi was laid on her stomach with her hips elevated. Her legs were straight and closed. I laid on top of her, my dick deep inside her.

"This … this.. is called, its' called the flat iron position."

Chapter 28
Zin
The Law Office of Zinfandel Carter
The Finebaum Building
18th and M St. NW

"I love the new digs, Zin. Really, this is nice," Nikki Locks stated, effusively.

I smiled inside and out, The best revenge was success. My suite exuded success. Damiyah James, my assistant, and my newly hired paralegal, Megan Doyle, a pretty young white girl fresh out of law school, moving around the offices gave the desired effect I wanted it to. The office looked busy and prosperous.

"Thank you, Nikki. I'm glad that you like it. None of this would be in existence if it wasn't for you."

"Me? Nonsense. Jen maybe, but not me. I just provided you with the right nudge in the right direction. You did the rest, and I'm really proud of you, Zin."

"Thank you, Nikki."

"But then again, I always knew you'd be great. I really didn't want to lose you. But I guess life has a way of dealing its hands when there is no one left to deal. Enough of that, though. Let me get to the real reason for my impromptu visit today. Actually, there's two reasons. You're still representing David Battle, right?"

I motioned Nikki to sit in the chair opposite my desk. I walked behind my desk and took a seat in my comfortable chair. "I do."

"Well, I have a client named Javon Jarrett who's just been charged by the Metropolitan Police Department for stabbing David a couple weeks ago. I don't—"

"I was there, Nikki. I kind of witnessed the attack. David was on a legal visit with me. As he was being escorted out of the visiting hall, he was attacked and stabbed. I was there that day."

"I'm sorry that you had to witness that, Zin. Apparently, the guy who David stabbed at the jail was a close friend of Javon's. He's not denying what he did. Do you know whether or not David plans to press charges? Or is he gonna give a statement or become a witness the case?"

"Are we talking lawyer to lawyer, Nikki, or are we having this discussion as two friends who just happen to defend two clients?"

"Depends."

"Depends on what, Nikki? Because you came *here*, I didn't come to you."

"You're right, Zin, and I apologize for the ambivalence. I'm here in a friend capacity, surely. Let's talk as two friends, please.

"Okay. You were David Battle's lawyer before I came onto his case while I worked for you. You know him just like I know him. He's not making any statements about any stabbings. Nor does he plan to press charges or be a witness against Mr. Jarrett. You know as well as I do that David doesn't operate like that. Between you and me, as two friends talking, Mr. Jarrett should be more concerned with the people outside the jail that love David, if you know what I mean.

"I know exactly what you mean, and as two friends talking, I would have to agree with you. I can't tell that to my client, though, but he'll be glad to know that the man he assaulted is not cooperating with authorities. You also represent a young man named Anthony Williams, right?"

"Right again. Why?"

"I asked because Anthony Williams slipped out of his handcuffs and tried to stab Javon Jarett in the South One. housing unit, the Max unit where they're both being housed. According to Javon, Anthony Williams is a friend of David Battle's. Did David send Anthony Williams to try to kill Javon?"

I shrugged my shoulders. "How could I know that? I'm just David's lawyer? He wouldn't confide in me with information like that. This is news to me. All of this is. I knew that Javon stabbed David, but not that he was charged recently or about the attempted assault by the client, Anthony Williams. I haven't seen or talked to Anthony in weeks. Maybe it's time I do a visit with him? David too."

"Yeah, maybe. But I told you there were two reasons I came here today. I just told you one reason. The other is really to give you a heads up before you went home and found Jen in bed with your man. It was obvious to us – me and Jen – that Quran Brashir was into you, and as a woman I could tell that over time those feelings became mutual. Jen told me what Jermaine Mendenhall..."

"How do you know Jermaine's full name, Nikki?"

Nikki Locks dropped her head and shook it. "I know Jermaine's name because him and Jen are now an item. Have been since you left him. He told Jean that you left him for a street thug named Quran. Is that true, Zin?

I nodded.

"Okay, cool. I was right to assume that. Wait! Are you in Quran still together?"

"We are," I smiled. "And I'm pregnant with his child." I added that part just so Nikki would go back and tell Jen, who'd share the news with Jermaine. The news of my pregnancy would break his heart. *FUCK HIM*

"Oh my Gawd! Congratulations, Zin. I'm so happy for you. I mean, damn, Quan Bashir is one handsome man. A man that gorgeous has to make beautiful children."

"Uh, I happen to think that I might also have some input on the good looks of my child."

"Of course, of course. I'm sorry, Zin, I never meant to imply otherwise."

"No need to apologize, Nikki. I'm just kidding. I know you didn't mean anything by what you said."

"I didn't, and now I'm even more happy that I came to give you the heads up. Someone in Gamble's office wants to reopen the David Battle case and investigate Quran for the murders of the three witnesses, including his brother. Quran is also being investigated in Maryland for several murders, one being the recent murder of a woman named Tosheka Jennings. A woman who I am hearing used to be his girlfriend before you. I have friends in every office of government and law enforcement, so the news I'm giving you now is good intel, Zin. It's been corroborated, so do whatever you can with it."

***

I dialed Quran's phone for the tenth time after Nikki left the office. But for some reason, he wasn't picking up. Nervous energy raced through my body as I imagined Quran in jail somewhere. I racked my brain for someone else I could call to check on Quran, but I could think of no one. I called Quran's cell phone again. Still no answer, so I sent him a text, hoping that he returned my call sooner than later.

//:Where are you Quran, and why aren't you answering your phone?

Chapter 29
Quran

I kept hearing the faint sounds of phone vibrating, but I didn't know if it was my phone or Kiki's husband's calling. It seemed like he had an uncanny ability to know exactly when I was inside her body. The suite was dimly lit and the curtains were closed, allowing no light in from outside. The heat being on in the suite made for hot, sticky, sweaty, long hours of sex. My body ached a little from muscles being used that I hadn't used in months. My dick was starting to get sore. I tapped the bed in submission. "You got it. You win. Can't take no more."

Kiki was on her knees, leaned over me with my dick in her mouth with both hands stroking and twisting it as she did her best deepthroat impression of Roxy Reynolds. My dick was freed from her throat.

"Tap out, then, nigga. I got your ass. Finally got your ass!" Kiki gloated. "And we still had two more positions left. The Corkscrew and the Wheelbarrow".

"Next time, baby girl. You wore my ass out," I said and got out the bed. "Somebody's phone. been blowing up like hell." I had to stretch my limbs.

"Probably wasn't nobody but Juice. Niggas -in jail be bored as shit. Either that or he could sense that I was with you. I'm starting to think that nigga is psychic." Kiki got out of bed and grabbed her cell phone from her purse. She looked at the phone. "I got a few missed calls, but nobody blew me up. Definitely not Juice."

Making the trek to the living room area nearby, I picked up my coat and removed my phone. I had thirty missed calls. Mostly from Zane and Jahid. A couple from Sean, Dave and Tomasina. Panic set in. I called Jahid's phone first, but it went straight to voicemail. The calls were from more than two hours ago. Zin's most recent call was only 30 minutes ago, I called her as I headed towards the bathroom.

"Where the fuck have you been, Quran? I was worried sick about you," Zin screamed into the phone. "Are you okay? Where are you? I thought you were in jail."

"Whoa, whoa. Calm down, Zin. I'm good. I'm on Howard Rd. in the spot. I was in here, knocked out, sleep. I was dead to the world. Never heard the phone vibrating. What's up? Why would you think I'm in jail?"

"Don't want to talk over the phone? Meet me at Ms. Debbie's in thirty minutes. We need to talk."

"Alright, bet, I'll see you in thirty. I love you."

"Love you too. Bye."

"Aww, ain't that cute. I never heard you tell somebody you love them before, Que. She must be a wonderful woman," Kiki called out.

"She is more than you'll ever know," I replied as I headed to the shower.

***

Ms. Debbie's Soul food and Seafood Café
District Heights, MD

"Don't nothing come to a sleeper but a dream. Ain't that what you always tell me?"

"The body's gonna do what the body wants to do. You know that. I never realized that I was that tired," I lied.

193

"What's up, though? Why all the secret squirrel shit? Why did you think I was in jail?"

Zin dug into her crab cakes platter before speaking. "Damn, this is good." She chewed and inhaled, then exhaled. "Nikki Locks came by the office today and told me that Jen Watts and Jermaine, my ex, are a couple."

"Who the fuck cares?"

"I know, right? But that wasn't the reason for her visit. It seems that dude that stabbed David...."

"Javon Jarrett."

"How do you know that? Wait…nevermind. Yes, him. He's Nikki's client. She asked me was David going to press charges and testify against her client now that he's been charged with assaulting David."

"My man ain't doing no fucking telling."

"That's what I told her. So you can calm down. I made that motion clear. Then, she told me that a friend of David's, a guy that David needed me to represent named Anthony Williams slipped out of his cuffs and tried to stab Javon Jarrett at the jail a couple days ago. I told her that I hadn't seen or spoken to David or Anthony Williams in weeks. But the most important thing, she told me, was the reason for my calls to you and the impromptu lunch we're having. Nikki says that you are being investigated by law enforcement in D.C. and in the state of Maryland for murder. One in particular is the murder of that woman I asked you about. The one from the scene on Howard Road."

"Tosheka?"

Zin ate more of her food and then drank from the glass in front of her. "Yes, her. Tosheka Jennings. Quran, why would Maryland be investigating you for that woman's murder? I asked you repeatedly, did you kill that woman? And you told me—"

"I told you the truth." I lied with a straight face. "I didn't kill Tosheka. Think about it. I haven't lied to you about anybody I killed. In fact, I confessed to you about murders that I shouldn't have. But I trust you with my life, my secrets. I don't know why Maryland is investigating me for Tosheka's murder. All they can have is the Tosheka's phone. There has to be pictures of her and I in the phone, my name or contact information. They probably have text messages, threads of her call logs that show that she called me every day, even on the day she died. I talked to her and tried to explain to her that we were done. She had clothes of mine in her apartment. I was at her place a lot before you came into my life.

They probably have my fingerprints or something. My DNA was probably there somewhere, but all of that can easily be explained. I was intimately with Tosheka off and on for a lot of years."

"Nikki said something about an investigation in D.C. as well."

"Can't be nothing but the same shit you told me about Tammy, Landa and my brother. They still think, well, you already know I killed them, but *they don't know that*. I'm not surprised that I'm a person of interest in their investigation. I do have one question though. How the fuck does Nicky Locks know about their investigations of me in Maryland and D.C.?"

"Said something about her having friends in every circle. And where your name came up, she decided to stop by and give me a heads up. She kind of figured that you and I are an item. Plus, Jermaine told Jen that I left him for street thug named Quran, and Jen told Nikki, I told her that we're having a baby."

I smiled at that. Zin was an open book that I had read several times. "You think you're the sharpest knife in the drawer," I said. You did that knowing Nikki would tell Jen, and then Jen would tell your ex. You wanted to hurt him deeply. Me doing in eight months what he couldn't do in six years – get you pregnant. Your horns are showing, girlfriend."

Zin laughed and then sipped her drink again. "Am I that transparent?"

"Yes." I laughed.

"Okay, you got me. Wait." Zin looked at her phone. "Damn, I almost forgot. Gotta go, baby," she said, standing up. "I got a hearing at two in federal court, and then I gotta go to the jail and see a client."

"What client?"

"His name is Marthell Dean. You don't know him…"

"Marthell Dean? He got locked up for killing a cop back in the '98 or 99, right?"

Zin slipped her coat on and grabbed her purse. "You know him?"

"No, but I know *about* him. He's a rat. When he got locked up for the murder, he told the police that a dude named Juan Wilson, not him, killed the cop. Juan was a friend of mine back in the day. When Marthell blamed him for the cop's murder, he went to court and testified against Marthell, saying that Marthell did the killing."

"You're absolutely right. Marthell is back from the feds on a 23-110 motion. I was appointed by the courts to do his motion."

"Not anymore. Withdraw from his case. We don't do rats."

"Consider it done," Zin said and embraced him.

"I love you, Zin with all my heart."

"I love you more, Quran. I love you more."

* * *

Downtown Locker Room
Minnesota Ave
Northeast, D.C.

I lifted one distressed Rockstar jeans pants leg see to how the new black and silver New Balance 990V tennis shoes looked on my foot. They looked great. I pulled off the ACG Nike boot from my other foot and slipped the other New Balance on. I placed the Nike boots into the shoe box. As I did, I felt someone sit down next to me on the bench.

"I caught you slipping," Sean whispered to me.

"Never that," I replied. "I had eyes on the door the whole time. I saw your Porsche pull into the parking spot. The paper tags gave you away. That and that big ass beard you rocking. Out here looking like a lil ass Arab nigga."

"Rather be an Arab than all them white people you got in you."

"I ain't mad at that. Fuckin' with them white people got me this curly hair and light grey eyes. And because of it, I fucks the baddest bitches in the city and beyond."

Sean laughed. "And beyond? Kiki Swinson from weak ass Virginia Beach ain't nowhere near beyond. You act like you fuckin' chicks from Dubai or England. Wild as nigga. Where you been at all day? I been calling you."

With my beyond bitch from weak ass Virginia Beach."

"Slim, you gotta stop fucking that bitch. She gone write a book about your stupid ass."

It was my turn to laugh. Sean was funny as shit. He motioned to one of the women who worked at the shoe store. "Can I see the new silver and black Foamposite in an eight and half, please?"

The woman nodded and disappeared into the rear of the store.

"All jokes aside, slim, I went to Troy Fortune's funeral. I thought maybe Rodney would show up to pay his respects."

"He didn't go, huh?"

"Nope. That joint was held at the Steve Young Church on Nannie Heleb Burroughs. It was packed like hell but no Rodney. Had he showed up, I was going to smoke his ass on sight in front of everybody."

"Did you get out the car and go into the church?"

"You better know it. I thought maybe Rodney might've got there early. I had to go in and see for myself if he was in there or not?"

"Had he been in there, you was gone crush him in front of God?"

The woman returned with the Nike Foamposites for Sean. He opened the box and pulled out a shoe.

"God? Youngin, I was in a church. God wasn't in there. They think he's there because of all them pictures they got hanging on the walls. The white people in them portraits be looking like country music singers."

I couldn't contain my laughter.

"Real talk, though. Word on the street is that Rodney's gone underground. He knows I killed Tony and he knows I'm on his ass. And he also knows that I ain't gon stop until he's dead."

"Aight, so what now? If we can't get to Rodney, who's next on your list?"

After trying the shoe and deciding it was a good fit, Sean said, "The two bitches, Ren Tyler and Crud's sister, Biana. You didn't think I forgot about them did you?"

Smiling, I replied "Shit, I forgot about them."

"Well, I didn't. I'm on there ass and I gotta get that nigga Moe Best. He done grew his hair out; got long ass dreads now. I'ma knock them shits straight off his scalp. What about you? You got the three that was on your list. What's next for you?"

Somebody… anybody I can catch that's close to Javon Jarrett?"

"Javon Jarrett? Remind me who that is."

"A dead man, ock. A walking dead man."

"I get that part, youngin, but who is he?" Sean pressed.

"That's the dude that's over the jail, who stabbed my man Dave a minute ago? I'm about to visit his family and make him understand that touching my partner wasn't a good idea.

Why do I feel like I've told you all of this before? Just had a feeling of Deja vu.

Sean shrugged. "You might have. I can't remember shit but the people I need to kill and the ones who crossed me before."

"I can dig that. After I do that, though, I'm gonna fall back for a while. My name is ringing in all the wrong places. I'm allegedly under investigation in D.C. and Maryland. Nikki Locks told Zin and Zin told me."

"Join the club then, youngin. I'm sure that they're probably investigating me too. That's why I never leave witnesses. No face, no case."

"Bullshit. You left a witness in that house on Longfellow when you smoked Reese. You left Tinaboo alive after killing Kenny Sparrow. You left Doo Doo alive after we killed Whistle in Crud. Need I say more?"

"See what you done did, ock. You gon make me fuck around and smoke Trinaboo's ass Booze ass, then find that girl and get rid of her, too. Doo Doo's already dead..."

"And you left Rodney."

"Not for long, youngin. Not for long." Sean stood up with the box of shoes in his hand. "Gotta go, youngin. I got a lot of work I gotta do. Be safe."

I followed Sean to the counter. Without another word to each other, we paid for our shoes and left the store.

***

I reached into my pocket and found the paper that Tomasina gave me. I read the address on the paper and then looked at the address on the house on Varnum Street 4315. Slowly, I drove down the block and parked the car. I screwed the sound suppressor on the Glock 40. In the winter months in D.C., the sun started to set around 5:00 or 6:00 PM. It had just begun to set, but it was practically broad daylight still. I could leave and come back or I could stay and finish what I came there to do. I thought about what Zin said about somebody trying to get at Javon Jarrett at the jail and missing. I thought about my promise to Dave. His blood had been spilled. My decision was made. Pulling my mask down over my head. I got out of the car and walked back to 4315 Varnum Street. I entered the gate, walked to the front door and rang the doorbell. A young dude with dreads answered the door. He had tattoos that covered his arms and neck.

"Is Javon home, bro?" I asked.

"No, my brother locked up..."

That was as far as the dude got before I lifted the .40 and shot him in the face. I leaned in and hit him twice more for effect. Then, I turned and ran.

***

"I need to see you, baby girl, for a little bit of loving, hugging and touching."

"Quran, baby. That's pretty tempting, but not tonight. Tomorrow, I promise you we'll do whatever you want, but tonight is out of the question. I have a lot of work to do. I'll probably be up late getting it done, and then I'll need all my beauty rest."

"Are you cheating on me, Zin?" I asked.

"Are you really asking me some stupid shit like that, Quran. I can't believe you just asked me that. Why the fuck would I... You know what? I'm not even going to dignify that question with a response. I'm pregnant with your child and you have the audacity to—"

"Okay, okay, I'm sorry. Forget I asked that."

"Already forgotten. I love you, Quran. And there's no one in life that could do for me, what you can do for me, on any level. Trust that."

"My bad, Zin. I'm just a little stressed, I guess."

"Stress is good in some cases. It means you need to fall back some. I can't tell you how to live your life, but you gotta change eventually, Quran. For the baby, for me and yourself."

"I'm already hip. It's a process, Zin. It'll happen, trust me. It will."

"I' ma hold you too that. Let me get back to work. I'll call you in the morning."

"Alright baby, I love you."

"Love you more."

The call ended.

"Whew," I exclaimed and tossed the phone on the dresser. I had dodged a bullet. There was no way in the world I could have Zin and her not know that I had been fucking all day. My sore manhood throbbed, to reminding me of the vigorous workout it had sustained that day. Smiling to myself, I laid across the bed in my condo, and seconds later I was fast asleep.

Chapter 30
Tomasina

"Come into my office and sit down, Tomasina. Your father's gonna be a little late picking you up. But he's on his way," Principal Muriel Davis said.

"Can I finish drawing my picture, Mr. Davis?"

"Sure you can, Tomasina. Sit at my desk and draw."

"Thank you."

"What are you drawing, Tomasina?"

"A family picture of my brother and my father."

"That's nice, baby. Go ahead and draw."

An hour later, I was whisked out of the office by my father, who had red eyes and looked to be crying.

"Daddy, were you crying?" I asked my father.

He nodded his head as he walked up the hill.

"Why were you crying, Daddy?"

"Because... Because your brother is gone, Tommie. Your brother is gone and I'm sad about it."

"Gone? Gone where, Daddy? Where has my brother gone?"

"He's gone to Paradise, baby. Your brother is with all the angels now."

"But how? How can he be with the angels?"

My father stopped walking. He kneeled to face his 10-year-old daughter. The tears ran down his face. He said, "Your brother is dead, Tommie. Somebody killed him last night."

I kneeled at the grave of my brother and put fresh flowers near his tombstone. With tears in my eyes, I traced the curved letters of his name in the granite stone. Images of the day I found out he had been murdered, continued in my head. I remembered the pain and the intense sadness I felt as a kid to learn of my brother's tragic death. He had been shot to death by one of his friends. My young mind understood that he was never coming back to me, but my young heart couldn't stop from breaking into pieces. I was so devastated by my brother's death that I acted up in school and rebelled against everything and everyone at home. With the death of my brother, my entire life changed.

I picked myself up off the ground and brushed off my knees. Grass and dirt fell along with my tears. I wiped my eyes and stiffened my resolve. "Soon, brother. Soon," I said to myself and hoped that my brother could hear me. I walked. Harmony Cemetery's winding roads back to my car.

***

"Gimme a me a bag of Takis, a Rock Creek grape soda, a pack of Tropical Fruit Starburst and some Grape Bubblicious gum," I told the man behind the glass at the Valero gas station. I pulled a $20 bill out of my purse. Then, I heard a familiar voice behind me.

"Damn, you look good as shit. Get a box of gold pack Magnums, one of them Mojo pills, and a orange juice Nantucket."

I placed the order as instructed. I paid for everything and grabbed the bag from the man behind the glass. I turned to face Quran. He was dressed in Hugo Boss, head to toe and looked like a snack. He smiled his award-winning smile. My hormones raged. I handed him the bag and walked past him to my car.

"Did you do what I asked you to do?" Quran asked as he approached.

"I told you I would, didn't I? He didn't tell you?"

"I haven't talked to him in a minute, but if I did, he know better than to mention you on the phone."

"Glad to hear that, Que."

"You fuckin' with a nigga that's trained to go and know exactly what to do. And on some real shit, I appreciate you fucking with me, Tom."

"What can I say? I'm a real bitch and real bitches do real shit for real niggas. But fuck all that, Que, cube who you about to fuck off that Mojo pill?"

"Guess."

"You... Me?" I asked, pointing to myself.

Quran smiled and nodded his head. "Follow me to the spot."

"Damn, do the dick come with breakfast?"

***

1851 Howard Road
Southwest D.C.

As soon as I stepped into the apartment, my clothes started coming off.

"You are not about to be in my ass for no hour. Or none of that geeking ass shit. You tryna kill a bitch ass off of Mojo."

Quran was in the process of undressing as well. "Who said anything about fucking that pretty fat ass."

"I'm just saying because the last time I was here I left with a sore ass, wet pussy, and lock jaw."

"The last time you was here was a wonderful thing, but I never hit that pussy before. Ever. It's time to change that."

"Out the blue, Quran? I ain't going for that. Your man Dave told you about this fire pussy."

"By Allah, he didn't. I just decided to sample it on my own."

204

"Alright, then Que, let's get to it."

***

I can't explain the feelings I felt. My feet were on both of Quran's shoulders. I could see the bright pink polish on my toes. I couldn't help but to curl them every time Quran went deep into my canal. It felt as if his dick was trying to stroke through my stomach area. Quran's sweat fell from his forehead onto my face as he slowly grinded himself deeper into me. Loud moans escaped my mouth, no matter how hard I tried not to scream out in pain. The pounding I was taking felt so painfully good. I wanted it to stop but couldn't deny the pleasure I was getting. The shit confused and scared me at the same time. The Mojo pill had kicked in, and it had Quran's stamina on *1000*. It seemed like he had been inside me for hours. After all the intimate moments we shared, this was the first time that Quran had ever been inside my pussy. I had sucked his dick on too many occasions to count. As I squeezed my eyes shut and gave in to the crescendo of ecstasy that was building inside my core,

I remembered the first time I touched Quran. We were all at Tosheka's apartment, drinking and smoking. Well, actually only Tosheka and I were drinking. After one too many drinks, she passed out drunk in her own vomit. Suddenly, I was alone with Quran and all I could think about was all the times she bragged about his dick. The size. The length and girth. It was something that she was addicted to. Seeing my opportunity, I wanted to know if she'd been exaggerating or not. Quran came out of the bathroom. I cornered him by the door and ripped at his zipper while staring in his eyes.

Once his dick was out and in my hand, I stopped to see if he protested at all. Like the typical male with his dick in a woman's hand, he looked at me lustfully His mouth never moved, but his eyes said *make me cum*. Delighted to see that

Quran's dick was as big as Toshekka proclaimed, I did what his eyes beckoned. I dropped to my knees and made him bust in my mouth. I swallowed his semen gladly, and I wasn't done.

I sat on my knees and licked Quran's nuts and soft dick until it rose again. Then, I ate him until he came again.

After that, Quran and I hooked up, often without her knowing. But for some reason, we had never fucked. He had never been inside me until last week when we fucked my ass. Today, he was in my pussy and if I had any control over our trysts, it would be no time turning back, he'd always love to fuck me. No more just getting his dick sucked. As if he could read my thoughts, Quran's fingers closed around my feet. His powerful body pressed me down and his midsection rose. My pelvic area rose with him. As my feet went closer to the pillow, my pussy rose. Then, Quran grinded forcefully into me. All I could do was bite my lips and moan loudly. I squeezed his neck tightly. I felt too satisfied, too full of dick. I had already come twice, but a third orgasm erupted minutes before, Quran filled his condom with his seed.

"I ain't gon lie, Que, that was well worth the wait."

"I always knew that pussy was probably torch. It's in the way you walk, I could tell."

"Is that right? And your man had nothing to do with this happening, huh?"

Quran set on the dresser, fully clothed, while I tied my boots. "I told you earlier that me and Dove never discussed what you did, either time. But I do know that he enjoyed it. As for what made me want to do that after all this time, I don't know? When I saw you earlier at the gas station, I got super turned on. It was as if I really paid attention to how sexy you are for the first time. I tried my hand and you went for it."

"I went for it? Damn. That sounds kinda strange. Like you tricked me or something."

"Never that. I just didn't know if giving me the pussy was part of the plan for us. Every time we hooked up in the past, it was all about you getting me. I thought that was all you ever wanted. Well, until you gave me that phat ass."

"Uh.. Sir, didn't you mean until you *took* this fat azz? All I did was give in after you had half of it already in me. Wasn't no use in fighting it after it was all the way inside me, the shit felt bomb and the next thing I knew, I was coming. I never came from anal sex before you did it last week. Real talk, my inner voice was screaming for you to stop because my ass was hurting but my outer voice betrayed me when I begged you not to stop until you came in my ass and now the pain in my pussy matches the pain I felt in my ass days ago. Thank you for all the pain, Que."

Quran chuckled. "Stop what you doing, Tom. That was pleasure too. Besides, don't blame the pain on me. Blame the Mojo pill. And damn, your pussy was so good I almost forgot why we met up in the first place". He left the room and I could hear the apartment door open and close. I heard the door open again and seconds later Quran was back in the room with a bag. He handed the bag to me.

I peered inside the bag. It was filled with small individual packages of weed.

"That's a whole pound of weed broke down into ounces. I need you to get that to Dave and my brother. Not all at once, but whenever you can. And I gotta ask you this..."

"Ask me what, Quran?"

"Would it be too much to ask you to get my brother out the streets?"

Are you asking me to fuck, Jahid?" I asked.

"To be honest Tom, I don't give a fuck how you do it, or even if you do it at all. If you got a buddy over there that will get him together, that's cool with me. If not, I don't care how you got him, I just need you to get him; hand job, head, pussy, ass— it doesn't matter to me. I want lil bruh to be good on every level while he's there, feel me?" Quran went under the bed and pulled out a Timberland boot box. He opened it, removed several wads of cash and put the lid back on the box. Quran pushed the box back under the bed. "Here, take this. That's five bands."

"I put the money in my purse. I'm gonna make it happen. I got you, Que. I don't know for sure what's gonna happen but Jahid's gonna be straight. Anything else?"

"Yeah, let Dave know that I visited Javon Jarrett's family. His brother sends his regards."

***

"Ohh. Ohh, shit. Tomasina stop. Shit. Shit. Shit."

Marissa Parson was laid on her back on her couch as I kneeled between her legs and tasted every inch of her pretty pussy. I licked her inner thighs, tongued her clit passionately, and stuck my tongue in her ass while I fingered her.

"I'ma cum. I'm coming, about to come, Tomasina."

Marissa ended up being a squirter. Her juices hit my lips in a stream and ran down my chin. I had no clue what the shit was— cum or piss, but it turned me on like hell to make it happen. So much so, that I ate her some more then reach under me and rubb my own clit through my panties, I could feel the wet spot at the center of my panties. Eating Marissa made me wet as fuck. I moved a finger into my panties and before long, I was coming along with Marissa.

***

I was laid out on Marissa's couch, completely exhausted. Two different sexcapades in one day was almost too much. *Almost.* I could smell the freshly showered Marissa before I laid my eyes on her. It had to be the scent of her body wash, or maybe the shampoo she washed her dreads with. Marissa was a dark-skinned beauty. She gave me Lupita Nyong's vibes. But she was much prettier. Her teeth were white with braces. Her dimples were even more prominent when she smiled. Marissa sat on the loveseat across from me. Her robe opened to show her shaved pussy when she put her foot up on the couch. I noticed that her feet were pretty. Her toes were painted a bright red color and there was a gold anklet around her right ankle. Her skin was beautiful. The robe covered her stomach but opened to reveal a peak at one of her ample breast. Marissa looked at me and I looked at her.

"Damn, Tom, bitch. I really needed that," Marissa said.

"Glad I could help because I really need you," I replied.

"Need me how?"

"Your post is the MDV tonight, right?"

Marissa nodded. "Tonight, tomorrow and Friday. On the first shift."

I sat up and grabbed my purse off the floor from me and extracted one of the wads of money I got from Quran. I pulled out $500. "You trying to make some easy money?"

Marissa eyed the big faces in my hand. "What do I gotta do to make it?"

I made a show of peeling out five more $100 bills. I need you to do three things: Let me in your unit tonight and I'll man the office while you pop a friend of mine out of his cell. I need you to show him some love. Either fuck or suck him. But you gotta make him cum. Then, you'll put him back in the cell. And you man the office while I do my thing with another dude. You can take him in the exam room. When you finish, I'll take my guy in there and get him together.

"By my count, that's two things you said three."

"You're right. After you do your thing, I need you to give him some weed for me. What's up? You with it or not?"

"Just one time right?" Marissa asked.

"If you want it to be. These niggas got rich friends though, Rissa."

"I need my fucking job, Tomasina."

"And you think I don't need mine?"

Marissa crossed the room and took the money out of my hand. "I'm with it as long as you don't get me in trouble."

"Think positive thoughts, bitch. You'll be fine."

"Do you do this all the time?"

"What? Getting niggas pulled out or eat pussy real good."

"Both," Marissa said salaciously.

I stood up. Put my purse across my shoulder and said. "Wouldn't you like to know?"

"Who are we popping out tonight? Who am I popping out for me?"

"You have a date with Jahid Bashir and I have a date with David Battle.

***

Center Treatment Facility,
1901 E St. Southeast.

The metal door to the medical unit opened and I walked int with purpose. Marissa was writing in the log book as I entered the office. She looked up at me before she could say a word. I said. "I'll be right back. I gotta use the restroom real quick."

In the restroom reserved for officers, I pulled down my pants and panties then squatted over the toilet. One push of the pelvis brought the condom covered package of weed out of my pussy. I tossed the weed into the sink next to the toilet. With a grimace and a deeper push, the compressed package of weed also wrapped in condoms, came out of my ass. Tossing that package into the sink as well, I thought about the process I had undergone to get myself ready to smuggle. the weed into the jail in my ass. I had taken a wicked dump and then an enema to clean my rectum out. I repeated the enema process twice before declaring myself ready to tote. I wiped both off with wipes provided by the facility. Both packages were washed off with soap after I fixed my clothes,

I pocketed the weed after washing my hands in the sink. I looked into the mirror and almost didn't recognize the person who stared back at me. My weave was tight, and the hairstyle Iwas rocking was one of my favorites. My full lips were accented with Fenty lip gloss. My brown eyes seemed a bit dull. My caramel complexion wasn't as bright as it usually was. At 5't5 and 150 pounds, my weight was mostly in my thighs and titties. I looked good, but I didn't feel good about myself. I looked for the old me in the mirror but couldn't find her. The old me laughed loudly, enjoyed life and dreamed often. The old me vowed to grow into the strongest woman, never settling for less or ever disrespecting myself. That *me* had been gone for a long time. That me died not long after my brother was brutally murdered and my father died of a drug overdose. That me view the world through tinted lenses. That me was a remnant of the past, now replaced by the woman who stared back at me in the mirror. I left the restroom and reentered the office. I pulled at one of the weed packages and passed it to Marissa. "Has the lieutenant made his rounds yet?"

Marissa nodded her head.

"Alright then. Go ahead and pop out Jihad."

Marissa buzzed into Jihad's cell and summoned him to the office.

Minutes later, he walked into the office. "What's up, CO?"

"Don't say a word, Jahid, just go with her," I directed.

"Come on," Marissa led him out of the office.

I took the chair that Marissa had just vacated, leaned back, and smiled.

***

"It seems to me that you're tryna make a habit of this, Battle," I said as soon as I was inside the exam room with David.

"Am I wrong for that?" David asked.

"I guess not," I replied, and bent over to untie my boots. After they were untied, I pulled both Nike boots off. Then, I took my pants and panties off. Dressed in nothing but my uniform shirt and socks, I said, "Get up on the exam table and lie all the way back. We don't have a lot of time." David did as I told him. I pulled at his uniform pants and boxers until they were huddled at his ankles, Leaning over, I kissed his dick and it sprang to life. Using the chair beside the table, I climbed up onto the exam table. I positioned myself to squat on his erection. Grabbing it, I placed it at the entrance of my wetness and slid down his pole.

"Gotdamn," David moaned.

"Shut up and enjoy the ride, nigga."

I placed both hands on David's chest and looked directly into his eyes. Then, I bounced up and down slowly. My pussy was still sore from the beating that Quran had put on it, but I ignored the pain. I focused more on the pleasure that was building up. Music that only I could hear played in my head as I moved from side to side, and front to back. I moved up and down, then ground myself onto the length of him, all while never losing eye contact at all. David bit down on his lip to stifle a moan. I put my finger on his lips to quiet him. David opened his mouth and sucked on my finger. That turned me on enough to where I squeezed the muscles in my pelvis and made myself tighter on his dick.

David tried to speak. I pulled my fingers out of his mouth. "I'm about to come in you," he said.

"Go ahead then," I replied.

He grabbed my hips with incredible strength and held me down on his dick. I could feel him pulsating inside of me. I knew that he was coming. His warm flood splashed all over my inner walls. Quickly, I got up and climbed down from the table. I grabbed tissues from beneath the sink in the room, balled it up and used it to stop the cum that would run out of me later. I slipped on my panties and pants, then put on my boots. Pulling the packaged weed from my pocket, I gave it to David. "Here, put this up."

David took the weed and checked it. "You gonna make a nigga fall in love with your sexy ass."

"Don't do that. I'm a heartbreaker."

"Yeah, I bet."

"Oh, before I forget, Que told me to tell you that he hollered at the dude who stabbed your peoples. He said to tell you that his brother sends his regards. Said, you know what he means by that."

"That's what's up. Bruh must really fuck with you to tell you that. So, do me a favor and relay a message to him for me. I know we got the phones, but I still don't trust them like that. Tell him that Jay was tryna call him yesterday but couldn't reach him. He almost got caught with the phone, but he flushed it. Tell him that Jay's lawyer told him that he is under investigation for bodies in D.C. and Maryland. He thinks they looking at him for the joint on Oxon Hill. Tell him he got to fall back and lay low. Got all that?"

"I got it. I'll make sure he gets the message."

"One more thing; is bruh really getting you for what you're doing for me. Because if he ain't, I'm tryna really look out for you."

"I'm good, boo. Quran takes good care of me in more ways than you can imagine. Thanks for the offer, though. You can go back to your cell now and be sure to enjoy the rest of your night."

"I will. You can bet on that."

***

Downstairs on the first floor of the jail, I was back at my post. I sat inside the Central bubble and thought about what David Battle said to me....

213

"... Tell him that Jay's lawyer told him that he's under investigation for bodies in D.C. and Maryland. He thinks they looking at him for that junk on Oxon Hill."

Bodies. Oxon Hill. Investigation. Quran. Tosheka. David Battle didn't know that. I know Tosheka, a lot of people probably didn't know that, but Quran did. The only murder that happened in Oxen Hill, MD, recently was Tosheka's murder. David had to be telling me to tell Quran that he was being investigated for *that* murder. A strange feeling descended over me. Why would Maryland police be investigating Quran for Tosheka's murder? Had I been right before when I suspected of Quran being the person who killed Tosheka. I thought again about the last conversation that I had with her. She was going outside to see Quran. It was more than logical to assume that Quran was her killer, but the question of why he'd do it always came back to me and I couldn't answer it. Now the police had put two and two together and come up with Quran. Again, why? I thought back to the first time I'd seen Quran after Tosheka's death.

"Tom. How are you, baby girl?"

"Considering all the wild shit that been going on the last couple of weeks, I'm good, Que, and yourself."

"Fucked up about Tosheka, but you already know that. I'ma body any and everybody that was with that shit. Believe that."

"I already know, Que. Say less. My girl didn't deserve to go out like that."

"What the fuck was Tosheka into lately, Tom?"

"I've been working sixteen-hour shifts for the past 5 months because CTF is short of staff. I talked to Tash all the time, but I hadn't seen her in like 2 months. Since you curved her, she was always ranting and raving about your new woman. She told me that she had somebody new but never told me his name. I should have pressed her for more information about the dude…"

"You think he did it? Killed Tosh?"

"Who knows? Maybe, maybe not. But right now, whoever he is looks suspect."

Quran paid for Tosheka's entire funeral. I took the money to her mother myself, but Quran never showed up to the funeral or the repast. I had asked him about his absence and he just explained it away. I had never paid it any real attention until now. Had Quran really killed Tosheka. If so, why?

Chapter 31
Michael Carter
Central Detention Facility. D.C.
DCJail.
1901 D St. Southeast.

"If you ask me, the whole city is just lost, bob. No bullshit. Shit, is just different now. It's fucked up. We lost our way somewhere. You used to be able to pick real D.C. niggas out of a crowd. But now you can't. If you take some niggas from Baltimore and Virginia and brought them here and put them with the young niggas out there in the streets nowadays, you wouldn't know who is who. All the young niggas got dreads. Remember it was cornrow braids. Remember that?"

"I remember."

"Ain't no more of that. It's all dreads now, men and women. And the clothes— don't let me get started on the clothes. Shit sad, Bob, real talk, everything is small as shit, tight as fuck. Pants, shirts, coats, jackets… everything tight. You ain't gon believe that shit when you get out there, bob. Them young niggas' pants so fucking tight that you can see their thigh and calf muscles through the pants."

"Get the fuck outta here, slim," I laughed.

"If I'm lying, I'm flying. God, take the breath out of me right now. You could be riding past somewhere and see an ass that look good as shit in some jeans and get up on the person, and it's a man."

216

I bust out laughing super hard.

"You think I'm bullshitting, bob? No homo. Them young pants got their butts fat as shit. Then they got the nerve to have the tight pants hanging off their asses, showing their draws. I'm telling you, bob, shit is crazy. And don't let me get started on the colors. Shid. Them niggas lil ass outfits be bright as shit. Lime green, orange, yellow, pink, light blue, light purple. Wild as shit and let them niggas tell it, they fly as shit. They influenced by BET., Kenya West goofy ass. Ain't no more. *MCHUNU. Hobo. AllDAZ, We R'One. Madness. Shooter's Sports. City life*, or *Squash All Beefs*. All that *Zoton* shit played out. Urban Streetwear is some 'Bama shit now. They into all that foreign shit. *Versace, Gucci, Prada. Louis Vuitton, Dior. Valentino*. And *YSL*. I like some of the shit, but..."

The door to the cell opened. I got out of the bunk and looked up the tier. I saw the CO in the bubble popping cell doors on both tiers – mine, and the one upstairs. Then I saw a big orange cart being pushed in the inmate workers. The cart was filled to capacity with plastic bags full of commissary items.

"What's that OG Mike? Trays."

"Naw, slim. That's commissary. Just come in the block."

"That's what's up," My celly said and hopped down off the top bunk. "I'ma fuck one of them lemon pound cakes up before I get back to the cell.

***

"Don't walk away from this table without checking your bag. If somethings is missing let us know now. If you leave this table, you're dead. Ain't no coming back talking 'bout *I'm missing something*," the female CO that ran commissary announced.

A few minutes later, my name was called.

"Carter, thirty-eight cell."

I stepped up to get my bag.

"Let me see your armband, Carter."

I showed the woman my armband.

"Give Carter his bag," the woman instructed.

I grabbed the bag and busted it open. The inmate worker grabbed the receipt in the bag and called out everything that should have been in there. While he called the items out, I placed the items into a different plastic trash bag. Satisfied that all items were accounted for, I stepped away from the table with the bag.

I heard somebody say. "Damn OT. Big, big shit."

Suddenly I was approached by three young dudes. All three had dreads and tight ass orange D.C. Jail uniforms on. I smiled to myself as I remembered what my celly had just said.

The three dudes varied in size and height. I assumed the one in front was the ringleader. I'd seen him around the block several times but had never acknowledged him or the two dudes with him. They appeared to be just along for the ride.

"Your bag, big as shit, OT," the ringleader said. "What you got for me?"

I set the bag down and smiled. "Youngin, the only thing I got for you is pain, misery and death. A whole lot of it?"

The ringleader scowled and stepped an inch closer to me. He was about my height and weight. "Fuck that supposed to mean?"

Taking two steps towards him, our faces were inches away from each other.

"It means that if you think you or your men with you are going to take anything out of this bag, you're mistaken. This bag might look like it contains food and snacks, but like I said, it's full of misery, pain and death if you take even one item out this bag, everybody that you love gon be dead in a week. I promise you that. That's where the misery and pain comes in. So, let me make sure I heard you correctly. "You want something out of this bag?"

The young boy ringleader looked into my eyes as I looked into his. What he saw was anger and death. What I saw was fear.

"You want something out of this bag, youngin?" I asked again.

"Naw, I'm good, O.T," Ringleader capitulated. "I was just fucking with you. I got my own bag over there."

"Cool. I see that you ain't as stupid as you look. I'm in thirty-eight cell if you change your mind." With that said, I walked through the trio of young dudes and went back to my cell.

***

"Carter. You need to go to the Medical," the CO came to the cell and said. He put a small hall pass in the opening of the cell door. "Stick your arm out and you'll be ready to go."

I brushed my teeth and washed my face. I ran water over my hair to soften it, then brushed it. I got dressed into my two-piece orange uniform, stuck my arm out the door and waved it. Seconds later, the cell door popped.

***

"Let me see your pass," the big black African CO said in English that I could barely understand.

I handed him the pass.

"Go straight back to the left. Doctor Ruiz is already in there."

I hadn't put in a sick call slip or requested to see a doctor, so I was surprised by the impromptu summons to medical. In the room. I was instructed to go to, a short Hispanic doctor stood at a desk writing on the pad.

He looked up. As I walked in. "Michael Carter?"

I nodded my head.

The doctor pulled a white paper prescription bag out of his white hospital coat. "Here's your medication," he said, crossed the room and gave me the bag.

"Medication?" I replied. befuddled. "I ain't on no medication."

"A friend of yours says you are. Take the bag and leave. No questions asked. There's a note inside the bag for you. Wait until you're back in your cell to read it. Go. Now."

I turned and walked out of the room, then left Medical.

***

Inside my Cell

Inside the bag was a small smartphone and a charger. A small piece of paper was there too. Unfolding the paper, I read the note.

Turn the phone on. There's one number programmed into the phone. Tap the number and it will dial. Someone will answer on the other end.

Balling the note up, I tossed it into the toilet. On my face was a look of pure confusion. I powered the phone on. And saw that it had three bars indicating that it was fully charged.

"Celly, stand at the door and watch out for the cops for me."

"Gotcha, bob. Say less."

Scrolling to the contacts in the phone, I saw one number programmed in. As instructed, I tapped on the number. The phone automatically dialed it.

The phone on the other end rung twice and a man answered.

"Mike." The voice was familiar, but I couldn't place it.

"Yeah, this is me. Who is this?"

"Your old friend, Mike. Carlos Trinidad."

"Carlos?"

"He laughed, It's me, Mike. I know that it's been a long while, but I've kept tabs on you for years. We have to talk, but not on the phone although it is clean. Use it however you like. In a couple days, you will be called to a certain place inside the jail. I'll be there waiting for you. We need to talk about life and death. Do you remember Victor Martin, Mike?"

"Of course, I do. How could I not remember him?"

"Do you remember our trip to New York?"

"Again, how could I forget anything about that incident?"

"Good. I'm glad that you haven't lost your memory. You'll need it when we talk. See you in a couple days, Mike."

"Alright, Carlos."

The line went dead. I put the phone up and laid back on my bunk. What the fuck could Carlos Trinidad want with me after all these years? A weird foreboding washed over me.

Chapter 32

Sean Branch

Trinaboo was driving a new modeled CL63 Mercedes-Benz. I smiled in admiration of her hustle. I got out of the car and met her in the parking lot of Applebee's on Donnell Drive. We embraced.

"Hey brother, how are you?"

"I'm good, baby girl."

"Glad to hear it. Well, I got good news. I was able to get in touch with Moe Best. My girlfriend Shawnie, from Hillside, got a cousin named Lynn. Lynn has three kids by Kenny Best…"

"I know Kenny and all those brothers and sisters. We grew up together."

"Cool. Anyway. Lynn called Kenny and got Moe's cell phone number. I called Moe and told him that I've been in his lines since the go-go's in the 90s. I said a whole lot of shit that he ate up like food. To make a long story short, I set up a date with Moe for today."

"Where?" I asked Trina.

"You told me to find a place that is seedy and discreet; a motel like the old Motor Lodge across from Crystal's Skate? Well, I found the perfect place. I just left there booking a room. It's a small motel on Allentown Rd. next to the larger Quality Inn. The way it's made, its way off of the road. And there's woods surrounding it. There's no cameras on the building and nothing next door to it but a wall of the Quality

Inn. You can reach the room from the parking lot." Trina pulled out two key cards. "Here's the extra one."

I accepted the room card.

"So how do you want to play it? Just like we did, Kenny or a different way?"

"A different way. Mo-e is a lot different than Kenny. He's a killer with killer instincts. He knows the game and the art of the setup, although he dishonored himself and became a rat, he's still crafty. He understands that his days are numbered and that people are going to come him. I believe he knows that *I* am coming for him. For you to get at him out the blue is definitely gonna raise a red flag in his head and he'll be ready for a backdoor move. He'll be strapped and watching you and the door to the room, I think he'll be prepared for a move. So we have got to preempt him. You have to pull up to the motel office and act like you're just getting the room. Then take him to the room. I'll already be inside the room, hiding. You get him inside the room and work your magic. Don't be shy either. I've already seen you naked and in action. So, just act normal. Get him to let his guard down. And then I'll pop out on him and do the rest. I pulled the wad of money out of my coat pocket and handed it to Trina Boo. "That's two bands."

"Two thousand dollars," Trina said, and her eyes lit up.

"It's a reward, Tee because you always do what I need you to do and you can be trusted on every level. I respect that and appreciate you."

Trina pocketed the cash. "You already know I fuck with you the long way, Sean. I'm about to pick Moe up and take him to the room. See you later."

***

I found the Roadway Inn exactly where Trina said it would be. The key card had the room number on it. I found the room with no problem as well. Letting myself into the room, I searched it and moved around every inch of it. It didn't take long for me to find the perfect hiding spot. I could see the room door and the window next to the door. Removing my coat, I pulled out both of my sound suppressed weapons. I settled into my hiding spot to wait for the victim.

***

"Did you bring condoms?" Trina asked as soon as the motel room door was closed. She immediately started to undress.

Moe Best looked around the room furtively before pulling out a gun. He smiled and laid the gun on the dresser. "Of course I did. Extra-large Trojan joints with ribbed contours and a warming sensation gel on 'em. I only got the three in the box joints though. Is that gonna be enough?"

Trina smiled. "I think that should be more than enough. As good as this pussy is, though, you might only make it through one. I've been known to put niggas to sleep like babies, snoring and shit."

Moe laughed. "So I heard. I been wanting to see what you working with for years."

"Likewise. I heard about you. You and that dope dick."

"Since you already know my secret, I ain't gotta hide what I do." said Moe Best. He pulled a small bag out of his pocket, opened it, and dumped out a portion of powder onto the back of his hand. He brought his hand up to his face and used his nose to sniff it. He repeated the process and sniffed powder into the opposite nostril. "Ohh. Shit. Damn, that's good shit."

The look on Trina's face was one of disguised disgust. Moe began to undress down to his boxer briefs Trina was standing in nothing but lace panties, the matching bra she had just removed. She moved to the bed.

"C'mon on. Show me what you can do with that dope dick."

Moe pulled off his boxers and walked naked to the bed. Trina lifted up and removed her panties. She laid on her back and opened her legs. She motioned for Moe to enter her in the missionary position. Moe ran back to his pants and removed the box of condoms. He tore the condom pack open with his teeth and removed one. On the way back to the bed, he slipped the condom on. The lighting in the room was dim.

I watched climb onto the bed and between Trina's thighs. They began fucking and I came out of my hiding spot., thinking, *there's no better way for a nigga to die than in some pussy.* Trina saw me first. I upped the gun and shot Moe in the back of the head. Then with the second gun, I shot Trina right in the face multiple times.

"Sorry, baby girl, but I couldn't leave you around this time," I said aloud and shot Moe in the head repeatedly. "Stinking ass rat."

Quickly, I rifled through Moe's pockets, found his cell phone and pocketed it. I searched through Trina's things quickly; I found her cell phone and the money I'd given her earlier. I pocketed both, grabbed my coat and walked into the night.

***

International House of Pancakes.
Saint Bartles Road
Thirty minutes later.
"Aye dawg, do you love her?"

" Leave her out this, Sean... please dawg! She's innocent in this. She ain't but 20 years old, and shorty is thorough. If you let her go, I swear to you, she ain't gon tell nobody about this. Let her go dawg, please!"

"Shorty, thorough, huh? What's your name, boo?"

" Yoni"

"Are you really thorough, Yoni?"

The girl nodded.

"It's your lucky day then, Yoni, But let me make one thing clear to you. My name is Sean Branch. Ask your family about me. If you breathe one word to anybody about what happened here tonight, I'ma find you, then I'ma kill your whole family. Old people, kids and all. I'ma wipe out your whole existence. Do you understand that?"

The young woman nodded as tears ran down her cheeks.

The chicken tenders at the IHOP we *p* re my favorite. The batter, the texture, the taste. I picked up a tender and moved it around in the syrup before eating it. Then Iforked a generous amount of waffle off the plate and into my mouth. My mind was still on the woman whose life I spared the night I killed Reese. Her name was Yoni. I'd done everything I could to find her, but had come up empty handed. For now her life would go on without her knowing how close she'd come to losing her life not once, but twice. If only I knew where to find her. Quran's words to me inside the shoe store had hit home. I had been too proud to admit it, but in my arrogance I had left too much to chance. I'd left too many people around who could one day be a witness against me. And those were chances I couldn't afford to take. I thought about Trina Boo lying dead in that hotel room on Allentown Road and shook my head. If I had a heart, this would be the part where I'd cry for her, but I had no heart, and all the people left on my list would come to learn that irrefutable fact— the hard way. As I stood over their bodies and took their lives, I thought about Rodney Shaw. I thought about Ren Tylor. I thought about Biana Clark. Then, I thought about how I'd fell after I killed them all.

Chapter 33
Ren Tyler

"Oooww shit."

"You gotta hold still, boo," Jada, the tattoo artist scolded.

"I'm trying to stay still, but the needles feel like they're penetrating my bone," I pleaded.

"Back pieces are the worst, Ren.. But if you don't, hold still, the portrait of Brian won't come out right. Let me see that picture again."

I handed Jada the picture of Brian. Seconds later, she passed it back to me. I stared at the picture and my eyes watered as tears fell down my cheeks. I rubbed the picture of it as if it was his actual face I could feel his smiling face stare back at me as if he could see me and wanted me to feel better about his absence. At least that's what my mind told me. But there's no way that I could ever feel good again— Brian Clark meant the world to me.

"Am I putting wings on both sides of the portrait?"

"No, no wings. Wings imply something angelic. Heavenly. My baby was the furthest thing from an angel, Jada. I would never disrespect his memory that way. Instead of wings, put flames on both sides. Brian represented fire and if there is a such thing as heaven and hell, I understand that he's in hell and one day I'll join him there. So that we can be together in the next life for an eternity."

"Ren, are you sure you want me to put flames around the portrait?"

"I'm sure, Jada. Put flames and make them colorful. Bright and realistic."

"It's your body, boo. Whatever you want, flames it is."

***

"I love the tattoo, Ren," Bianca said.

"Thanks. I love it too."

"But you gotta explain the flames on the both sides of my brother's face. Why is he surrounded by fire."

"Do you believe in Heaven and Hell, Bianca?"

"Uh. I guess so, yeah."

"Well, which of the places do you think Brian is at now?"

Bianca put the leftover food on her tray in the trash. "Guess you got a point there."

"Were you able to get in touch with Tomasina?"

"I've talked to her a couple times since the last time we saw each other. Tom says that Quran's last name is Bashir, same as his brother, Jihad, who's at CTF in the medical unit. I tried to get any info I could on Quran and told her why I needed it."

"And?"

"Nothing. That's all she knows. I asked her about Sean Branch. And all she knows is his history. What the streets say about him."

"And what's that?"

"What? We already know that he's a cold-blooded murderer. Kills whoever, whenever, for whatever reason. Heartless. Cold. Brutal. Insane. The usual."

"Well, I have good news. I got a possible line on his mother and daughter. We couldn't find the daughter because her name is not Branch. There was a story on the news a while back about a woman who was killed and her body tossed in the river. That body was recovered by a fishermen near the wharf. The woman was identified as Raquel Dunn. The name rung a bell in my head. So I went back through the articles I read from Sean Branch's trial back in 1993. That's where I saw the name before. In one the articles, it mentioned that Sean's baby mother testified at his trial as an alibi witness. That's how I found out about the daughter, too. I had a thought and searched for anything Raquel Dunn. Appears she loves social media and had an Instagram page and Facebook. There are pictures of her and her daughter on there. I kept digging and found out that the daughter's name is Shontay Dunn. Shontay Dunn also has a Facebook, Instagram and Twitter account. I sent her a friend request on Facebook and she accepted me. I got to see all of her pictures that she's posted. Most of the pictures are selfies, some are with her and her mother, but a few are Shontay with her father. She posted the jail pictures of Sean Branch as well. I took screenshots of all of those photos of Sean Branch." I pulled out my cell phone and unlocked it. I pulled up the photos and passed the phone to Bianca. "Say hello to Mr. Sean Branch."

Bianca stared at the photo before swiping to the next. "That nigga is gorgeous."

"I know, right? It's gonna be a shame to make an ugly mess of such a hard, handsome face. But before I do that. I'm gonna take away someone that he loves. The way that he took Brian from me."

"He took Brian from *us*, Ren."

"You know what I mean. In the pictures on her page, Shontay is sometimes wearing a Chipotle uniform. Again, I dug around until I could pinpoint familiar places in her photos. I came up on the Chipotle near Galleria Place. I called the restaurant and asked for her."

"It wasn't the one, huh?" Bernice asked.

"Oh, its definitely the one. She works there on the closing shift on Sunday through Thursday. Every other week, she works on Friday."

"So you're gonna kill Sean Branch's daughter?"

I nodded my head.

***

Chipoltle
7th Street NW.

Bianca exited the Chipotle and walked to the car. She climbed in the passenger seat. "She's in there working hard as hell."

"Good. If we're lucky, her father will pick her up from work, and I'll kill two birds with one stone."

"Don't you mean one gun?"

***

"Here she come, and I don't see any cars nearby. that seem like someone about to pick up somebody," Bianca said.

I watched the woman named Shontay zip up her coat and exit the Chipotle. She walked down 7th Street. I got out on foot to follow her. At G Street Shontay turned the corner, and just as I hit the same corner, I saw her turning into a parking garage. I walked faster to catch up with her, entering the garage shortly behind her. I could hear her footsteps as she climbed the stairs to a level above the ground floor. I heard a door open and close. I took the steps two at a time and exited the stairway. I saw Shontay had reached a red Infinity. The Infinity beeped twice as it recognized her key fob. I called out the woman's name.

"Shontay!"

"Who…?" Shontay said as she saw me approaching her. "Do I know you?"

My hand was on the gun in my coat pocket, finger already around the trigger. "No, but I know *you*."

"What do you want?"

"To send a message to your father."

"What message?"

"This one," I said, and pulled the gun. I shot her repeatedly until her body dropped, then I walked up to her and shot her some more.

***

As soon as we walked in the door of my apartment, Bianca said. "We've been talkin' shit and planning shit, but things just got really real! You just killed Sean Branch's daughter."

Calmly, I took off my coat and put the gun I'd just used on Shontay on to the dining room table. "I thought it was we who killed Sean Branch's daughter."

Bianca stopped pacing the floor and removed her coat. "You know what I meant, Ren."

"I heard what you meant, but you telling me shit that I already know. We differ on one thing though, sis."

"And what is that?"

"For you, things just got real. For me, they've *been* real. Shit became real the moment that Brian died in that parking lot. I don't give two fucks about Sean Branch or anybody else that he loves and cares for. I'ma kill everybody that he loves anyway. His mother is the next person on my list."

"Do you know exactly where his mother lives?" Bianca asked.

I shook my head.

"Do you know anything about his mother?"

"Nope, but I found his daughter. I'll find his mother."

"We should have just followed his daughter to wherever she was going. She might have led us to either the mother or Sean himself."

I sat in one of the dining room chairs and removed my shoes. Then, I stood and wiggled out of my jeans. I headed to the bedroom.

"Where the hell are you going?" Bianca called out.

231

"If you must know, I'm going to get my bullet and use it to make myself cum. Killing always makes me horny.

"Killing makes you horny? Damn, Ren. How many people have you killed?"

"If I told you that, I'd have to kill you."

TO BE CONTINUED...

COMING SOON

IF YOU CROSS ME ONCE 5
Vengeance is mine

IN THE BLINK OF AN EYE 2
AMEEN (The Beginning)

NOW TURN THE PAGE FOR A SNEAK PEEK AT
ANGEL 5 THE FINALE

Chapter 1

Najee

"Put the gun on the ground! Now!

"Drop the gun, sir!"

"Put the gun down!"

I stood in the crowd and watched the scene unfold. Gunz stood not far from the Benz. The expression on his face was distant. One of his hands clutched at his side. It appeared to be covered in blood. What had happened before I walked up? Had Gunz been shot? If so, by who? I looked at guns as he stood there motionless. Cops were on every side of him with their guns trained on him. I wanted to call at him and tell him that it was over and to get down. I wanted him drop his gun and we'd find a way to get him out of this jam. But I didn't. I couldn't. I silently prayed that Gunz took one last look around and saw me standing in the crowd. But he never turned, never looked. I tried to understand what he was going through as she stood there, then his facia expression changed and it told me all that I needed to know. I watched the tears fall down Gunz' cheeks. I knew what he was going to do.

A loud scream pierced the night as Gunz raised the gun and fired at the cops. Gunshots rang out from all directions, I watched my best friend go out in a hail of bullets. Tears filled my eyes. I turned and walked away. My heart was forever broken. Gunz and Tye were gone forever. Two of the most important people in my life had died hours apart from one another and I had no idea who was inside the Toyota. I saw the result of the crash, but it was impossible to know if the driver had been Aziz Navid or not. I walked slowly back to the porch, eyes full of tears I refused to wipe them away. I didn't care who saw my tears. My pain was on display for the whole city to see. I wanted the universe to understand that someone would die for every tear I cried. All of a sudden, a song came to mind. It played in my head with alarming clarity. As if my head was a speaker, it vibrated through my entire body...

"Day after day seems like I push against the clouds./They just keep blocking out the sun. It seems since I was born./I wake up every blessed morning./Down on my luck and up against the wind./Don't you stop? Don't you run, don't you cry/. You'll do fine. You'll be good./You'll get by./Right after Night. Seems like I Rage Against the moon./But it don't never like the dark./I cursed the falling rain./But I won't stop for my. Complaining./Down on my luck and Up Against The Wind./Don't you stop, Don't you run, Don't you cry."

The song "Up Against the Wind" that played out in the movie "Set It Off" after Cleo and Frankie died was cemented inside my head, and I couldn't believe the parallel circumstances that caused it to fill my head. I thought about the scene in the movie where Cleo refused to surrender and was shot down by cops. It was the exact same scene that had just played out in front of my eyes with Gunz. At the Porsche, I tried to ignore all the broken glass inside the car. The blood that stained the seat. Aminah's blood. I tried not to think about her, but I couldn't *not* think about the fact that just like Gunz and Tye, Aminah was gone to. I sat in the Porsche with no driver's side window to keep out the cold. I cried like a newborn baby.

Eventually, I started the car and drove through the streets of Newark. It was the city that birthed the animal in me. I realized then just how much everything had changed. Nothing was as it had been years ago. I rode past the White Castle on Elizabeth Ave and saw it filled with dudes wearing purple bandanas. I rode past Shabazz High School and Branch Brook Park Skating Rink. The past could never return to confront the present. And the future was a naked bitch walking to and fro, uncertain of where she was headed. The cold wind that smacked me in the face as I drove couldn't keep my tears from staining my cheeks. The end of my journey found me right back where it started. Brick Towers. Yellow crime scene tape cordoned off the area where Amina's body had been. Where I had left it. Plain-clothed and uniformed officers were still at the scene. I parked the Porsche and then proceeded to the projects on foot. Minutes later, out of nowhere, marked and unmarked police cars, swarmed the area, . The cops jumped out of their cars and surrounded me. A black detective that I knew personally emerged from the crowd.

"Take your hands out of your pocket, Najee," Detective Curtis Dobbs said. "And get down on your knees and put your hands on your head. If you do anything other than what I just said, I will shoot you."

I complied completely with every command. I was frisked and my gun was taken off my waist. As I was being handcuffed, I tried to remember all that I had done with the gun. It was clean as far as I could remember. After I was lifted from the ground, I was led to a nearby squad car. The detective I knew walked up and said, "Najee Bashir. You're under arrest for the murder of Richard Giles. You have the right to remain silent. Anything you say can and will be used against you in a the court of law…"

***

Later that day...

After the processing, I was placed in a large holding cell. One that I hadn't been in since being arrested for shoplifting as a teenager. I pulled off my coat, balled it up and used it as a pillow on the metal bench. Laying there, I thought about what the cop said. I was charged with killing Richard Giles. Without having to be told, I know what Richard Giles was "Rich", the dude me and Gunz bodied at the gas station. The murder must've been caught on video.

"Najee Bashir?" A voice called out.

I opened my eyes and looked up to see an Asian detective at the bars.

"Yeah, what's good, yo?"

"Wanna step up here for a moment?"

"Naw, talk"

"Do you want to talk about what you're charged with."

"Naw, I'm good."

The detective left quickly and minutes later, a uniformed lady cop appeared. "Bashir, come on, you get a phone call."

I was released from the holding cage and led to a phone. I dialed the number I had remembered by heart. It was answered on the second ring. "Carlos?"

"Najee?"

"Yeah, it's me. What's good, Pops? I'm in a jam. I'm in jail for murder."

"When did you get arrested?"

"This morning."

"So, you're still at the police station?"

"Yeah, I'm about to be transported to the Essex County Correctional Facility. Then, tomorrow I got to court."

"Okay, just sit tight and be cool. I'm sending someone up there today. They'll be at your court hearing. I'm gonna get you out of there, so don't sweat anything. No worries. Do you need anything else besides freedom?"

"No, I'm good. But Gunz and Tye ain't."

"Are they in jail too?"

"Naw, they're dead. And Aziz ain't."

"Say no more. Call when you get to Essex County."

"I will. Let Angel know where I am."

"I will talk to you later, son. Let me get the ball rolling."

"Aight, pops. One."

***

Essex County Jail
354 Doremus Avenue
Newark, NJ

"Gentlemen, welcome to the Green Monster. Take off all of your clothes and form a single file line. As you pass through this door here, stop and stand in front of an officer. That officer will search you. If you have any contraband on you, please leave it in this room somewhere. Because if we find it once you go through the door we are going to beat your fuckin' ass. Understand, gentlemen."

No one in the room spoke up and said a word.

"Okay, good," the correctional officer said. "Now, strip!"

***

"Najee Bashir?" A man called out.

"Right here," I replied.

"Step in that room over there and see the Lieutenant."

I stepped into a small room and saw an officer seated at a table. "Sit down, Bashir. I'm Lieutenant Tafuri?"

I sat in the seat across from the Lieutenant.

"Where are you from in Newark, Bashir?" Lt. Tafuri asked.

"Brick Towers."

"Brick Towers?" The Lieutenant repeated and wrote down what I said. "And what gang are you affiliated with?"

"None."

"No gang?"

I shook my head. "No gangs."

"Religion?"

"Muslim."

"Figures. Well, Mr. Najee, I've read your arrest report and you have the unfortunate luck of being charged with the murder of Richard Giles. Everybody here was familiar with Rich but we are even more familiar with Giles' brother, Mase- Kilah Stafford also known as Homicide. Homicide is the leader of the largest gang housed in this facility. The Grape Street Crips. Richard Giles and Mase- kilah Stafford are both from the Baxter Terrace projects, which also boast another 100 or so inmates who are not Crips, but love to put on for the hood. These inmates are housed all over this facility and I can't let them kill you here. So, unfortunately, you'll be going to 2C1, the Protective Custody Unit...

"I'd rather die."

"Is that right, Bashir?"

"It's death before dishonor. Always."

"If you're refusing protective custody, you gotta sign off on it."

"Where's the paperwork I got to sign."

"I'm gonna get it for you, Najee. And for what it's worth, I respect your decision. But it's *your* funeral. Wait here...."

Stay tuned for
Angel 5: THE FINALE

Lock Down Publications and Ca$h Presents
Assisted Publishing Packages

BASIC PACKAGE	**UPGRADED PACKAGE**
$499	$800
Editing	Typing
Cover Design	Editing
Formatting	Cover Design
	Formatting
ADVANCE PACKAGE	**LDP SUPREME PACKAGE**
$1,200	$1,500
Typing	Typing
Editing	Editing
Cover Design	Cover Design
Formatting	Formatting
Copyright registration	Copyright registration
Proofreading	Proofreading
Upload book to Amazon	Set up Amazon account
	Upload book to Amazon
	Advertise on LDP, Amazon and Facebook Page

***Other services available upon request.
Additional charges may apply

Lock Down Publications
P.O. Box 944
Stockbridge, GA 30281-9998
Phone: 470 303-9761

Submission Guideline

Submit the first three chapters of your completed manuscript to ldpsubmissions@gmail.com. In the subject line add **Your Book's Title**. The manuscript must be in a Word Doc file and sent as an attachment. Document should be in Times New Roman, double spaced, and in size 12 font. Also, provide your synopsis and full contact information. If sending multiple submissions, they must each be in a separate email.

Have a story but no way to send it electronically? You can still submit to LDP/Ca$h Presents. Send in the first three chapters, written or typed, of your completed manuscript to:

LDP: Submissions Dept
P.O. Box 944
Stockbridge, GA 30281-9998

DO NOT send original manuscript. Must be a duplicate.
Provide your synopsis and a cover letter containing your full contact information.

Thanks for considering LDP and Ca$h Presents.

NEW RELEASES

BLOODLINE OF A SAVAGE 1&2
THESE VICIOUS STREETS
RELENTLESS GOON
RELENTLESS GOON 2
BY PRINCE A. TAUHID

THE BUTTERFLY MAFIA 1-3
BY FUMIYA PAYNE

A THUG'S STREET PRINCESS 1&2
BY MEESHA

CITY OF SMOKE 2
BY MOLOTTI

STEPPERS 1,2&3
BY KING RIO

THE LANE 1&2
BY KEN-KEN SPENCE

THUG OF SPADES 1&2
LOVE IN THE TRENCHES 2
BY COREY ROBINSON

TIL DEATH 3
BY ARYANNA

THE BIRTH OF A GANGSTER 4
BY DELMONT PLAYER

PRODUCT OF THE STREETS 1&2
BY DEMOND "MONEY" ANDERSON

NO TIME FOR ERROR
BY KEESE

MONEY HUNGRY DEMONS
BY TRANAY ADAMS

Coming Soon from Lock Down Publications/Ca$h Presents

IF YOU CROSS ME ONCE 6
ANGEL V
By Anthony Fields

IMMA DIE BOUT MINE 4&5
By Aryanna

A THUGS STREET PRINCESS 3
By Meesha

PRODUCT OF THE STREETS 3
By Demond Money Anderson

CORNER BOYS
By Corey Robinson

SON OF A DOPE FIEND 4
By Renta

THE MURDER QUEENS 6&7
By Michael Gallon

CITY OF SMOKE 3
By Molotti

BETRAYAL OF A G
By Ray Vinci

CONFESSIONS OF A DOPE BOY
By Nicholas Lock

THA TAKEOVER
By Keith Chandler

Available Now

RESTRAINING ORDER 1 & 2
By **CA$H & Coffee**

LOVE KNOWS NO BOUNDARIES 1-3
By **Coffee**

RAISED AS A GOON I, II, III & IV
BRED BY THE SLUMS I, II, III
BLAST FOR ME I & II
ROTTEN TO THE CORE I II III
A BRONX TALE I, II, III
DUFFLE BAG CARTEL I II III IV V VI
HEARTLESS GOON I II III IV V
A SAVAGE DOPEBOY I II
DRUG LORDS I II III
CUTTHROAT MAFIA I II
KING OF THE TRENCHES
By **Ghost**

LAY IT DOWN I & II
LAST OF A DYING BREED I II
BLOOD STAINS OF A SHOTTA I & II III
By **Jamaica**

LOYAL TO THE GAME I II III
LIFE OF SIN I, II III
By **TJ & Jelissa**

IF LOVING HIM IS WRONG…I & II
LOVE ME EVEN WHEN IT HURTS I II III
By **Jelissa**

BLOODY COMMAS I & II
SKI MASK CARTEL I, II & III
KING OF NEW YORK I II, III IV V
RISE TO POWER I II III
COKE KINGS I II III IV V
BORN HEARTLESS I II III IV
KING OF THE TRAP I II
By **T.J. Edwards**

WHEN THE STREETS CLAP BACK I & II III
THE HEART OF A SAVAGE I II III IV
MONEY MAFIA I II
LOYAL TO THE SOIL I II III
By **Jibril Williams**

A DISTINGUISHED THUG STOLE MY HEART I II &
III
LOVE SHOULDN'T HURT I II III IV
RENEGADE BOYS 1-4
PAID IN KARMA 1-3
SAVAGE STORMS 1-3
AN UNFORESEEN LOVE 1-3
BABY, I'M WINTERTIME COLD 1-3
A THUG'S STREET PRINCESS 1&2
By **Meesha**

A GANGSTER'S CODE 1-3
A GANGSTER'S SYN 1-3
THE SAVAGE LIFE 1-3
CHAINED TO THE STREETS 1-3
BLOOD ON THE MONEY 1-3
A GANGSTA'S PAIN 1-3
BEAUTIFUL LIES AND UGLY TRUTHS
CHURCH IN THESE STREETS
By **J-Blunt**

PUSH IT TO THE LIMIT
By **Bre' Hayes**

BLOOD OF A BOSS 1-5
SHADOWS OF THE GAME
TRAP BASTARD
By **Askari**

THE STREETS BLEED MURDER 1-3
THE HEART OF A GANGSTA 1-3
By **Jerry Jackson**

CUM FOR ME 1-8
An LDP Erotica Collaboration

BRIDE OF A HUSTLA 1-3
THE FETTI GIRLS 1-3
CORRUPTED BY A GANGSTA 1-4
BLINDED BY HIS LOVE
THE PRICE YOU PAY FOR LOVE 1-3
DOPE GIRL MAGIC 1-3
By **Destiny Skai**

WHEN A GOOD GIRL GOES BAD
By **Adrienne**

A KINGPIN'S AMBITION
A KINGPIN'S AMBITION II
I MURDER FOR THE DOUGH
By **Ambitious**

THE COST OF LOYALTY 1-3
By **Kweli**

A GANGSTER'S REVENGE 1-4
THE BOSS MAN'S DAUGHTERS 1-5
A SAVAGE LOVE 1&2
BAE BELONGS TO ME 1&2
A HUSTLER'S DECEIT 1-3
WHAT BAD BITCHES DO 1-3
SOUL OF A MONSTER 1-3
KILL ZONE
A DOPE BOY'S QUEEN 1-3
TIL DEATH 1-3
IMMA DIE BOUT MINE 1-3
By **Aryanna**

TRUE SAVAGE 1-7
DOPE BOY MAGIC 1-3
MIDNIGHT CARTEL 1-3
CITY OF KINGZ 1&2
NIGHTMARE ON SILENT AVE
THE PLUG OF LIL MEXICO 1&2
CLASSIC CITY
By **Chris Green**

A DOPEBOY'S PRAYER
By **Eddie "Wolf" Lee**

THE KING CARTEL 1-3
By **Frank Gresham**

THESE NIGGAS AIN'T LOYAL 1-3
By **Nikki Tee**

GANGSTA SHYT 1-3
By **CATO**

THE ULTIMATE BETRAYAL
By **Phoenix**

BOSS'N UP 1-3
By **Royal Nicole**

I LOVE YOU TO DEATH
By **Destiny J**

I RIDE FOR MY HITTA
I STILL RIDE FOR MY HITTA
By **Misty Holt**

LOVE & CHASIN' PAPER
By **Qay Crockett**

TO DIE IN VAIN
SINS OF A HUSTLA
By **ASAD**

BROOKLYN HUSTLAZ
By **Boogsy Morina**

BROOKLYN ON LOCK 1 & 2
By **Sonovia**

GANGSTA CITY
By **Teddy Duke**

A DRUG KING AND HIS DIAMOND 1-3
A DOPEMAN'S RICHES
HER MAN, MINE'S TOO 1&2
CASH MONEY HO'S
THE WIFEY I USED TO BE 1&2
PRETTY GIRLS DO NASTY THINGS
By **Nicole Goosby**

LIPSTICK KILLAH 1-3
CRIME OF PASSION 1-3
FRIEND OR FOE 1-3
By **Mimi**

TRAPHOUSE KING 1-3
KINGPIN KILLAZ 1-3
STREET KINGS 1&2
PAID IN BLOOD 1&2
CARTEL KILLAZ 1-3
DOPE GODS 1&2
By **Hood Rich**

STEADY MOBBN' 1-3
THE STREETS STAINED MY SOUL 1-3
By **Marcellus Allen**

WHO SHOT YA 1-3
SON OF A DOPE FIEND 1-3
HEAVEN GOT A GHETTO 1&2
SKI MASK MONEY 1&2
By **Renta**

GORILLAZ IN THE BAY 1-4
TEARS OF A GANGSTA 1/&2
3X KRAZY 1&2
STRAIGHT BEAST MODE 1&2
By **DE'KARI**

TRIGGADALE 1-3
MURDA WAS THE CASE 1-3
By **Elijah R. Freeman**

THE STREETS ARE CALLING
By **Duquie Wilson**

SLAUGHTER GANG 1-3
RUTHLESS HEART 1-3
By **Willie Slaughter**

GOD BLESS THE TRAPPERS 1-3
THESE SCANDALOUS STREETS 1-3
FEAR MY GANGSTA 1-5
THESE STREETS DON'T LOVE NOBODY 1-2
BURY ME A G 1-5
A GANGSTA'S EMPIRE 1-4
THE DOPEMAN'S BODYGAURD 1&2
THE REALEST KILLAZ 1-3
THE LAST OF THE OGS 1-3
By **Tranay Adams**

MARRIED TO A BOSS 1-3
By **Destiny Skai & Chris Green**

KINGZ OF THE GAME 1-7
CRIME BOSS 1-3
By **Playa Ray**

FUK SHYT
By **Blakk Diamond**

DON'T F#CK WITH MY HEART 1&2
By **Linnea**

ADDICTED TO THE DRAMA 1-3
IN THE ARM OF HIS BOSS
By **Jamila**

LOYALTY AIN'T PROMISED 1&2
By **Keith Williams**

YAYO 1-4
A SHOOTER'S AMBITION 1&2
BRED IN THE GAME
By **S. Allen**

TRAP GOD 1-3
RICH $AVAGE 1-3
MONEY IN THE GRAVE 1-3
CARTEL MONEY
By **Martell Troublesome Bolden**

FOREVER GANGSTA 1&2
GLOCKS ON SATIN SHEETS 1&2
By **Adrian Dulan**

TOE TAGZ 1-4
LEVELS TO THIS SHYT 1&2
IT'S JUST ME AND YOU
By **Ah'Million**

KINGPIN DREAMS 1-3
RAN OFF ON DA PLUG
By **Paper Boi Rari**

CONFESSIONS OF A GANGSTA 1-4
CONFESSIONS OF A JACKBOY 1-3
CONFESSIONS OF A HITMAN
By **Nicholas Lock**

I'M NOTHING WITHOUT HIS LOVE
SINS OF A THUG
TO THE THUG I LOVED BEFORE
A GANGSTA SAVED XMAS
IN A HUSTLER I TRUST
By **Monet Dragun**

QUIET MONEY 1-3
THUG LIFE 1-3
EXTENDED CLIP 1&2
A GANGSTA'S PARADISE
By **Trai'Quan**

CAUGHT UP IN THE LIFE 1-3
THE STREETS NEVER LET GO 1-3
By **Robert Baptiste**

NEW TO THE GAME 1-3
MONEY, MURDER & MEMORIES 1-3
By **Malik D. Rice**

CREAM 2-3
THE STREETS WILL TALK
By **Yolanda Moore**

LIFE OF A SAVAGE 1-4
A GANGSTA'S QUR'AN 1-4
MURDA SEASON 1-3
GANGLAND CARTEL 1-3
CHI'RAQ GANGSTAS 1-4
KILLERS ON ELM STREET 1-3
JACK BOYZ N DA BRONX 1-3
A DOPEBOY'S DREAM 1-3
JACK BOYS VS DOPE BOYS 1-3
COKE GIRLZ
COKE BOYS
SOSA GANG 1&2
BRONX SAVAGES
BODYMORE KINGPINS
BLOOD OF A GOON
By **Romell Tukes**

IF YOU CROSS ME ONCE 4 | ANTHONY FIELDS

THE STREETS MADE ME 1-3
By **Larry D. Wright**

CONCRETE KILLA 1-3
VICIOUS LOYALTY 1-3
By **Kingpen**

THE ULTIMATE SACRIFICE 1-6
KHADIFI
IF YOU CROSS ME ONCE 1-3
ANGEL 1-4
IN THE BLINK OF AN EYE
By **Anthony Fields**

THE LIFE OF A HOOD STAR
By **Ca$h & Rashia Wilson**

THE STREETS WILL NEVER CLOSE 1-3
By **K'ajji**

NIGHTMARES OF A HUSTLA 1-3
By **King Dream**

HARD AND RUTHLESS 1&2
MOB TOWN 251
THE BILLIONAIRE BENTLEYS 1-3
REAL G'S MOVE IN SILENCE
By **Von Diesel**

GHOST MOB
By **Stilloan Robinson**

MOB TIES 1-6
SOUL OF A HUSTLER, HEART OF A KILLER 1-3
GORILLAZ IN THE TRENCHES
By **SayNoMore**

BODYMORE MURDERLAND 1-3
THE BIRTH OF A GANGSTER 1-4
By **Delmont Player**

FOR THE LOVE OF A BOSS 1&2
By **C. D. Blue**

KILLA KOUNTY 1-5
By **Khufu**

MOBBED UP 1-4
THE BRICK MAN 1-5
THE COCAINE PRINCESS 1-10
STEPPERS 1-3
SUPER GREMLIN 1-4
By **King Rio**

MONEY GAME 1&2
By **Smoove Dolla**

A GANGSTA'S KARMA 1-4
By **FLAME**

KING OF THE TRENCHES 1-3
By **GHOST & TRANAY ADAMS**

QUEEN OF THE ZOO 1&2
By **Black Migo**

GRIMEY WAYS 1-3
By **Ray Vinci**

XMAS WITH AN ATL SHOOTER
By **Ca$h & Destiny Skai**

IF YOU CROSS ME ONCE 4 | ANTHONY FIELDS

KING KILLA 1&2
By **Vincent "Vitto" Holloway**

BETRAYAL OF A THUG 1&2
By **Fre$h**

THE MURDER QUEENS 1-5
By **Michael Gallon**

FOR THE LOVE OF BLOOD 1-4
By **Jamel Mitchell**

HOOD CONSIGLIERE 1&2
NO TIME FOR ERROR
By **Keese**

PROTÉGÉ OF A LEGEND 1&2
LOVE IN THE TRENCHES 1&2
By **Corey Robinson**

BORN IN THE GRAVE 1-3
CRIME PAYS
By **Self Made Tay**

MOAN IN MY MOUTH
By **XTASY**

TORN BETWEEN A GANGSTER AND A GENTLEMAN
By **J-BLUNT & Miss Kim**

LOYALTY IS EVERYTHING 1-3
CITY OF SMOKE 1&2
By **Molotti**

HERE TODAY GONE TOMORROW 1&2
By **Fly Rock**

WOMEN LIE MEN LIE 1-4
FIFTY SHADES OF SNOW 1-3
STACK BEFORE YOU SPLURGE
GIRLS FALL LIKE DOMINOES
NAÏVE TO THE STREETS
By **ROY MILLIGAN**

PILLOW PRINCESS
By **S. Hawkins**

THE BUTTERFLY MAFIA 1-3
SALUTE MY SAVAGERY 1&2
By **Fumiya Payne**

THE LANE 1&2
By Ken-Ken Spence

THE PUSSY TRAP 1-5
By **Nene Capri**

DIRTY DNA
By **Blaque**

SANCTIFIED AND HORNY
by **XTASY**

BOOKS BY LDP'S CEO, CA$H

TRUST IN NO MAN
TRUST IN NO MAN 2
TRUST IN NO MAN 3
BONDED BY BLOOD
SHORTY GOT A THUG
THUGS CRY
THUGS CRY 2
THUGS CRY 3
TRUST NO BITCH
TRUST NO BITCH 2
TRUST NO BITCH 3
TIL MY CASKET DROPS
RESTRAINING ORDER
RESTRAINING ORDER 2
IN LOVE WITH A CONVICT
LIFE OF A HOOD STAR
XMAS WITH AN ATL SHOOTER